L M Ryan was born in Ireland and is convent educated. She lived there for eighteen years before leaving to live and work first in Staffordshire, then moved permanently to Chiswick in West London. She met and married her husband William and brought up her four children there. Sadly she lost her eldest daughter in 2012 and then her husband in 2019. She has two sons who are engineers and a younger daughter who is a PA. She also has one grandchild, a boy, Jude. Lucinda now lives alone in a sheltered housing unit and, as well as writing, is a keen gardener.

For my children, Niall, Aidan and Clodagh who are so special and whom I love with all my heart.

L M Ryan

THE GATHERING PLACE

AUSTIN MACAULEY PUBLISHERS™

LONDON * CAMBRIDGE * NEW YORK * SHARJAH

A CIP catalogue record for this title is available from the British Library.

ISBN 9781528993678 (Paperback)
ISBN 9781528993685 (ePub e-book)

www.austinmacauley.com

First Published 2021
Austin Macauley Publishers Ltd
Level 37, Office 37.15, 1 Canada Square
Canary Wharf
London
E14 5AA

Thanks to the entire publishing team at Austin Macauley Publishers, for their patience and understanding.
Also to my daughter, Clodagh Ryan, for her help and support.

Two tall pale men, dressed in white suits appeared, seemingly from nowhere, on the country road between the village of Barton Trinity and the town of Great Barton. They stood by the old, decaying fallen tree and waited. All who passed were carefully scrutinised and rejected. Twilight came and they were gone as suddenly as they had come. They would return at dawn each day until the man for whom they waited came. And he would come, of that there was no doubt and the gatherers would be waiting. But so too would other, darker forces and they would be equally determined to have him.

****

Chapter 1

Thomas Beck lay, sleepless, on his bed. He was seventy years old, quite a handsome man for his age, but his appearance was marred by a perpetual scowl and two deeply scored lines of discontent by the sides of his mouth. Even in sleep they did not soften. He turned over on to his side and stared into the darkness. His thoughts irritated him, his body irritated him, he was uneasy, had been for days now. There was something he had to do. Something simple, but dangerous maybe. He had to drive the car one more time. It was probably not the right thing to do, but it had to be done, before it all came to an end.

Thomas was not a friendly man. When he was young there had been two good friends. Both dead now. One had been James, red-haired and fiery, angry and mistrusting of most people, but with a deep affection for Thomas. The other was Robert, tall blonde haired and treacherous, rotten to the core, who betrayed him. He tried not to think about Robert.

Thomas had once been open and friendly, if a little reserved. Life had changed that. Staring into the darkness, eyes slowly becoming accustomed to it, he saw the shape of his wife, Valerie, sleeping in the other single bed. She was pleasant and friendly, people liked her. That annoyed him. What had that woman ever done to deserve friends? A small voice in his head told him he was wrong to think of her like that. Thomas was good at ignoring such thoughts.

Thomas listened to her slow, deep breathing. Why should she sleep when he could not? That woman deserved to lie awake in the night. She was the one who ruined his life. She and his so-called friend, Robert. If it had not been for the conversation he heard between them on the twins fifth birthday, he would have continued to believe everything was right in his world. Back then he thought the twins were his sons and life had a bloom to it. That bloom came back later when he had Kate, his daughter. His only child. The other two cuckoos were Roberts's children. All trust was gone. Now he was not allowed to drive his beloved

Triumph. Her fault again. Everything was her fault. Resentment filled his thoughts.

The small voice that struggled so hard inside his head to make itself heard was stilled, "Go away," he told it, "I know, who caused my life to fall in ruins. My wife." *So, why did you not divorce her?* the voice was quite clear and sharp, "Shut up," he told it, and turned on his side.

Now, he lay there brooding on how shabbily he had been treated by life. He had trusted his wife then. It was not just the twins. His sons. The man smiled bitterly into the darkness. They were not his sons. When they were born, he thought life could not be better. Yet, there had been a tiny doubt. A thought that the timing was not right. Thomas wished he had listened to the thoughts inside his head. But then he would not have listened to anybody, he loved her so much. The thoughts were stilled the moment they started. He only listened now to his own bitter, angry mind.

The business of not being able to drive had all started when he got those occasional feelings of pressure building up along his neck and inside his head. With it came a slight darkening of the world around him and a coldness. If he turned his head too quickly, he staggered, had to hold on to something. He could cope with that. It was age, Thomas thought, everyone grew older.

The odd feeling along his neck and his head began to come more often. He made the mistake of telling Valerie, after a surprisingly bad attack when he blacked out and promised to see his GP. Later that day, he had another. He asked her to make an appointment and was shocked when told to come in straight away.

He thought the doctor would say that his wife was just being over anxious. He was getting older. Things happened when people got older. It was all perfectly normal. Thomas was not happy when he saw that he was seeing the new chap, not his regular man and consoled himself with the thought that this one might be more up to date. To his shock and horror, the new young doctor agreed with his wife and examined him thoroughly.

Valerie kept butting in and the doctor took everything she said seriously, and then said he would send him to a Neurologist. Thomas, dazed and numb, heard his wife say they had private medical insurance and asked if he could be referred privately. Of course, he could, he would refer him to someone in London.

As they left the surgery, Thomas had been so angry. She had shrugged helplessly and said, "You know very well that whatever is happening to you cannot be right. People do not have black-outs without good reason."

She was nervous, knowing he would be angry with her for interfering in his life and he was. "You always damn well have to interfere, don't you?" he snapped, "Can't keep your nose out of my business?"

She muttered, "Sorry." No matter what, he was still her husband. Thomas was referred to the big Hospital on Fulham Palace road in London. He saw the consultant, had all the tests and was seen a second time for the results. He had a spur of bone growing on his cervical spine the consultant said, and it was very close to the artery, too close. Surgery was not an option. Too dangerous. He would have to be careful turning his head in case of loss of consciousness. The consultant would make his report and return Thomas to the care of his own GP.

That was when Valerie had committed the unforgivable once more. She mentioned driving. It was not advisable the consultant said. In fact, he should not drive at all. Thomas felt a fury so intense he was unable to speak. Her interference was bloody unforgivable. He adored that old car, loved driving. The consultant looked at Valerie. Did she drive? She did. Good.

Thomas clenched his jaw tightly as he shook the smooth white hand and they went down in the lift and out through the circular doors, past the teeming fish ponds to where the car was parked. "I can drive," he snapped, "I can drive. I am driving my car home."

"You are not," Valerie said calmly, "Get in that driving seat and you are in trouble. You are not allowed to drive."

She knew; however, he would not let it go. Thomas was livid with rage. How dare she. How dare she tell him he was not allowed to drive?

Valerie drove home and he made sure she was shaking by the time they drove the short distance to the traffic lights on the Broadway. She had driven out from the hospital car park, on to Fulham Palace Road, towards the Hammersmith Broadway, and with her husband snapping at her to do this, watch that truck, that bus, don't do that, she did not get in the right lane at the lights and ended up driving around the Broadway a second time. She managed it eventually and then they were driving toward Chiswick and on toward home.

They made to Barton Trinity without incident, but with Thomas sitting almost menacingly beside her. When they arrived, he jumped out of the car and examined every inch of it for any mark of dust or mud, anything he could find. There was nothing wrong but it did not stop him making her evening a misery.

In the days that followed, he was silent and sullen. He was determined to drive one last time along the seven mile stretch of road between the village of

Barton Trinity and the market town of Great Barton. She hid his keys a few times but he found them and yet he did not take the car out. He waited, knowing she was afraid and seemed enjoy her fear, playing cat and mouse. He was very good at that. He would drive it in his own time. Let her sweat. She started this. He would finish it.

Now in the early hours of Saturday morning, he determined that this was the day to drive the car one last time. Lying awake, smouldering with rage, he made his plans. This day he would drive along that stretch of road come hell or high water. It would be his swan song. She would not get the car though. Oh no. He would sell it, even if it broke his heart. Selling it would be a small assuaging of his anger. He got up and pounded downstairs.

A while later she opened the kitchen door peering around it, "What are you doing?"

"I'm hungry," he said, "I need a cooked breakfast."

"It's only six o'clock," Valerie brushed back her still auburn hair. "What was he up to now? Something going on." She walked to the fridge freezer, opened the door, "There's bacon and eggs. Help yourself. I am going back to bed." She walked out of the room. Whatever he was up to at this time of day she was not getting involved. He scowled as the door closed softly behind her, he was not really hungry, just wanted to annoy.

Later, dressed and ready to go out, Valerie asked to borrow the car to do the weekly shop, but Thomas said he was working on it; she'd have to get the bus into town and take a taxi back. She shrugged, knowing there was nothing wrong with the car. He always had to get his own back, sometimes even waiting for months.

Valerie sat on the seat of the eleven-thirty bus looking out of the window. Why do I stay with that man, she wondered? What is left? I know how much I hurt him all those years ago, but I did try to tell him. I really did. He refused to listen.

Marriage was a big step. He was so insistent, she had said yes and tried to forget what she'd done, but of course, in the end, it all came out. Well it had to really. Valerie had not known; she was pregnant by Robert then. I should have insisted that he listen to me. I did try. I did, she thought. It was amazing how he held that anger and resentment against her for so long. It was still there now. The boys, her twin sons, had suffered also. She smiled grimly. Talk about the sin of the father being visited on the children, only in this case it was the sins of the mother. A few years later, she thought, he had forgiven her and she became pregnant with Kate. He had not, nor would he ever.

Now Valerie walked around Great Barton looking into shop windows. She bought a beautiful black jacket, so elegant, just in case. The thought came unbidden. She stopped short. In case of what, Valerie wondered? She was uneasy. It seemed like a portent. She went to the supermarket and did her shopping, but the unease persisted. She needed to get home. Something, she did not know what, told her to go home. She called a taxi.

The car was still in the short drive and she felt the relief, but his face when he came into the kitchen looked odd. Sly. "Would you like some lunch?"

"No." Came the curt reply.

Valerie took a deep breath. What was he going to do? Then she knew. He was going to drive the car. He would drive it and in his present mood, something might happen, anything, an accident.

She stared at her husband of over-thirty-five years. Years of misery at times. A few moments of happiness but they were so rare. Why did he stay with her? More to the point why did she stay with him? She had fought so hard to keep this marriage going and for what? It was not worth it. If he wanted to drive let him go ahead, drive into oblivion, but then she had a fleeting moment of seeing the future on her own. It was so real and, in a sense, a relief, then she felt a sudden whisper of guilt and something else, a glimpse of the future alone. "Thomas, don't drive the car today," she said urgently, "Please, you might have a crash, kill somebody."

He snorted, "Step in front of the car then and it could be you." He juggled the car keys from hand to hand, laughing as he walked out the door.

She stood stunned and wretched with misery, and then a few moments later heard the car start, the sound of the engine fading away. Valerie stood in the silent kitchen. There was only the clunking tick of the old grandfather clock. She pushed the kettle on to the big ring of the Aga cooker, standing waiting for it to boil, then made tea, and sat in the old rocking chair sipping the hot sweet brew slowly.

There was a knock on the back door and Mel from next door came in. Mel was a handsome man the same age as she, hair silver grey and always pleasant. He looked after his ninety-six-year-old mother, who he said, was sleeping. She had dementia; she would be quiet for a while. He sometimes slipped in for a cup of tea if Thomas was not there. He was aware Thomas should not drive. He was also aware of the man's dislike of him.

Later, Mel went back home. He too was uneasy. Valerie put away the shopping, and then decided to prepare supper. It was now gone half past three. She looked through the window at the sound of a car but it was only the carer for next door. She tried to think of normal things, and set about stuffing a chicken, leaving it in fridge in a dish covered with foil, ready for roasting; they would have it for supper with peas, carrots and roast potatoes. Thomas liked his roast potatoes and lots of gravy. What was left over would do for supper on Sunday. She stared at the dish; her hands fluttered helplessly.

She looked through the window and saw Mel on the pavement staring along the road. He too was watching and waiting. There was a curious feeling in the air; a stillness. It had rained a lot yesterday but today it was pleasant. Yet, no bird sang this mild April day. There was not even a gentle breeze. It was as if the world held its breath.

She watched as Mel walked back inside the house. Valerie sat in the rocking chair. The ticking of the clock seemed so loud. She stared at the face of the old clock. Seven minutes past four. The hands seemed not to move for ages, then it clunked loudly and the big hand jerked forward a little. She jumped nervously at the sound. A cold draught of wind came from somewhere. There must be a door open.

She made more tea and at six o'clock hearing the sound of a car, stood up and went to the front of the house to look out of the window. Relief so intense swept over her as it passed by that she had to sit down on the window seat for a moment to let the strength come back into her legs. She looked to the left and right. Something was so very wrong.

A little later the police car drove in slowly through the gate. A tall young officer stepped from the car, a young WPC emerged from the passenger seat. Both put on their uniform hats and looked toward the house. They walked across the gravel to the front door. Valerie smoothed her skirt and then her hair, and took a deep breath. This was it then. He had done it. Crashed the car, hit somebody maybe? Her mind would not allow her to think that it could be the worst and yet she expected the worst.

She felt strange. It was almost as if she had two people inside her head. Two voices, one saying it would not be too bad and the silly man was in hospital with a broken leg, the other saying, he had gone and done it this time. You are now a widow, one voice whispered, and the other said no, he's just had a bump. She told herself she would not move until they rang the doorbell, but at the same time rushed forward to open the front door. "Mrs Beck?" the young officer asked, she nodded and saw Mel come swiftly, stepping over the low link fence, "Do you have a friend or relative in the house with you?"

She stared at the young police woman whose clear brown eyes were filled with sympathy. "I'm on my own," she babbled, "My husband is out. Is it him? Did he have an accident, he shouldn't be driving you know." She pointed to Mel, "This is our friend, from next door. These officers are from the police Mel."

The tall young officer looked towards Mel who now stood near and nodded "A friend," Mel said, "a neighbour."

She heard their voices but the words made little sense. She heard the words, accident, badly injured, thought she heard him say something about unfortunate, nothing they could do, Identification. Those words seemed to come clearly but the rest were jumbled. What did it mean? Fear swept along her spine, went away, came back in waves, its icy fingers stroking her neck.

Valerie heard Mel say something about making tea and the young policewoman nodded. The worst thing of all had happened. Curiously, it was almost a relief. The thing she worried about these past weeks had happened and it was over. The fear was gone, but bewilderment and the beginnings of grief had taken its place. The poor, angry foolish old man had done the stupidest thing of all and it had all been so unnecessary. He was dead and then the thought hit her. He had never forgiven her. How could she bear that? She felt the tears begin to roll down her cheeks. Valerie Beck cried for her bitter angry husband, for herself and for the thought that he had died hating her. His final act of revenge.

Chapter 2

Thomas walked across the road that ran between Barton Trinity village and the market town. What on earth was going on? Unusually, there were several cars parked at odd angles along the grass verges and he wondered if there was a car boot or a gymkhana in one of Colin Black's fields, though he had not seen the usual notice pinned to a tree.

As he looked further on, he saw two police cars and then heard the siren as an ambulance sped along the road from town. There must have been an accident, he thought, turning back to look at his car but could not see where he had parked it. Thomas stopped, feeling a little confused. Where had he parked? Where had he been going? He could not remember. He felt curiously light and unconcerned. The dull ache in his knee which had troubled him for days was gone. Suddenly there was buzzing in his ears and a man seemed to be bending over him putting something over his mouth and nose. He struggled to put a hand up, could not, and then he was back on the road again looking around anxiously. What was that all about? Such an odd feeling.

Why was he here? Then he remembered, he was driving to Great Barton, and then decided to drive further on, before turning back, making the most of his last drive. What did I do then he wondered, Yes, he had driven back and had something to eat in the café just outside the town? Then he had driven out of town, had almost made it home, changed his mind, then turned and drove back again.

He remembered coming to the bend, had almost forgotten to slow down. He did not remember what happened then, but he had parked the car, was sure of that. I parked it here, opposite the old fallen tree, he told himself, and then changed it to a question. Did I? He suddenly felt odd and light-headed again and walked across the road to the old dead tree to sit down. The ground was a little higher there and he could look around as he waited for his head to clear. Then he heard that strange buzzing noise again and the flash of a face close to his, but as quickly as it came, it was gone. He looked toward the curve of the road which was called Five Mile Turn and was known to be an accident black spot. He was always careful here and yet today, he'd almost forgotten.

Thomas turned and looked across the fields towards the paddock where Colin Black's two girls trained their ponies. The two of them were out there now, where they had erected a couple of low jumps. He liked the two girls. They always waved. Pony mad, the pair of them and totally unalike. The elder was tall, thin, and with almost white blonde hair. The younger girl, plump and small with thick black hair tied in plaits, which stuck out from underneath her black riding hat, like inverted question marks.

Thomas turned his head and saw Colin sitting on the fallen tree beside him. The man did not appear to notice him. "Morning Colin," he said, but the big quiet man sat, and stared ahead looking distressed and did not reply. Thomas shrugged. Something was definitely up. The man was upset. Another man came over and sat beside Colin. Thomas recognised him as a farmer from outside town. "A bad business, Col," the man said. "Terrible, terrible." Colin's lips trembled, "Someone said, he was killed outright. I wonder who's going to tell his missus."

Thomas felt detached. He watched now as the cars were turned on to the back road by the police. He decided to sit and wait for the traffic to take itself off to wherever it was going.

Eventually, their work was done, police, ambulance and fireman, who had arrived with cutting gear and an officer who videoed the scene, were standing around seemingly waiting. Thomas thought he had better make for home. No point now in finishing his drive. Tomorrow was another day. He would go back home. He glanced at his watch. The glass was broken and the hands stopped at seven minutes past four. How had that happened? He became aware the black mortuary van had taken someone away.

A car was being hoisted up on a tow truck. The parts of the car that were not scratched and crumpled showed a rich red colour in the rays of the sun. He knew that car and the number plate. What it was to be getting older. Yet he was in reasonably good shape still apart from the head problem, but that was nothing. A couple of pieces of glass fell from the car and tinkled on to the road. He looked at the plate again and then he remembered. Thomas stood stock still. That was his car, his classic Triumph. What was it doing here? What had happened?

He heard Colin Black and the farmer talking softly behind him. "I wonder if I should go and see his wife," Colin said.

"The police will do all that," the other man said, "Best to leave it to them."

"She's a very nice lady is Mrs Beck," Colin said, "It's going to be a sad time for her now he's dead and I hear he was only seventy. No age at all these days."

"Poor old man Beck. Went straight into that wall from I hear tell, they say he died instantly," the other man muttered.

Colin Black sighed, "Terrible, terrible."

Thomas Beck stood as if turned to stone. Dead? What? He was not dead. He was here. He was alive, had not felt better in years. He looked at his hands, then down to his feet. All the bits were in place. He was wearing his navy cords and blue sweater. He was here. He was. He was standing here, alive and well and they were saying he was dead. This was all a mistake. He reached a hand to touch Col Blacks shoulder but there was nothing, no response and he could not feel the man's shoulder. He did the same with the other man. Nothing. Thomas looked at his hand. No feeling.

He called, "Colin, it's me, Tom Beck. Colin?"

The man seemed to be looking straight through him. He turned to the other man, reaching out. Nothing solid beneath his hand. Thomas eyes opened wide in horror.

He walked over to other people, strangers, staring into their faces, trying to touch or speak to them. There was no response. He laughed then. This was a joke. They were playing tricks. He called and reached out to touch people again and again. Nobody could see him. He was about to scream, then stopped. Think. Think, but what to think?

He was dead, yet that could not be right. There was no memory of the accident. Yet the van had taken a shrouded body away. Was that him? He felt light and a bit giddy now and went back to sit on the fallen tree trunk. Suddenly frightened, goose bumps seemed to crawl over his body. The day was getting colder. The cold seemed to penetrate muscle and even bone now. He sat for a while not even thinking, on the crumbling, insect-filled tree trunk staring at the big truck, driving slowly away down the road, with his car strapped down, turning it all over in his head, trying to make sense of the whole thing. There was no sense to anything. He was dead.

Thomas felt a terrible weariness fill his entire body. He closed his eyes and all sound drifted away. After a time, he opened them again and it had grown darker. Nobody on the road. All were gone. He was alone and afraid. The broken ends of the blue and white tape the police used to tape the area whipped wildly and made a rattling noise in the chilly wind. Then all was still again. It was a cold place and he was very much afraid.

Thomas stared wretchedly along the grey concrete of the road. It was empty, apart from a huge arch in the distance which he had never noticed before. He stared at it. What was that? The only other movement came from a dead leaf as it lifted and jumped crazily along the greyness of the road, almost like a living thing. No human life here, no animal. Just the bleak emptiness of the road. There was only that great arch. What was that thing? He stood up and looked around. There was another great arch behind him in the distance.

When had they been put there and for what reason? He looked around wildly, he had to get home and sort it all out. If he really was dead then she would have to know. He laughed and the sound echoed all around. What a joke, if he was dead how could he tell her anything? It would be a long walk home too without the car, and yet if he was dead, how could he drive? Besides the car was gone. He laughed hysterically, and then tried to pull himself together.

Thomas tried to walk towards the village. Yet when he reached the big arch which spanned the road, it was as if there was an invisible wall between him and it, then he tried walking towards town but the same thing happened. He tried to climb the hedge to cross the fields but there was a barrier he could not see. He could only walk along a short stretch of about a half mile of the road. He was stuck here in this place and for some reason could only walk a little way in either direction and that was between those two arches.

Thomas went back to the fallen tree and sat on it, looking around. Emptiness. Cold emptiness. Was this all there was? A cold grey road? Was this an afterlife? He'd not believed in one, well maybe once, when he was a child. At his school they told you that you died and went to some place great or someplace terrible. In religious instruction class, the teacher said, good little children went straight to heaven, but then there was the other place. A scary place.

I used to believe that when I was a child he thought. When did I stop believing? James believed too, for a while, but Robert, who was the Vicar's son, said it was all rubbish. You lived. You died. They reasoned it all away. There was some guilt but, in the end, he closed his mind to all that stuff.

Thomas stared around, and then smiled grimly. The sting in the bloody tail was, that he was here, alone, dead, in an afterlife in which he'd not believed. He was afraid. He looked around searching for someone to tell him what to do. There must be somebody. Where were all the others who died? So, where did they go from this point on? If there was this afterlife, then where was everybody? What did they know that he did not? Or did they reach this point and then just fade away into dust? That could not be right. Why was he here if that was all that happened?

He shook his head. Thomas had been brought up a Catholic until teenage, albeit under some duress as he grew. Then came his fourteenth birthday. That was when he knew he was too intelligent to believe all that rubbish. He gave up any pretence at even being a Christian. He made his choice then. Who needed all that stuff?

His father Thomas Beck senior, had claimed he was agnostic and it caused rows when he encouraged the boy to forget all that nonsense "I know. I agreed, if we had children, to let them be brought up one of your lot." He told his wife, "Well he's fourteen now and can make up his own mind. I don't have to be one and the boy does not have to be one either He does not believe in a God. He's old enough now and he can think for himself."

Beck senior was too old to go to war and would not have gone anyway as he was in a reserved occupation. So, he was always there, to share his opinions with the boy. He shared them forcefully, particularly as Thomas began to grow into teenage. His mother did her best. She wilted slowly but surely under a barrage of mockery from husband and son. In the end, they wore her down so she only mentioned religion or God rarely. After that she only asked him to go to church at Christmas or Easter. Thomas did go to church once or twice, reluctantly, because he loved her and hated to see her unhappy. He yawned noisily and scratched his way through the service in places he should not be scratching, doing everything except lying down to sleep in the pew. He became an embarrassment to her. She went alone to pray then. In the end, she gave up speaking to her husband and son about anything to do with religion and they left her alone.

Thomas found it curious that in his old age his father joined his mother and became one of the congregations of the Catholic church of St Joseph in Great Barton. Funny that. Had the old man learned something? Maybe. He wished he had taken more notice of what his mother had to say. If he had maybe he would not be so bewildered right now.

Here now, alone in the gathering darkness and feeling helpless as a child he learned there was, most definitely, a life after death. There was, because he was dead and he was here, right in the centre of it all and was starting to fervently hope it was going to get better because right now it seemed to be a cold and wretchedly miserable place indeed.

He sat down on the ancient fallen tree and watched the night fall. There was not one single thought in his head as to what might be done, or even where to start? How would he find a way out of this? He was as helpless as a new born infant. A cold wind whistled around him and curiously he felt the chill. People said you felt nothing when you were dead, but how did they know? How did anybody know? It was all talk really, but then, there was the worrying fact that he was here, and frighteningly alone.

****

Chapter 3

Thomas sat and waited, and waited. Time dragged on. Nothing, nobody came along the grey road. The darkness came down quickly and with it a terrible loneliness. Dogs barked somewhere, breaking the silence. A vixen screamed, making him jump. There was curious rustling in the hedgerows. What were these animals doing in an afterlife? Yet what did he know? He wanted to sleep, and looking around for a place to lie down, saw beneath the fallen tree a space and wriggled into it. Sleep did not come and he felt colder still. What he would not give for one of Valerie's warm furry throws.

The wind seemed to work its way into every part of his body. He should never have turned the key in that car, because if he had not, he would be home in his own comfortable bed under a warm duvet instead of lying under a dead tree on a bitterly cold night. "I wish I had not driven the car," he muttered aloud. "Well now, that's a start," said a pleasant male voice from somewhere nearby.

Thomas startled, wriggled out from under the tree and stared around but could not see anybody. He peered into the gathering darkness. Ah, there was something, someone there. It was only a vague shape, a mistiness. "Who are you? Why don't you show yourself properly?" he called nervously. "Forgotten me already," said the voice.

Thomas peered into the darkness, "I don't know, whether I have forgotten you or not. I don't know you. I can't see you properly." Thomas said. "He did not like this at all."

"OH, come now Thomas," the voice said, "I have been with you all your life. Mind you did not listen to me then, so why would I expect you to remember me, or even know me now. If you cannot see me properly it is because you never really wanted to know me."

"Where are you? Stop trying to frighten me," Thomas whispered.

"Sorry, I did not mean to startle you," said the voice, "I suppose, I had better explain. You cannot see me properly. Sadly, you will only see me as a mist, which is a pity as I look somewhat like you. I am part of you, the part you always ignored. Remember? I am conscience. That small voice in the back of your head, easy to ignore because we are just a small voice. Unless of course, you care, and you did not. However, once you pass through the Portal you have no choice but to listen, if I choose to speak. Here, you cannot ignore me."

"I don't have to listen to you if I don't want," Thomas snapped childishly.

He did not like this business of a disembodied voice or, that he was speaking to something he could not see, "Anyway, what do you mean by the Portal? What is this Portal?"

"Yes Thomas, you do have to listen. That huge arch is the Portal," the voice said, "Let me tell you about it. The Portal, Thomas, is the doorway between life and death, death of the body that is. Once you have entered in and the Portal glows and throbs with its own life, there is no going back to earthly life. Then one of the gates will be opened for you."

Thomas sighed, "Look, I don't want to know about gates, all I want to do is find out where I have to go now, but I cannot get off this blasted road."

The voice tutted softly, "Listen and learn then. Mind you, you never listened did you, not to me or anybody. You always knew best and were always right. No point in hissing and snapping now, Thomas. So, do not interrupt and let me finish speaking. This is the Portal space; there are two arches, one at each end. You are in the middle. It is a state, not a place, or if you like, a plane. You cannot leave it. It is simply a place between two entrances. You enter in and then you enter in again to another place. There is no going back. All is forward from this point. You have not yet been found. Someone will come and find you."

There was a pause. Thomas thought he heard the voice chuckle. This conscience thing was enjoying his fear and misery. But then the voice went on, "You must wait patiently for this to happen. In fact, you may even find a gate to enter before they find you. Some who have passed through do find their own way in."

"What do you mean I have not yet been found? Who is supposed to find me? Where is this gate? What is this all about?" Thomas was shouting now.

He was confused and angry, and did not like this thing. No face, no body. Only mist and a voice going on about things he did not understand. The voice was silent for a while then gave a little cough, seeming to clear its throat, and went on. "OK, please listen carefully, and I mean carefully. Do not interrupt and I will endeavour to explain. You were expected here the day before yesterday.

You did not come. The Soul Gatherers, who should have met you, had to go away to their respite. They were told to come back in the morning, but you, being you, did not come then either. So, when you finally decided to make your move, they had gone on to gather in another soul. They thought you would live out your allotted span so they did not come to meet you. Got that?"

"No." Thomas snapped.

A long breath was expelled from somewhere in front of him and the voice said, "I dunno why I bother. Contrary. Miserable. Bad tempered and you do not listen. Give me strength."

Thomas stared silently into the darkness of the night; he did not know what to make of all this. Somebody to meet him and he wasn't there and then he was to meet them again and they thought he was not coming, and these people were who? What were they? Oh, why had he driven that car? He turned his back on the misty shape and sat down on the old tree. He could not move forward or back. He was stuck on this road and it was cold and miserable. What were these soul gatherer people, who were supposed to find him? His body began to tremble.

Stop now, and think this out, he told himself. So now you know there is an afterlife. Well, be honest man you always thought there was even though you denied it to anyone who ever mentioned the word. Suppose, just suppose, these people who were coming to meet you were not from a good place. His body stiffened. Oh no. Oh no…. That did not bear thinking about.

Suppose he was going to be sent to that other place, the place people said was down under the earth somewhere. There, he had thought it. Suppose it was like in that film Ghost and the dark shadows were coming for him. Terror struck at his heart. No, not that. He jumped to his feet and walked up and down as far as he could and back again. He was panicking.

The voice said, "Oh, stop that, Thomas. I can hear your thoughts you know. If you were going there, you would have been taken the second you left the earth. You would barely have had time to get through. You might not even have passed the Portal. Mind you, they too can sometimes get past the Portal. As far as taking souls goes, they don't waste any time. They are impatient to take their own, although they do not get many. Since it now seems you are not one of theirs, you can just sit and wait. Whatever happens now the darkness cannot take you. They might try, but you are protected. The people who lost you will find you."

Thomas sniffed crossly, then squeezed back in under the fallen tree and curled up. He was going to ignore this voice thing. He lay there but did not sleep as he hoped, yet at the same time felt a small sense of ease and was less frightened. He was not going to that place. Now the only thing to do was wait until whoever it was came for him. He knew his life had not been the best and he could have been a nicer person but maybe, just maybe, they would not be too hard on him, whoever *they* were. Thomas wrapped both his arms as tightly as he could around his cold chest and sides. He wished they would hurry up. Imagine being cold forever. Imagine lying under this log forever. Imagine anything you like Thomas, he told himself. You have done a lot of things you should not have done and at this moment in time, or whatever it is called, you have no choice at all. None.

The little voice spoke again, "That's it Thomas, make a start, because when you are found you will have a lot of making up to do. There is a mountain of work. You think you could have been a nicer person, do you? Oh ho…, you could. I will leave you now and see if I can find your people and direct them to you."

There was a deep silence all around now. Then the wind suddenly blew hard as if trying to blow him out of his resting place. He heard whispered voices and his heart jumped. Was it them, the people who were to find him? He looked up and could see only darkness, but there was a smell. Faint. Unpleasant. It was a smell of musky dampness and decay. Something rotten. The smell became stronger. A stench. The wind blew it in and around him and he almost retched.

Something was moving out there, something frightening. Thomas sensed the evil, could almost touch it. He could not hear footsteps, but there was an odd rustling as of something was brushing past leaves. He stared out from under the tree, eyes watering from trying to penetrate the darkness of the night. Then a shadow moved, shimmered in the darkness and took shape. What was odd was that it was so dark and yet there was this odd lightness around the edges. A shape like that of a big man stood on the road, and just behind was a smaller shape. A woman? Something told him: "Stay here. Do not go to them." He moved in further, frightened. This was something bad, very bad. He swallowed painfully.

The shape of the big dark shadow turned its head swiftly in his direction, then so did the smaller. They sniffed like an animal, as if scenting him, moving stealthily and then he could see them properly. To his horror they were without faces. The body shape was there, thin and not clothed and yet, not naked. Shapes, clothed in darkness. No faces. Just a dark space where it should be.

The female shape moved closer, "It is here. I smell it." Her voice was harsh.

The male laughed. Not a laugh really. A snigger. "Is it ours?" the female asked, "Let us take it. It could be ours. Can we take it?"

"It is not, but we could always try to take it," said the male voice of the big dark shadow and laughed.

The small female shrieked with laughter and running forward seemed to reach for Thomas. He screamed, "No." curled up and put his arms around his head. They reached toward him and he pushed himself as far in as he could. Yet they did not touch him. The male laughed and the female screamed and hissed at him, then suddenly as if they had tired of a game, they were gone and he could hear their howls of laughter fading into the distance.

He lay trembling for what seemed like hours, then at last a light showed in the sky and a cold grey misty dawn showed itself. He stood up and looked around feeling wretched. Then he saw them, two tall slender men dressed in white, coming towards him smiling, pale faces glowing. "Thomas, we have found you," one said.

He stared at the men fearfully, "Do you belong to them? The ones with no faces and the awful smell." he asked. "Ah. You have seen them. The Scavengers. No. We are Gatherers; we will take care of you now. You are safe. They could not take you. We are sorry it took so long." Both smiled kindly. The frightened man looked into their serene pale faces and the calm eyes and knew he could trust them. "Where are you taking me?" Thomas shook, he was freezing with cold and the terror of the night "Do not fear Thomas." said the first, "No harm will befall you. We have told you; you are safe."

"We take you to The Gathering Place," said the second.

"What is The Gathering Place?" even his voice shook.

"It is a place." said the first, "where you will rest and be safe while you work through how you have lived your life."

"You will also have to undo some things that should not have been done," said the second.

He stared at them, "How will I know what to undo and how will I work through my life. I can't remember most of it." His teeth chattered with cold.

One of the men spoke gently: "It is not for us to tell you. You will know in time. We are simply the gatherers of souls. We search and find those who have left the earth and who may be lost. Some find their own way. You Thomas have been lost and are now found. Come. There will be another to tell you what must be done."

They smiled at him and he felt warmth as they placed protective arms on his shoulders, leading him away from the fallen tree towards a gateway he had never noticed in all his years of driving along this road. It was a big heavy wooden gate banded with copper. He stared at it as one of the men put a finger to it and pushed it open. Brilliant light poured out.

****

Chapter 4

Thomas stood in the light and stared in through the gateway, and felt the warmth pour on to his poor cold body. The two men guided him in gently and he passed through the gateway. From behind a shrub a small golden head appeared. A child? "Hallo," the little creature said smiling. then said to someone he could not see, "They are here. They have found him." The child lifted a hand gave a little wave, lifted a small set of pan pipes to its lips and began to play, then it disappeared but the music continued.

They walked a short distance along a blue and gold mosaic pathway edged with flowers and came suddenly out into the open. The heat was glorious after the numbing cold of his time between the arches of the Portal. Thomas head swivelled as he tried to see everything at once. It looked like a beautiful garden, yet was so big he could not see where it ended. It was vast. He felt warm, safe and peaceful, without anger or fear for the first time since he died. Looking across the vastness of this place, Thomas could not take it all in and for the life of him could think of nothing but the Land of Oz, in the film of that name. The colours were so bright, so sharp, the pathway so beautiful. It was wonderful to be away from that cold and frightening road and the dark shapes.

The men took him further inside and led the way to a small row of seats, in a little arbour surrounded by flowering shrubs, where a small waterfall poured crystal clear water into a little rock pool. "Please sit, Thomas, this is a waiting room." It was like no waiting room he'd ever seen, "We go to find your guide."

He felt apprehensive again, "Do not fear Thomas. Your angel guide will soon appear."

Angel guide? As his daughter Kate would say, Yeah, right. Oh well, he would sit here and wait and see. He sat, loving the warmth, staring around trying to see everything. There seemed to be flowers everywhere, of the kind he had never seen before, and the colours were astonishing. Then there was the scent. What was it? So beautiful. It was difficult to pin any one scent down.

Someone, a long time ago, Thomas could not remember who but it might have been his grandmother, who said that sometimes a gift was left in place of a deeply loved person who was truly good. The gift was the scent of flowers she said. He could smell violets now. There had been a huge patch of them at the bottom of her garden on a piece of moist ground, and it brought her back.

Outside the little garden he could see another waterfall of crystal-clear water which poured from a rock, falling into a large pool. There were trees in the distance, dotted here and there in groups. He wondered about food. Many days had passed but, he'd had no desire for food or drink, nor had he slept. Perhaps there was no need for any of it when you were dead.

Thomas sat and looked out over the vast plain. It went on and on until all the colours blended together into a single colour, a deep purple line on a distant horizon. Little wooden houses were dotted around in small groups all over the place. Some were beneath the trees. They were dazzling white with a veranda and a picket fence surrounding tiny green lawns. What exactly was this place? Little houses and gardens, like a miniature town, but spread out across the plain, they too fading into the distance. He turned and looked off towards another path, then caught his breath.

He stared in astonishment at a tall pale shape that shimmered and moved slowly towards the two men who had found him. They pointed towards Thomas and apparition turned and looked towards him and it was if electricity poured through him. Something he never thought he would ever see in reality seemed to float toward him. It was so incredibly beautiful Thomas felt tears prickling his eyes… It had huge silver blue eyes, and pale translucent skin. Long silver hair flowed down over its shoulders. It wore a long robe which seemed to flash white, silver and pale blue as it moved, but incredibly, it had wings. Wings? Great white feathered wings pointing upwards, moving gently.

Then the apparition floated rather than walked towards him and smiled at him. The huge glowing eyes were filled with gentleness and the smile was of infinite beauty which filled his mind and he felt as if he had been opened out like a flower to receive all this wonder. An angel? What else could it be? Thomas asked himself. It reached a long slender hand toward him and as the slender fingers gently touched his, he could feel the most amazing sensation of intense love and caring and wonder. Surely, he was dreaming. That was it. This was all a dream. Any minute now he'd wake and see Valerie's shape beneath the duvet in the next bed. Thomas tried to pinch himself to make himself wake up, but could not even feel the pinch. This was no dream. This was an angel. Then to his surprise he saw another smaller shape behind the first. It looked like a girl. Were there girl angels? This one too was incredibly beautiful with long dark curling hair and glowing amber eyes, but that one kept its distance. The two men in white suits waved a hand to Thomas, "You are safely gathered in now," they assured him as they walked away.

Thomas looked at the angel. He wondered how he would speak to it, what to say, indeed what to call it. Was it a him? He only knew *of* angels, not about them, was vaguely aware they were supposed to be beings of some kind who had a halo around their head, and wore white. There was a memory of angels with names, of one who was called Gabriel who announced things and one called Michael. Then there was one who went bad. He remembered that one was supposed to be the greatest angel of all, but who was put out of heaven and sent to the other place. Memories from his long distant childhood teachings came to him.

He watched now as the angel came closer. The face, the eyes, so beautiful seemed to glow as if a light shone behind. He thought that they all looked the same when you saw them in pictures, peaceful and good, without expression, though. But this one sort of shimmered with light, seemed to be made of light. "Thomas you are welcome," smiled the angel, the voice soft, gentle and full of kindness.

Should he shake hands?

The Angel spoke again, "I Thomas, am called Cadamiel. Your angel. You will see many of us here as we await souls to direct on their way and this, the dimension in which you find yourself is called The Gathering Place. You have passed through the Portal into this. You might call it a place. It is not. It is a state. Your journey of life as you saw it, is over. You are now on another journey. This is a journey to true life and eternal love. You call it Heaven. Mankind of differing faiths call it by different names, but for you it is heaven. Some of these journeys are short, some do not have a journey, but some are long, as yours will be. Yet, time here has little meaning. You will find as you go through this state that it appears not to exist, in the same sense of your earthly time. But you will see as you go through this dimension."

The angel moved closer. It did not sit but seemed to hover just above the ground. He stared at it. Did he say it was a he? Were angels' men? Did they have a gender? Thomas did not know. He looked at the hands, long and slender, almost translucent. He'd caught a glimpse of the one who looked like a girl. It still hovered near the end of the pathway. Thoughts and memories from the distant past flitted into his mind. "An angel," said a far-off voice of memory, "is a spirit created by God and is all Spirit. They were there when God laid down the earth's foundations and before the creation of mankind."

There had been arguments about that. Someone a long time ago, trying to sound intellectual, said they helped sustain the cosmos. They hardly knew what the cosmos was, much less what it meant. Robert Verne, who thought he knew everything, had dismissed the idea, "That's a load of rubbish," he had sneered. Robert sneered a lot. He did it when there was something he did not understand. They all did. "Please sit Thomas," the angel said, "and we will speak of what is required of you. Your journey may be difficult but you can make it less so, by working through your past life. The choice is yours; always remember that you have free choice. It is expected of you that this free choice is well used."

Cadamiel beckoned to the second angel who came forward a few steps, holding a book. It was a strange looking book. Mouldy, blackened as if by flame, Thomas thought. In width it looked like an ordinary book, but in length it was almost three times as long, and it was covered in dirty brown filigree work, "This book is your Book of Life," Cadamiel said, "It will be placed on the table in your shelter and it is your duty to return it to its former glory; as it was given you at birth."

Thomas stared at the odd-looking book, puzzled. "I see you are puzzled," Cadamiel said, "Do not worry, have patience, all will be revealed with time. Now, you have much to do. The choice of how you do it lies with you. Please understand that what I say to you I say without criticism or judgement. That will be for the ultimate judge. If I say you have done something that is not right accept it as well meant and that I simply tell you that as fact. It is, as it is. When I was created, within me was placed only love and obedience to the will of my Master and I was then given to the caring of mankind. Do you understand what I tell you?"

Thomas nodded but was not at all sure that he did and was beginning to feel about seven years old. "Then we begin," Cadamiel said, "First, let me say I do not make the rules. I deliver to you the word of my Master. So, accept what I say without rancour. The book of your life is writ large Thomas and there is much there that is written with a poor hand, a cold uncaring hand. You created anger and discord where it was not necessary. You also created fear and a punishing harshness. Kindness, gentleness and love became alien to you."

Thomas bit his lip. This was like being back at school and he did not like the feeling. The angel nodded and there was a hint of a smile, as if it knew his thoughts. He pulled himself together. "You made too, a judge of yourself over others, indeed, over many. You had no right to that judgement, Thomas. As you passed the Portal those who searched in the books of life for you, found little to commend you. They searched hard, because losing a soul is a deeply saddening thing here. When all life has passed from your body, your spirit remains and we want you here with us."

Thomas was growing cynical again. Do you now? Well I don't want to be here. I want to be back at home, he thought. The angel looked at him. It seemed to know his thoughts. "I would ask only that you listen, Thomas. Your book is not good and yet, something within took you from the downward spiral and lifted you high enough that we were able to keep and hold you here. They who scavenge for souls wanted to take you. We are the Gatherers; we cleanse and purify. The Scavengers, they harvest swiftly and destroy. You did enough, Thomas for us to hold you. We are glad, but, you do not seem happy with this?"

Thomas bent his head feeling sudden shame for his cynical thoughts and his life filled with anger.

Cadamiel said, "Come, I will take you to the place reserved for you here. The angel, Fariel, too will watch over you." The smaller angel smiled came closer, "You may earn some privileges, small ones, but not yet. When your time here is done, the Great Angels will come for you, but that will not yet happen. Though, when you see them, you will know why they are called Great Angels."

The angel Fariel still held the strange book. It said in a gentle voice, "There is also danger too, here in the gathering place. We will protect you Thomas, at all times, but you also have a part to play in this. Outside of here you met two who would have you. Be aware, they sometimes gain entry. There are many more, not always recognisable for what they are. They cannot take you if you do not reach out to them. You are ours. You have not been easy to hold and keep, but if it is necessary, we will do battle for you, 'The great amber eyes' held his, 'We may yet have to do so.'"

Thomas bit his lip. Had he been so bad that it was hard for them to hold on to him? He did not think so, felt a touch mutinous. Blooming angels, thought they knew it all. The angel, Cadamiel, inclined its beautiful silver head and smiled as it heard the thoughts of the man. This soul would soon discover they did know it all, as had many before. It was to be expected, but then as it was said upon the earth: Rome had not been built in a day. Thomas Beck would have to be protected from himself, as much as from any other, and there were many of these others in many guises.

Thomas walked with Cadamiel and Fariel across the vast plain. He could now see various people being led by angels, some too by Gatherers, all heading in the same direction. He looked all around, then looked upwards over the distant purple line. Something flashed in the air above. He glanced up. There was something up there. Something misty, he squinted. Huge gates, which gleamed and glittered with great flames on either side, but it was all blurred. What was that up there on its own in the air? He thought, what a place this is.

The angel Fariel spoke, "That which you seek to see now in the far distance and beyond the great gulf, you will not yet see properly. It is to that place behind the Great Gates you will be taken when it is time to pass onward into life. It is there each soul will go when they have removed all obstacles. Then the veil beyond the great gulf will lift for you. That is your goal. Remember too, it will take time to reach your goal and must be all your own work. Nobody can do this but you." Cadamiel spoke then, "We will leave you now to find your way to your goal." Then, both the angels shimmered and were gone.

Thomas stood and looked around, puzzled. What was happening here? The plain was gone. Nothing. There was nothing, just the emptiness of space all around and the square of rich green grass on which he stood. Everything else was gone. It was as if he stood on a carpet in outer space. He turned to call for help. Nothing. He sat on the patch of grass wondering what should he do now. After a while he got up and began to walk around trying to find a way to somewhere, anywhere. Yet he could not see a door or gate. Just the square of green grass. All around there was nothing, just sky above below and beneath and all around and the place up there. He watched it. It was still there, shimmering behind a mist. Yet no matter how he sat or lay, or stood, the great gates could still be seen, still behind the mist so he could not see it clearly. That was the place he had to get to. That was his goal. He had to work to get there. That was it.

What was it the angel said? "That is your goal, Thomas."

He took a deep sighing breath. This was worse than being alive. At least there were some roads and paths and maps there. He could do with a map. He stood and stared upwards to that place in the distance and shook his head. "My goal," he said, "but how do I get there. That is my goal and…" he stopped because as soon as he said that everything changed.

He was no longer on a patch of bare green grass, but standing before the veranda of one of the little houses he'd seen earlier. A small rocking chair rocked gently back and forward as if inviting him to sit.

****

Chapter 5

"Well now, you've done it at long last and isn't it time you found yer way in here." said a distinctly Irish voice, "You've been lying down and standing up and rolling around the grass for hours. I thought you were never going to get the hang of it at all. I was nearly dizzy from watching yer contortions and machinations. Still, you made it in the end. Good man yourself."

Thomas turned and saw a small man sitting in a white wooden rocking chair, on the veranda of another little house. He stared. The man was smoking a pipe, which he took from his mouth, waved it at Thomas, grinned broadly and said, "Hello there."

He had reddish grey hair, twinkling blue eyes and a small neat nose. Nodding a greeting to Thomas, he returned the pipe to his mouth then clenched it firmly between his teeth. Thomas scowled and sat in the rocking chair determined to ignore the small man. It had taken him ages to get here. He had not known what he had to do. Nobody said. Nobody bothered, neither had this grinning little jackass.

Thomas snapped, "You could have told me what to do and so could those angels but did any of you bother?"

"No, they do a disappearing act and you sit there sniggering to yourself."

"Oh dear me." the small man said, "Well, as my granddaughter Laura would say, you seem to have had a sense of humour bypass and me name's Mike Kelly, by the way. Now tell me, did you not get a clue when them angels of yours was going on about your goal? That was it. Still, I suppose you haven't got yer mind in gear yet, as regards this place. I mean, you got yerself in this pickle. Nobody else at all. You have to get yerself sorted out, not them. It's your problem. Right? There's no help, yer on yer own now, but I suppose there is the odd bit of advice available."

Thomas turned away scowling and angry and sat in his own rocking chair, refusing to acknowledge Mike or introduce himself. "Look," said the little man eventually, "Just take a bit of advice from someone who has been here a very long time. Get yer nose down out of the air. That attitude will get you nowhere, there's no point in getting all aerated up here, nobody here pays any attention to all that stuff. Don't take offence. We are all in the same boat, all of us here for the same reason. What makes you so special that you have to have the guided tour before you decide to stay?" He raised bright red eyebrows at Thomas, who sniffed and pursed his lips.

The little man did not take offence and went on: "Of course, they do have helpers for them that have no knowledge of this place or choose to block it out for some reason best known to themselves. The likes of you and me who knows it's here are lucky, we are sometimes allowed to be helpers and guide them in, later on of course. Oh, and a word to the wise, remember this my bad-tempered friend. We are all equal here. The fella's with the wings is the ones in charge. Not you or me. We are here to listen and learn and do."

He puffed happily on his pipe. Thomas still scowling, hunched his shoulders and sat, sulking in his chair said nothing, "In this place," said the little man, "everything has to be worked at you see. Now you know the way in to your little patch is just by realising you have a goal and you have to achieve it. You will not be able to tell anyone else either, because, they will not notice you until they realise what it is they must do. You have to work at things here. So, don't go getting your underpants in a twist over nothing."

He puffed away on his pipe sending up great clouds of smoke. Thomas ignored him, but the little man was having none of that. "So, now you know my name is Mike," he said, "and before you ask, which you will, I'll give you a potted history of me life. Lived my childhood and teenage years in Ireland. Got thrown out by my always angry Father when I was seventeen. I had a mother too but she never dared open her mouth, otherwise she got a walloping from the old fella. When she passed on, she went straight on I believe, never set a foot on the green grass here. A saint of a woman." He smiled beatifically and puffed again on his pipe which was beginning to annoy Thomas. "Well anyway, I nearly starved to death but a nice lady in Dublin found me, gave me work and food and a nice home. When I was twenty-one, she died. Left me a bit of money and I went to live in London. I married a lovely English lady and had a daughter. I was not as good as I should have been to the pair but they still loved me. God bless them." He sighed, "Anyway, I behaved myself fairly well and when the daughter got married there was only me and herself. We were planning to go and live by the seaside in Cornwall. Even took a trip to look at a place. It was nice too."

He sighed even more deeply, took the pipe from his mouth and for a terrible moment, Thomas thought the little man was going to spit. He did not, but inserted the pipe between his teeth for another puff. Thomas clenched his fists and his jaw. "Didn't I make a terrible mistake though," Mike Kelly looked sad, "I hadn't had a drink for years and then I fell off the wagon. Hit the ground with a terrible bang, so to speak. Got drunk and fell under a train when I was sixty-three. So here I am. I'll never get the pension I worked hard for to keep me and herself, but I have to say I did leave her a nice big insurance and now I'm trying to find me way in through the big gates." There was a pause, "You know what? I was always afraid of dying but it was terrible easy when the time came for me to go. It was over in a second. Now isn't that a funny thing, although I suppose you know that now."

Thomas looked at him through clouds of smoke and gave up. He listened to the little man. "I have to say something to you though," said the little man, "It's not easy peasy here. To find your way through them gates is hard. You don't see them, but there's big fella's with huge wings hanging around with the book, you know. The big Book of Life thing. They see everything you do and they never miss a trick." Mick pointed the stem of his pipe into the distance towards the huge gates, "If you want to get in there you have to work. Some stay here a long time and I'm afraid I am one of them. I was foolish but that's another story. Anyway I'm tired of drifting around this place. I want to be on my way, so I am working towards that as fast as I can."

Thomas Beck stared at the small Irishman. The man was sitting back in his chair and smoking contentedly. He thought, this man is smoking a pipe. Thomas sat up quickly. Where did he get a pipe if he is dead? He asked, "Where or how do you get a pipe and tobacco here?"

Mike took the pipe from his mouth and stared at in wonderingly, "Well now, that's the oddest thing. I don't know, but I always loved a good pipe of tobacco. I had it when I fell under the train. I had it when I come through the Portal. It's always alight and always full to the brim. Maybe it's a privilege. It could be that somebody up there likes me. Yes, it could be that." He smiled and got up easily from his chair, "I better be off. There's a long road ahead of me and its littered with rocks. To tell the truth some of them are very heavy to shift. Bye, now. I'm sure I will see you again soon." He waved a hand and ambled off into the distance.

Thomas watched the little man until he disappeared, he smiled ruefully, then sat on the little white rocking chair and stared around. He was here now and might as well get used to it. There was no going back, or was there? The little man's small garden in front of the building was filled with flowers, some of them really exotic. They seemed to grow and open as he watched. A faint perfume wafted up from them. He seemed to breathe in peace with their scent. His own garden was bare. It was surrounded by a white picket fence and there was a gate leading out to the plain beyond. He could see figures walking along guided to the angels by men in white suits. He could see two with a very shabby looking young woman, who seemed to be chattering happily and pointing at everything.

He decided to take a walk and look around before he started doing whatever it was, he had to do, so he walked down the short path and tried to open the gate. It would not open. Thomas tried to clamber over but there seemed to be a barrier of some kind. Another bloody barrier. He kicked at the gate feeling angry and frustrated. "Oh man who is so swift to anger I wouldn't do that if I were you," said a small voice.

Thomas turned so swiftly he almost fell. There was no sign of anybody. Then he realised what it was, "Oh, it's you again." he snapped crossly, "What do you want?"

"Dear me, I must be a very un-interesting conscience. I am your small voice Thomas, your conscience. Remember me. You cannot get rid of me so easily," It gave a chuckling laugh "Where did you get to?" Thomas asked.

"I told you. I went to find the Gatherers and I sent them to you. You know Thomas, you forget your friends so quickly. Thankfully we do not all have your memory lapses."

Thomas snorted and turned to go back to sit down, but stopped and thought for a minute, then asked quietly and with humility: "So what do I do now?"

"You know what you have to do. You have been told." said the voice, "You also know what it is you are going to do. You are going to start your usual carry on. You will shout and bully and try to make life as difficult as possible for everybody around you as you did when you lived. But my friend, bear this in mind. You are no longer alive. You are in the world of the spirit. You cannot bully or frighten anybody here. Each person who arrives here is equal under heaven.

Do you understand that? Your rudeness and unpleasantness on the earth will not work here."

Thomas looked shocked, "I did not do that."

There was a peal of mocking laughter from the little voice, "Oh really? So, you did not frighten anybody, were not vain, did not make excuses for your behaviour?" the voice mocked, "Think again, and for once in your miserable existence, listen. In this place humility is the best policy. You are not a body. You are a spirit, a soul. You have nothing. You own nothing. You have no control over any other soul. Another thing, nobody here is going to run around smoothing your ruffled feathers, or to keep you calm in case you make life difficult for them. Nobody."

There was silence while Thomas digested this, then the voice pressed home its advantage, "My dear Thomas, nobody here is going to work out your salvation for you. You and you alone must do that, and let me add. You cannot blame anybody here for anything. Everything you did in life; you did from choice. You chose, others complied. This is not Barton Trinity. I am no kindly gentle angel. I am conscience and here I come into my own. If I speak then you listen. Oh, and another thing, watch out for the Great Angels, the Seraphim. Heavens warriors. They take no nonsense. That is something you should not forget, although they will protect you from harm should they need to, they will let you have it in the neck if you start playing up. Besides, I will have to leave you soon. I have to go now to get my instructions. I will be back for a time, although I'm not sure how long they will let me stay with you."

****

Chapter 6

Thomas sat stunned. He had been humiliated by someone or something he could not see. He said aloud, "My wife never spoke to me like…" He stopped, sat back in his chair thinking. She did not speak to him like that even when they were children. Rarely contradicted him, even when he was wrong and he had been wrong, occasionally. She knew better. Thomas remembered how desperately he'd struggled to have her as his wife. They'd had a few good years and then it fell apart. Her fault, all of it. Yet, was it all her fault? The question hung in the air.

Valerie. His wife. His choice. They grew up together. He had loved her more than life and yet he pushed her away. More than pushed. A curl of something akin to shame washed over him. She was afraid of him sometimes. That was obvious after he'd found out what she did. Oh, she hid it well. Small as she was, she had courage. Not so afraid as she grew older though. Stood up for herself in the last couple of years. He knew that. Yet, all those years. Were they a waste, he wondered?

The boys, too. Those small fair-haired twin boys who adored him. Called him Dad until he told them not call him that. He frightened them and stood shocked at the thought. Had he enjoyed their fear of him so much. No. Surely not. "Surely you did, so work that one out, man of straw, man of no substance," muttered his little voice, though he did not hear it, "You are safe here, not that you deserve it. It is you who must bear the shame, not I. I tried. Did you listen?"

Thomas sat and stared out across the plain deep in thought. His little voice had not returned, and he knew it was gone. He saw nothing, heard only in his memory the voice of what he knew now was his conscience. He thought, if only I had listened when I was… when I was what? Young? When I was alive? Too late he had heard the voice. No, it was not too late. That was why he was here. He saw everything like a film inside his head.

Valerie Simmons was always beautiful. She was one of those who grew from childhood to womanhood without going through an awkward phase. An only child, she lived in a large detached house in its own grounds on the outskirts of the village with her mother Amalie Simmons. Amalie's husband was an officer in the navy and she always said she would not have children. They got in the way. Then, as she said, the best laid plans and all that. Of course, that was when she was old and only too glad to have her daughter to lean on. Amalie had thought the pregnancy was just her age, and when she realised otherwise, it was too late to go into the private clinic to get rid of what she called 'the thing'. No Doctor would help her when she was so far on in her pregnancy. She made sure too that everyone knew how angry she was, including her husband. Out of sight and out of mind most of the time, the small girl sometimes wondered who the beautiful woman who lived in her house might be. Someone told her Amalie was her mother.

Valerie's father was twenty years older than her mother, who at the time of her child's birth was forty. There would be no more children. Then Valerie's father died suddenly of a heart attack at sea when the girl was five and Amalie began to spend long periods of time in London with friends. She suddenly married someone else who was surprised to find he had a step child.

Thomas remembered Valerie telling him the house always seemed to echo around her. She never really liked it. It was too big. There were a least five empty bedrooms. Sometimes she was alone in the house at night. The nurse would go out with the housekeeper on their nights off. They did not care if her mother and stepfather were away. They never even put the tip of their noses around the bedroom door to check on the child.

Sometimes there were parties when she used to sit on the bend of the stairs and watch through the bannister rail, but that was before Dada went away forever and Mama began to cry a lot. Then there was a new Dada who shook hands with her if they met. She liked him. He was kind. Then the parties began again and he was not happy and left. She told Thomas all this in the early years. These were different, noisy parties with people who screamed with laughter, got very drunk and locked themselves in the empty rooms. There were odd smells from the cigarettes they smoked and some of the people who came sniffed powder up their noses and rubbed it on their gums. They screamed with laughter and offered it to her. Those people frightened her. Then Mama brought home an Uncle, but then they went away for ages. She was alone again with the staff. What was interesting to Thomas then was that she told her story as if she was still a child.

When he, James and Robert first became aware of her, she was an eight-year-old with long auburn curls and big green eyes. They tried to ignore her but the girl followed them everywhere. She watched from behind bushes or trees as the boys pretended to be Robin Hood or played cowboys and Indians. When they needed someone to tie up for a fight or a kidnap game, they let her in to the group. They were the big boys then, aged thirteen to her eight years.

She was allowed to be Maid Marion. If they got fed up with her, they tied her to a tree and left her. Once they forgot her and left her until dark. Eventually Robert remembered her and ran back to set her free. She had not even been missed. She was soaked to the skin and freezing and was ill for a couple of weeks. The three got a telling off for that and never did it again. James, the red-haired boy got slapped by his permanently grumpy mother and beaten by his father. "I told you girls were rubbish," James was scathing, "They tell tales. Tell-tale tits."

Robert was the one she liked best and he was the tallest, with fair waving hair and big innocent grey eyes, but there was little of the innocent about Robert Verne even then. As Thomas mother said, he knew more than his prayers. James was different, an unhappy boy with spiky red hair and angry green eyes who only wanted to fish in the river and play heroes and villains. "Girls not allowed. Go away," was his cry.

James had no interest in girls. Actually, he had no interest in any girls, ever. He had a sister, Gina, who was the same age as Valerie, and whom he bullied unmercifully. Doris Beck said it was not surprising since that was all the boy ever saw at home, yet he never touched Valerie. His sister Gina was a small nervous girl who always seemed to have bruises. It was odd how clearly, he remembered her She was not easy to be with. A difficult girl, yet he liked her. There was a sadness about her, a loneliness. She had tried to kill herself when she was sixteen, he had found her and helped. He was grown up then and aged twenty-one.

Thomas had given her salt and water to drink and she threw up a huge amount of tablets. Gina drank, had a reputation. She tried again later and he was there for her that time too. Eventually she disappeared from the village and he did not know where she went. She did not come to her mother's funeral, or her brothers when he died in that stupid accident. The father was never seen again.

James had grown from looking like a red-haired boiled lobster, into a good-looking young man, and was gay in a time when it was against the law to be so. He had a friend by then, an older man whom he adored. He was beginning to make a name for himself in films too. He got great reviews for his small part in that last film. Then he had that stupid accident and slipped on an icy patch off the edge of the pavement right under a bus and died instantly.

Robert too had grown to be even more handsome and Valerie loved him from the start. Thomas had never been other than he was as a child. Deep brown eyes and thick dark hair, fairly tall and slim with everything about him neat, even elegant. Yet it was Robert the girls turned to look at, but he did not appear interested. Of Valerie, he always said in his cool calculating way, "It is a well-known fact Valerie's mother is awfully rich and there is nobody else in the family. I intend to marry her when she is old enough, but of course, I shall wait until she inherits. No point in marrying her first. They might lose everything. It happens you know. I will wait until the old people are gone, when I shall propose and she will accept. of course."

James who had been alive then, looked scathingly at Robert and snorted. All he said was, "stupid git." Thomas too thought Robert was hard and calculating but said nothing.

Then suddenly, there was somebody else in the picture. There was her mother's new husband. Robert did not think of that. She had married for a third time to a very much younger man, Valerie was sent away to school. She knew she was in the way. In a sense it was a relief. Her new stepfather made her uneasy. He looked at her in such an odd way out of the corner of his eye. It made the girl uncomfortable. She was glad to be leaving.

The boys were by then young men and remembered her in passing, although Robert mentioned her once or twice, saying he was still waiting to marry the heiress, his nickname for Valerie. Thomas missed her, but there were other girls. James could scarcely remember what she looked like. He had no use for females apart from his little dog Susie. Then he was killed so tragically. After that Robert began to go away a lot. His grandmother left him a cottage in Barton Trinity and he had a small flat in London. He met another heiress a year later. This one was a lot older and bought him a sports car and money too, and gold jewellery. Doris Beck, Thomas mother called him a gigolo.

In the end, Thomas and Robert went their separate ways and were not to meet for a few years, and James was dead. Thomas grieved for his friend. Robert seemed not to care very much and went his own way after the funeral. Gina did not come back then. They did not see her again.

Thomas was now working for the Ministry of Defence. He remembered the first time he saw Valerie again as a twenty-three-year-old. Her appearance had not changed a great deal. Still the same Valerie. Still beautiful, but now there was something more. She was supremely confident and elegant, and if he was honest, incredibly sexy. Thomas had fallen deeply and passionately in love at first sight and for the first and only time in his life.

He sat now on his veranda, gazing out but seeing nothing, feeling angry and sad at the same time. He had wasted his life on her. He should have divorced her, gone out and found somebody else. Made a life. Yet in all honesty, had he ever thought about it? No. There had just been that simmering rage and it was almost as if he swam round in a pool of it and could not get out.

He thought back to the time when he eventually began to take Valerie out, becoming aware his mother was not particularly happy. "A girl like her is not for you, Thomas," she told him, "She's always had everything given her, not like those of us who had to work for everything we got. She's a rich girl. Rich and spoiled."

"Now now… Doris," his father laughed, "You are supposed to be a good Christian woman."

"I am a good Christian woman and you know it," she'd said, "but she's not for him."

His grandmother Beck, who was alive then and adored her only grandchild told him he had to make up his own mind, but even she was not sure.

Then, a short time later Robert came back to the village on what his father called his forays into the wilderness. Thomas saw him with Valerie in the cinema in town. They sat three rows in front of him heads together, and he watched as Robert put his arm around her shoulders. He saw them leave before the end of the film. Thomas, wallowing in misery could not even remember the name of the film.

A few weeks later Robert was gone and incredibly Valerie was back with him. He said nothing but was wary. A month later Robert came back again and they started going out together again. Thomas went back into his shell and decided to stay there. He would never meet anyone else, only wanted Valerie. She wanted Robert. That was the end really. He avoided them both. She rang a few times but his mother, at his request fielded the calls.

Just after Christmas that year his Grandmother Beck died in her sleep. She was over eighty and had been frail, but it was still unexpected. They were astonished to find she owned a lot of property in the village. The house in which she lived, some cottages on the back road and one of the newly built four-bedroom house on the Avenue, which she left to her grandson Thomas. The Avenue had only ten houses then, it was more of a cul-de-sac. Thomas sold all except the four bedroomed house on the avenue.

She also left a fabulous 1939 Riley saloon car to Thomas Senior and all her jewellery to Doris; the family were not even aware of what she had. The Riley had been covered and locked in the garage. They had no idea where she got it. It was hardly driven and was soon in perfect condition after a bit of work. His father passed it on to Thomas. "What do I need with one of them sports jobs. I'm too old to race around the countryside and I wouldn't dare drive it into town. I would end up wrapped around a telegraph pole. Scares the living daylights out of me, that thing does." he said. That was when Thomas discovered a love of old cars.

The house on the avenue was now empty. Thomas had it painted and decorated and decided to move in alone. He was pretty well settled and in his late twenties then. He moved in the early spring, living quietly and getting on with his life. Thomas was vastly amused to discover he was now very much sought after by the single girls in the village, but was not interested. The years passed. He travelled to town on the train each morning and home in the evening, living quietly and getting on with life. He was over thirty then and all thoughts of marriage or girlfriends were forgotten. He was reasonably content. Yet there was something missing.

It was early Summer when Thomas saw Valerie again. He had settled himself in his seat on the train and was opening up the evening paper when he saw the movement on the platform. A couple seemed to be having an argument just outside. Her back was turned toward Thomas. The woman flounced away toward his carriage. Robert, for it was he, shouted something after the woman. Was that Valerie? No. Thomas delved deeply into his evening paper, but he turned as a woman bounced into the seat beside him breathing heavily. It was Valerie. "Well, well, well," he said grinning, "Look who's here."

She turned, eyes snapping angrily, but when she saw who it was, began to laugh: "Oh Thomas," she said when they stopped laughing, "It is so nice to see you again. Robert has such a terribly cruel tongue. You would never be so unkind."

Then it began all over again. They started going out together and he hid it from his mother, whom Thomas knew would not be happy about it. She would say Valerie only wanted him now because he had a big house and money in the bank. His mother did find out and did go on about it. His father said Thomas should be careful and not take things too quickly. He had always liked the girl but she was a bit flighty: "Well, if you love her, why not, but wait a bit. Make her chase you, not the other way around. She might appreciate you a bit more if she has to work for you."

"Don't encourage him," his mother snapped.

Thomas thought about it for all of five minutes, but it was not his nature. He still loved her and wanted to marry her. She still took off at weekends. Then was gone again for three months. He felt desolate. Suddenly she was back and coming to the house to see him, seemed to want to be seen out with him. One more try, Thomas thought. If she said no, then it was forever, he would not let her back into his life. He asked her to marry him.

Valerie stared at Thomas for a few moments, turned and looked out of the window, then she turned to face him holding her hands out in front, as if to keep him at a distance and asked, "Are you sure this is what you want? I mean, are you absolutely certain? You see, you have to be certain. There are things you need to know. You have to know. It's important. I want to tell you certain things before you decide."

Thomas did not care about anything else except that he felt now Valerie was close to saying yes to his proposal. He heard no warning in her voice. Nothing. There was nothing else except the certainty she would marry him. "Please," she said, "I want you to think about this. You need to think about it. Take a couple of weeks, more if you wish. I am going to go away for a couple of weeks. Think it over carefully. There are things you should know."

Thomas would not allow her to speak, "There is nothing you have to tell me, nothing I want to hear. We will start from the moment you say yes. I know I want to marry you. I do not need time to think about it. It has only ever been you. Please Valerie. I love you so much. I love you enough for both of us if that's what you're worried about. Just marry me."

She sighed, but looked away, her green eyes seemed resigned to whatever it was she saw in the future, "You are sure this is what you want Thomas?"

"I'm sure," he said, "I have never been more certain of anything in my life."

She looked at him for what seemed a very long time. "Then I will marry you." she said.

Thomas Beck sat on his veranda and stared bleakly out towards the colours of eternity, towards the great gate behind the mist. The decision had been his. She wanted to tell him, had tried to tell him but he would not allow it. The only thing that mattered was that he had her for the rest of his life and that she was safely married to him. Robert was out of the picture, or so he'd thought.

Would it have been better if he listened to what she wanted to tell him. He was not sure. Would he still have wanted to marry her? Yes, he would. Nothing could have changed that. He might have been hurt but he'd have got over it in time. One thing was certain, he would not be here in this place working out his life if he had. One thought. Why, had she stayed and put up with everything he threw at her? For that matter, why had he? He had no answer to the question.

Thomas knew his mother was not a happy woman in those days. She said it many times. They were not suited. The girl came from a different world, a spoiled young woman who always had everything she wanted. That Robert she told him; he was always hanging around the village these days. He was trouble too. "You and Valerie would be better off without him here," she said Thomas was not aware then of what his mother knew. She discovered he was still around Great Barton and Valerie was meeting him, it was too late, and days away from the wedding. Doris kept it all to herself. She could not bear to burst her son's bubble of happiness. People had made marriages on a lot less than that. She could only hope, and men were such fools when it came to love. She hoped he would not regret it. She bore the guilt of not speaking out for many years. It was Cassie Chasen, the odd daughter of his mother's friend who told him after Doris died. Cassie and he sometimes confided in each other. She was his only real friend. So honest and open.

His mother's friend Rebecca Chasen and her daughter, Cassie, often came to tea in Te Olde Tea Shoppe with Doris. Rebecca did not like Robert, who had invited Cassie to a dance in the Town hall in Great Barton, "On the way back." Rebecca said in a lowered voice, "he tried to interfere with my girl."

Cassie had punched him and he threw her out of the car half a mile from home, "In the dark of the night too and anything could have happened out there on that dark road." Rebecca said angrily.

Doris looked at the girl and realised that was where Robert got the black eye and bruised cheek. Then she looked at the large but very pretty girl and thought,

48

anyone who tackled Cassie would make a big mistake. Yes, anything could have happened, but to Robert. "That Robert goes to Valerie's place nights too." Cassie muttered through a cream cake. "You sure?" Doris asked. "It's that car he drives. It roars. The engine noise is distinctive. Oh, its him all right."

Doris nodded, but did not comment. She spoke to her husband when she got home. "Why don't you mention it when she comes around next time," he said, "Ask her if she's seen him lately. See what she says. Then you can decide what you want to say to our Tom. That is if you want to cause trouble. Do you? Besides Cassie could be telling lies. Valerie is a beautiful girl. Cassie is a bit hefty. Could be a touch of jealousy."

She did not want to interfere and he had no intention of getting involved. In the end, neither said anything. It had all come out, of course, in later years, and the couple had the twins by then. Not that Thomas had said a great deal about the business, but he'd become a shadow of his former self. It had all gone so dreadfully wrong.

Doris often wondered if she had spoken out, would it have made a difference. She had asked once again before they married, where Robert was and made a mess of that. It came out badly, almost accusingly, she becoming flustered and embarrassed. Valerie smiled her cool smile and said, yes, she had seen him and they had a few words in passing. Doris, feeling a complete fool had closed her lips and her mind.

In her dying days, when she was barely able to speak, Doris had tried to apologise to her son: "I'm so sorry, so very sorry." she had whispered, holding his fingers, "I should have stopped it."

She had then closed her eyes to the world and concentrated on her journey to eternity. Thomas had not been sure what she was so sorry about then. He realised later when Cassie told him. She had known the truth. He wondered sadly where his mother was now, probably up behind the big gates. She was a truly good woman.

He stood up and looked out across the plain. Nobody walked out there now. It was funny how it seemed to become very quiet at times. Then again, a big crowd would come in all at once and there would be Gatherers and angels all over the place. He did not want to think any more, but could not help it. "Why did I never listen?" he spoke aloud. He shook his head, "Because," he told himself, "You did not want to hear. You would not believe. You locked all love behind a steel door when you eventually discovered what was wrong. If only you had not. Think about it. Love changes things, softens harshness, creates a beauty of its own. It changes sight sound, touch, taste. It can also send common sense out through the door pretty fast. If you had listened, and acted, you'd probably have been a real human being, instead of the iceberg you became. I made such a mess of it all."

****

Chapter 7

Thomas and Valerie married in the Autumn. Any doubts were put to sleep. Life was going to be wonderful, and for a while, everything was perfect. There was only one thing that worried him. She disappeared the weekend before the wedding, had not even bothered to mention it before she went. He could not find her anywhere. She appeared on the Monday morning full of apologies, said it was for a dress fitting. She meant to call him but he had left for the train and had suddenly realised she was way behind and had to dash. Did I really believe that he asked himself? Of course, he did not. He was blinded to everything except that he was marrying the love of his life.

The wedding day dawned mistily but the leaves on the trees were a rich brown and gold and at noon the sun came out and it was a glorious late October day. Thomas senior had gone to shave and dress in the early part of the day. All was well until he tried to get dressed in his best suit which had not been worn since the previous Christmas. "I told you, you had put on weight." Doris snapped. She wanted to get ready and he was in the way, "I said you should go into town and have a new one made. Would you listen? Of course not. Now we have to try and shoe-horn you into this one."

"Oh, for goodness woman be quiet and put in my cuff links. I can't do the damn things."

She sighed, helped him, then left him to, as she said, stew in his own juice. Her voice floated down the stairs, "Knows it all. Both of them know it all. Neither of them ever listens to a word I say. Don't care if he can't fasten his trousers. All his own fault, looks like he's wearing a strait jacket."

Thomas who had come home to see how things were going, left the house and called for Robert who was to be best man. They chatted for a while, then he asked Robert, "Where have you been these past months. I heard you've been abroad."

"No, I have been in London, just been very busy, got to work these days. Got to keep the coffers full."

"Valerie said you'd gone abroad."

Robert had smiled, but looked shifty and had not met his eye, "Got to keep the girls quiet. You know how they chatter to each other, so I tell 'em, I've gone abroad. They can't catch up with me then." he laughed, glanced at his watch, "It's early, let's go to The Inn for a couple of shorts."

Several times Robert seemed to be about to say something, but had not. Thomas thought it might be nerves, though he was not the one getting married.

The village church was filled with masses of chrysanthemums, white and yellow, and purple and white gladiolus. It was filled with the perfume of the flowers. All of the village were invited and were there, parents with children, a couple of infants who slept happily and a coach was waiting outside the church to take them to Wednsebury House for the reception.

The organ thundered into the wedding march. Valerie looked stunning, walking slowly up the aisle on her latest stepfather's arm. Her dress was three-quarter-length white lace over silk with a full skirt. The strappy top was covered by a tiny white lace jacket with a mandarin collar beaded with pearls. Her hair was piled high around a pearl and diamanté coronet and she carried a bouquet of silk lily of the valley and pink roses.

Her bridesmaid was a friend from London, dressed in an identical primrose dress. Robert seemed instantly drawn to her. Amalie's new husband looked young enough to be her grandson, as he happily led his step daughter, a year older than he, up the aisle. "Her mother must love wedding cake. Four times wed." Doris Beck whispered. Cassandra sitting behind with her mother giggled. Thomas senior dug an elbow into his wife's side.

Everything went well and Robert eventually disappeared with the bridesmaid. Doris was relieved to get home she said, to get out of her corsets, but agreed it had been a good day. She was still uneasy, but they were married now and it was their life. Let them get on with it.

Thomas sat on the rocking chair and thought back to the days before Christmas the first year of their marriage. They had been wonderful. They lay together at night before the blazing fire whispering and making love. Valerie was soon pregnant. A honeymoon baby she said. That Christmas day they spent together, loving every moment. Boxing Day was spent partly with his parents and later with her mother and the new husband. Thomas liked Amalie and was concerned for her. The new husband, she had married abroad looked very young, he also seemed very domineering. Valerie's mother must be at least seventy, possibly more. Anton Bailes was easily thirty-five years younger than his wife.

The twin boys were born the first week of June weighing six pounds and six pound three ounces. Full term the Midwife said to Valerie. Valerie smiled contentedly. They were not, she said emphatically. The babies were not due until the third week of July. The midwife's eyebrows hit her hairline but she nodded and smiled. I really will have to keep my mouth shut, she thought. Valerie's mother-in-law Doris smiled but said nothing. These were full term. Anyway, hers not to reason why. "They are premature darling." Valerie told her husband, "The doctor said, I could not have carried them much longer or they would have had to give me a caesarian section."

Thomas happily accepted that. He had two utterly beautiful sons, would not listen to his mother and her mutterings. Thomas adored Valerie and his sons. Life was wonderful and he was also a complete innocent about pregnancy and babies, premature or otherwise.

The years following were happy too. There was one shadow though. Valerie's mother seemed to fall over a lot. There were bruises on her face and some on her arms. Thomas was suspicious. He liked the older lady. Her husband wanted her to move away to London. Life was dull in the country he said. Amalie would not move. In actual fact she was afraid to move to London, insisting they live in the country. After all, he was very handsome and a little too attentive to any of the pretty young girls they met. She had laughed. Thomas stared hard at the husband who would not meet his eye.

They were the best years of my life Thomas thought. Robert came and went occasionally. He was working now in the film industry and often arrived with a bored and vacant looking starlet or model on his arm, who only came to life when the conversation was about them. They drove down from town in his sports car. He never drove anything else. Robert's fair hair was usually blown about and once, when he stepped from the car Thomas was amused to see his hairline receding and there was a sparsely covered spot on the crown of his head. His own hair remained a rich brown and was still as thick as it had been when they were teenagers. Valerie, if it was possible, seemed to grow more beautiful and was as slim and lovely as ever.

Amalie, her mother aged rapidly then and suddenly looked old and frail. Where she had once been an independent woman who would rush abroad at the drop of a hat, she became very dependent on her only child and spent hours every day with Valerie and the twins. She said she could no longer cope with the demands of her husband and left him alone in the house. He went off alone, sometimes, staying away overnight. Thomas and Valerie worried about Amalie.

The day came when Amalie rang soon after arriving home to say most of the antiques in the house were gone as well as all her jewellery. Her husband left a note to say he would not be back, had met somebody else and that she owed him for the time he spent looking after her. Thomas and Valerie took her to live with them and the boys. Amalie was devastated. She said, "I always put them first, the men I married, even before my child. I was so wrong in that."

"How could he be so cruel? I gave him everything."

Thomas insisted she live with them. She would not let them call in the police. That would be too humiliating. In a short time, Amalie became even more frail, In the end, it was all too much for her and they found one morning that she had slipped quietly from life, barely three months after coming to live with them. Amalie looking as if she had just gone to sleep, with her hand beneath her cheek looking peaceful and young again.

It was the twins' birthday that June. Valerie said they should have a little party for them, after all they did not understand that their grandmother had died. They just knew she was not living with them anymore. Valerie told them grandma had gone to live with God because she was very old and needed a lot of help, and since God had lots of helpers it was the sensible place for her to go. She said she was not able to give Grandma all the time she needed because she had her boys to look after and daddy too. The boys nodded in unison and seemed to accept what was said.

A few weeks later Robert came back for the children's birthday. Afterwards Thomas remembered that he had come for every birthday. This time it was just a small party with four other children from the surrounding houses in the Avenue. It was a lovely June day and he could not remember now what it was that made him go to the French windows to watch after the other children had gone home. Maybe it was the shrieks of childish laughter. Robert was laughing too, throwing first Jonathan in the air, then David. Valerie was looking fondly at Robert and the boys. Robert was laughing, head thrown back. He lifted David high in the air and the child threw his head back.

That was when he saw the likeness. The fair curling hair, neat small nose, the pink skin, like Robert as a child, where he was dark and Valerie paler skinned.

He turned to stare at Jonathan. No, it was only his over active-imagination. Robert kissed and hugged the children, then reached for Valerie and hugged her.

Thomas heard him say, "You have done an amazing job with them. You do know how much I love them. Everything I do now is for them. I have invested everything I have for our children's future."

Thomas stood, one foot over the frame of the French windows. He was cold suddenly, could not move. His heart seemed to have slowed down so it barely beat. Then his chest seemed to fill and his heart stop. Only his mind seemed clear sharp and alive, humming with the shock. His thoughts went back to Valerie's words to him before their wedding: "You have to know Thomas."

His heart suddenly exploded into a fast pounding beat. He had not wanted to know, had pushed everything to the back of his mind. He had not slept with her before their wedding and yet the twins were six weeks early. The midwife said they were full term. What had the doctor said. He could not remember. Then there was the way his mother had looked at the infants and then turned to stare at Valerie. All the time he had accepted that they were premature, made his own mind believe the lie and now to discover they really were Roberts's children. There was no doubt. He came to life, stepped into the garden, the boys shouting for him to come and play.

Thomas reached Robert's side. He pointed a finger almost to Robert's nose. "You," he said very softly, dangerously, "You hear me and you hear me well. Leave now and you never come back. Do you understand what I say? Never come back to this house again, you treacherous rotten bastard and you," he turned to his wife, "go inside with your two sons. Your sons, not mine. I will deal with you later."

If he had ever been unsure, had any doubts, they were gone. Her face deathly white, told him it was true. Robert was the father of his twins.

That night for the first time since childhood Thomas cried, bitter scalding tears. He slept in one of the spare bedrooms and woke the next morning with a core of ice in his stomach that had never gone away. He had not spoken to Valerie until the children went to school the following day. "I will not divorce you," he said then, "I will be civil to you, but that is all. I will not be humiliated by you. Do you understand?"

She had nodded, face pale and eyes swollen from crying and lack of sleep and that was how it was. A lifetime of bare civility in public. Privately, of course, it was another matter. Anger ruled.

Thomas sat still on his chair. The pain which used to fill his mind and body every time he saw those children was gone. There was only emptiness. That day so long ago, the most painful day of his life was etched in his memory. He had seen from the look on her face it was true. She had not said a word, made no denial. She had just taken the boys and gone inside on shaking legs, not even looking at Robert. The children, sensing something was wrong, looked bewildered but went quietly with her. It was almost as if they knew they would never be able to laugh and enjoy themselves again while he was there. That was, pretty much how it would be.

He had turned then to Robert then, fists clenched. He wanted to punch and cause pain, even to kill. Robert stood pale and quiet, hands by his side, waiting for the blows that did not come, accepting the consequence.

Thomas had spoken again, in monotone, "You leave now. You never come back to this house. You will never see my wife or my sons again. As far as everybody outside this house is concerned, they are my sons. I will bring them up. I will not be shamed by you, or her. Do you hear?"

Robert, who had turned to leave, stopped and turned back, "No doubt after today's little display all three of them will be made to pay. You always were an unforgiving bastard Thomas, even as a child."

He waited for the punch. It never came. "Out." Thomas snarled, "Out, and if I ever see you again, I will kill you."

Robert had left the village and Thomas never saw him again.

He remembered that day so clearly. It was burned deeply into his brain. Whenever he felt kindly towards her or remembered how much he still loved her he went over it all again, allowing the anger and resentment to fill his mind. Allowing it to poison his thoughts, killing kindness and love. In the end, killing him too, because that was what had happened. The final phase of his anger sending him out in his car. Killing himself.

That was so wrong. Of course, it was. It had all been spite and anger and that had killed him. He had allowed it all to make him so bitter and twisted he could see nothing except how she had wronged him. He had never forgiven her, never wanted to forgive her, because he might become vulnerable again. That could not be allowed to happen. So, he had got in the car to punish her, because he punished her for everything, and made sure she knew why. She could not be allowed to forget. Yet, who had he punished? Himself of course. Oh, it was all such a dreadful mess, a dreadful way to live and it was he who made it so. Then he laughed bitterly. It was an even worse way to die.

He remembered softening toward his wife, a mistake at the time but it brought comfort in the form of his daughter Kate. He had been to an office Christmas party and came home on the last train, a little drunk. Unusual for him. Eight weeks later Valerie said she was pregnant. Kate was born the following October. She was him, with rich brown hair, the same dark eyes, and long legs. He adored her.

Thomas could not be sure, but he always had the feeling his wife took the children to see Robert, especially during the school holiday. Kate was a baby when she began taking them away. He had no proof of course, and he'd be damned if he asked the question. It might look as if it mattered and that would not do. Thomas refused to take them anywhere. If they wanted holidays, it was up to her. She took them away every summer for a month, paying for it herself. They usually came back tanned and healthy looking. She also took them away at Easter too and for a few days after Christmas.

The twins grew to learn not to ask for help with homework, and you certainly did not ask Daddy to play. You just got shouted at. Mummy helped with homework. She mended broken stuff and if you fell and got hurt, he called you stupid or an idiot, but Mummy made it better. He did not like the idea of her taking Kate away. She was Daddy's girl. The boys loved her too but he would not let them near her cot or pram when he was at home. They looked at him warily, that man who always seemed so angry, snapping and shouting and they feared him, never quite knowing why, sometimes asking their mother what they had done. Then they simply avoided him.

The children never spoke to him about their holidays, but then he never asked. It was odd that they never mentioned it, where they went or what they did. That was her doing of course. He did not ask, so why would they say anything. He had lost so much. Valerie had always fiercely protected her children. But she made sure, that beyond all doubt her children knew they were loved by her. She did tell them he loved them too, but it was obvious they did not believe her. Yet she tried. The twins had grown to be surprisingly well-adjusted young men. Kate of course. was safe from his anger. Thomas adored her and she him.

When Kate started school, he had no way of keeping the children apart. Also, he felt she needed protection and he saw with fury her love for the boys she called her brothers. He knew he could not be with her always and the boys and

Kate grew close. Thomas remembered something that had happened one evening after they had come back from an Easter holiday.

He had his suspicions when they were all in the bathroom chattering loudly and cleaning teeth before bed and he thought he heard Kate mention the name Robert. He opened the door and stared at his wife. "What?" she asked. "Did I hear Kate mention that man?"

"What man?"

"Oh nobody." He had stamped down the stairs wincing at his stupidity.

Kate had come down in pyjamas and dressing gown to say goodnight and had given him a nervous smile. Yet again his pride would not allow him to question her. He knew Valerie had taken his daughter somewhere he could not go, would not go. As far as Thomas was concerned his wife had shot her last bolt. He would never, ever forgive her.

Thomas, sitting now on his rocking chair on the veranda knew he had been wrong. So very wrong. The woman he married had not loved him, had tried to tell him about her affair with Robert but he had not allowed her to speak. She had not lied. He gave a wry smile. She had been economical with the truth, yes. Add to that the fact he made sure she did not tell him because he did not want to know and he had the answer. Standing he lifted his arms to the great gates behind the mist, "I just did not want to know," he called, "I did not allow her to tell me. I was the one who was wrong."

"Well now. I am pleased to hear that," said his little voice.

"Oh, you're back again. Where have you been," Thomas snapped.

"On a sabbatical," said the little voice, "I will soon be gone from you. Will you miss me," there was a throaty chuckle.

Thomas snorted There was a long silence. Eventually he broke the silence. "Look, I was wrong not to let her tell me," Thomas repeated, "I did not have a choice because I was afraid of what she would tell me. But I suppose if I had allowed her to say it, I could have made the choice of whether to marry her or not. I could have let her go. Now I cannot forgive"

"Let her go. Let her go." said the little voice tartly, "That does not even come into the equation. You would not have let her go and you know it. You did not let her tell you. There are no ifs, ands, or buts. You made the choice. You made every choice in life all by yourself. Nobody forced you to do any of the things you said or did. You could have wiped it all out in a moment. You chose not to. The two boys had no choice. They could never please you. Is it so surprising they returned

58

home rarely after university? Your thinking is all about yourself as usual, how you feel and what you want. You, you, you. Let it go Thomas. If you want to go forward, let it all go. Forgive and forget, although I fear you have left it a little late. Look around you. Now you *have* to learn."

Thomas looked around. Something was happening. The great gates behind the mist somehow seemed further away than ever. They were slowly melting away. He looked all around. Everything was fading, even the plain. A great silence came down taking away the sounds he associated with the gardens. Although there was the sound of birds and sometimes music in the distance, birds were never seen, nor was there ever a sight of musicians. Suddenly all sound was gone. He was standing on nothing. There was now just emptiness all around. "What's happening?" he asked, alarmed.

Banks of white cloud suddenly began to roll up before him. He could not see or hear. He was enclosed in the whiteness of them. Thomas panicked, tried to fight his way out but could not, then he heard another voice. This voice was deep and matter of fact, "Do not be afraid child. You are enclosed in what you call clouds to make you think with singularity. You have reached a point where you must make a decision, and it is this. You will forgive and forget, or," there was a pause, "you will be sent back to the Portal to remain until you have made a decision. The Portal, in your case, because of your coldness to others, was a fearful and very cold place. It was the death of your body as you left the world. If you are returned to that place it will be even colder and much more fearful. Think, Thomas. You have a choice. There is no threat in this. It is simple. You go forward or you go back. Make the choice."

There was nothing then. No sight, no hearing, no feeling of the warmth of the Gathering Place. Total isolation. It went on and on and still he could not bring himself to make a decision. He wanted to shout that he needed help. He tried to call out the words but no sound came from his lips. He could not speak. Then when he could no longer bear it, he heard sounds. They grew louder. Music. Were they letting him out? The music went away. Nothing. His mind cried bitter tears. Then he decided. I could have stopped it all. I am so sorry. I forgive her. Yet he was not released from his isolation. He was being made to wait.

Thomas stood for a long time supported by the clouds. He felt very tired, then elated as if something had been released from inside his head. Now he felt as if he was going to sleep but surely there was no sleep in this place. It was not necessary here. He did close his eyes feeling he was peacefully drifting. It was a trance like state, yet for how long it went on he did not know, but suddenly he opened his eyes to find himself on the veranda of his little house and to his relief, out of that suffocating whiteness. It was a good feeling.

Thomas stood up and looked around. He felt light as a feather as if, so much weight had been lifted not just from his mind, but his whole body. He looked at the house, he had never been inside, had only ever sat on the veranda. It would be nice to go inside and see what it was like, but then he'd not been here anymore than a matter of days. "Days." queried the little voice, "Is that what you think? Sheesh. A bit longer than that, me thinks."

"Oh you're back," Thomas smiled, "Where have you been?"

"It smiled," the voice muttered, "It is still smiling. It is not snapping at me. Whoop de doo."

"Come on." Thomas said coaxingly, "Where have you been?"

"Oh, all right," the voice said, "I have been out in the great stillness beyond light and time looking around, seeing what is happening, replenishing myself, while you have been wrapped in your own misery."

"Misery?" Thomas was surprised.

"You call it clouds," said the voice, "They do it to make you think."

"Oh. I see." Thomas said, "So, this replenishing thing, how do you replenish yourself?"

"I get away from you," the voice chortled.

"Don't be so smart," Thomas said, then asked, "Why will you not let me see you.?"

The voice made a long humming noise, "Uuuum, well, you would not like what you see, because, you would see yourself as you truly are. In a way, it would be like the picture of Dorian Grey. I can assure you Thomas, you would not like that. I hold too much of your anger and fear. I hold your negativity and that is monstrously heavy. It is a big load. I hold some of your good but that is outweighed by the rest. I tell you truly. I look forward to the day when the load can be taken from me. Though I have to admit you have lightened it a bit lately. Thomas, do you not realise what heavy baggage I carry for you?"

Thomas was silent, digesting this, "Am I then, such a very bad person?" he asked in a small voice.

The voice sighed deeply. Thomas heard the indrawn breath and wondered again about what exactly it was, "You are not truly bad, Thomas. I admit to being sarcastic at times and annoying you, but that is one of your own little tricks. I am part of you, so you should not be surprised. I have told you often that you have done things that are not right, have tried directing you along other roads. Not easy. I have been a lone voice many times and it is sad when I could not re-direct you."

"How do you mean." He knew he was not going to like this. "So cold Thomas. So harsh and cruel and judgemental. You have rarely listened to me. Some listen but do not heed. Some heed but wish they had done something else, something more exciting than my dull safe offering. I know there have been others with so much more anger and a truly hideous evil inside them. Yet Thomas, in all my time serving mankind I have rarely known such anger as yours against one frail human. Your wife. Oh, and your children, they suffered too. Yet, against her you were relentless. You had a terrible need to punish her."

Thomas dropped his head, "I am sorry. So very sorry."

"At least you have said you are sorry. Try a bit harder."

But being Thomas, he could not let it end there. He grinned, then chuckled to himself: "and will an angel come along now and give me a gold star."

"Leave it alone Thomas," sang out his voice, "Leave it alone. Now, I have to leave you to your own devices. I need a break. Goodbye."

"Hey, come back," he called but the voice was silent. He was never sure where the thing was. It might be beside him or it might have gone off somewhere.

****

Chapter 8

He stood and walked to the white gate, leaned on it and looked out towards the great glittering gates behind the mist. He still could not see it clearly, yet there was a brightness and the mist did not seem so thick.

This was a good place, but there was something working inside him now, a need to get out of here and up to that gate. This was the most important thing of all but there were other things he needed to know, to understand. He turned and walked back to the veranda sitting himself on the rocking chair. If you did not ask you did not find out. "Little voice. Conscience. Where are you. Come back," he waited a moment, "Are you still with me?"

"Yeah, fool that I am," said the voice wearily, "I should have left you to your own devices years ago."

Thomas hesitated, then asked, "So, where did you come from? What place? Were you born? Or have you always been here? Tell me please."

The little voice did not answer for a while. Thomas had come to learn that it did not always answer at once. It sometimes seemed to consider, so he waited. When it spoke again it sounded different, gentler, wiser. The words were spoken differently, as if, of a time past. "I am not sure from whence I came Thomas. Nobody ever spoke of it. I simply came to be. I was created and given knowledge. I never asked, I just found myself with a shepherd boy, when he was born some two thousand years ago, to a woman of Bethlehem in Judea. It might be said I was born with him. He was named Jacob. His Father was a shepherd in the hills outside. The boy was born with the power to heal animals and men. He was born with a gift and knowledge. He cared for sheep and goats alone from the time he was eight years old. He had to keep the wolves away, with only his great hound and a big stick to protect them. He was a kind and good boy who spoke little. He loved to play music on a whistle he carved from a reed. It was an interesting time. Bethlehem was crowded with people." The voice faded for a while. Then spoke again. "They slept anywhere they could find room. The nights were chill.

The people had to come to that place to be registered on the orders of Rome. Herod the Great was king then. He was Rome's man. I do not know why they called him great. It may be that he built so much. He re-built the second Temple in Jerusalem. He did bad things too. He had a wife and child but put them aside. It is said he had them killed, to marry his niece, yet he married many times more. So many died in his reign."

The voice was still for a moment. Then, "On one night, I went down from the hills with the boy. It was so strange. It was very cold and clear. It does not snow often there, but there was a dusting of it that night. The hills were lit up and the stars in the sky so bright, it seemed as if it were day and as if the whole world too was alive with something unbearably, unbelievably beautiful. I remember the moon hung low in the sky, like a great lamp. The boy Jacob said he wanted to touch it, and reached a hand towards it. He sat a while gazing into the light. Then said he felt he should go down into the town to see a child he knew of, who was born there. He knew things without being told."

"We left an old man and the dog to guard the animals from the hungry wolves and went down from the hills. I did not know then what we were going to see. The place where the child was born was open to one side and the wind blew cold but it had a roof. The child was wrapped tightly and lay asleep deep in the straw. The child's father stood and watched as we came, he looked a little afraid but smiled. He was not young. The girl who was the baby's mother smiled but said nothing, just watched the child. My boy Jacob gave them fleeces of sheep to warm them and he played his music. He changed that night. He could talk of nothing else but the light around the child. He could see the light. The wonder of this night. I could not see the light, but I felt the wonder."

There was another short silence. Then said, "He knew, you see, that the child was born for greatness and goodness, and for the rise and fall of many. We went back to the hill together. The boy lay and watched the sky. He did not speak for a long time. It was the wonder he felt. In the weeks that followed, some men came with a camel train. Some said they were Kings of other lands but I thought they were priests, and yet they plotted the stars, so I do not think anybody knew who they really were, but they were very wise. They brought with them gifts and first went to pay their respects to Herod. He discovered they had come to find a King. Yet not him. He did not like that. He was afraid. Herod waited a while, then sent them out on their way to find this King. He urged them to return with news of his whereabouts so he too, could go and pay his respects. Later when they did not return to him, in his rage and fear he might be overthrown Herod sent out soldiers to find the child and kill him. The little family were warned to leave for Egypt where they lived until the child was twelve and they returned to Nazareth, to make their home, where Joshua, his foster father taught him to be a carpenter. Joshua died there but his mother Maryam lived on. She was still very young"

Another long silence. It was as if the little voice carefully gathering its thoughts. It seemed as if it did not want to say too much or too little, or perhaps, he thought, it might just want to make things clear.

Thomas asked tentatively, "Did you ever see, you know? Him. The one. You know who I mean. God."

There was a longer pause, then the voice answered, "It is said, none can see the face of God and survive the awe, the power, might and magnificence. I do not know. I have not seen the face of God. Though, how could I see the face of pure spirit? I do not understand it. I am a mere speck in the universe, a nothing, and yet, I have seen things. Great things and terrible things. I have seen some things so very fearful. One of the worst was on a night many years later when it was cold in Rome. Braziers burned over an arena. My shepherd and his wife were taken and brought to a place where they were put in cages with many others. This was because they followed him. The One, the child who was born years before and who was killed, nailed upon a tree. They preached his word you see, his peace and love. My shepherd and the followers were all sent out into an arena filled with sand, with nothing but their courage and prayers as a shield, then the fierce beasts were released and they stalked and killed. The people cheered. There was none who could save anyone that day, not my shepherd or his wife. She died quickly, he soon after, but not before he had seen the lioness leap upon her. As his tears fell, he too died. The Gatherers took all their souls and lifted them high away from all fear and pain. It was strange, but no Scavengers came that night upon the earth."

Again, there was the long silence, then, "Their children escaped to preach the word. They were young men then, and perhaps the cages were not well tied with the leather thongs. They escaped with some others as the cage they were in fell open."

The voice said slowly, "I stood and watched and was afraid because I felt something that night, like a huge presence. Like I know not what. It was a hugeness, a power and greatness which overwhelmed and frightened me and it was so immense I wondered if I too would have my existence taken. I wondered if I would become as nothing once more, as I was before my shepherd. I did not want to be as nothing, to be as emptiness again. Then I saw a great sweep of light cross the skies and a huge arm clothed in white swept a light across that blood-stained place where so many were torn apart and a voice of thunder promised that Rome too would soon be in her death throes. I think I may have seen a tiny part of the Master of all that night. I was so small and of so little importance and that presence so great. I was truly humbled."

Thomas felt as if his throat was filled with pain and tears.

The voice continued, "Then I was taken up too and given to another, a small infant just born in a wattle and daub hut. I was told the boy would be a king. He was for a time. The boy was a king in his seventh year, of a place of little more than a few mud huts and of thin cattle and sheep and a few fields of wheat. His people were small and squat but then he died of something strange. I went on then to many others."

"Do you remember them all?" Thomas wondered.

The voice said; "Oh yes. I remember all of them. Why would I not. They were mine for their time on the earth, I lived within them as I did with you and how could I ever forget you Thomas. I was once given a girl; her name was Jeanne a lovely and innocent girl who's goodness put to shame those around her. They tried her, burned her at a stake. because they feared her foresight and goodness. I am not sure which they feared most, the foresight or her goodness. She was young. Filled with a flame. They doused the flame within, but the flame without they used to destroy her. There were so many. Some lived long. Others lived short lives. I was sent back in time to the last days of Pompeii. That I do not understand. I had been with an infant only a little time. The mountain erupted with such force there was no escape. My infant died with her mother. Then came the deathly silence. It was no more."

"Many with whom I lived worshipped strange objects. I was in a land of green too, where they worshipped a snake god but then a holy man came. He ended all that. I was given a girl they said would be queen of part of that same country. She was called Maebhe. She was of those who were tall and dark and very intelligent. She died young. Poisoned. So many ages. So many centuries," said the voice, "One I can never forget. She practised the black arts. Such was her evil she destroyed herself and those things she brought up, those monstrous things, they terrified me. I was in fear all of those days. I have never known such fear."

This time, the silence was long and when it spoke again, the voice seemed sad. "Now Thomas, I must leave you. I would like to speak more with you, but I have little time left. I will soon be gone from you. I think you will find you may now leave your space. You will also have peace within yourself. You may also help direct souls who find their own way in. It is part of the work here. You know, my friend, you have been very hard work. I hope my next charge is easier Goodbye, Thomas. Try to be good," Thomas heard the voice fade away. "Goodbye," Thomas whispered. He felt surprisingly sad. The voice was his no more.

The voice was gone now. Strangely, he would miss it, but it seemed he was moving on, however, slowly, He opened the white wooden gate and stepped out on to the plain. It was quiet out there. Not one soul walked. It was so tranquil. Nobody sat on their veranda's. Sometimes he could see them there but they seemed to be so deep within their own thoughts he would never disturb anyone. The grass was like a green carpet. Even the scent of the flowers was less. No angel moved; no gatherers dashed about. Thomas stood and allowed all the peace wash over and through him. If this then was the gathering place, what then was heaven?

He was about to walk away when he noticed a figure coming towards him, someone in a white suit. As the man drew nearer Thomas realised it was Mike, but he had not previously worn a white suit. Thomas gestured towards it saying, "All dressed up, Mike and nowhere to go I see."

"The same as yourself." The little man grinned.

Thomas looked down and laughed. "I never noticed. I wonder when this happened?" he said. "They give you the white suit when they think you are ready for it. Of course, some get it straight away. I don't know how they work out these things," Mike told him, "I was told it is the big angel who says you can have it. You know the one I mean." He frowned, "It's the one who fights for the likes of us. You know, the battler for souls. Gods warrior. Look, maybe if I tell you, you might remember the name. There was this artist fella called Perugino who lived, I think it was in Venice, way back. I used to know a bit about art. The lovely woman in Dublin taught me a bit. Anyway, this artist did a picture of him dressed in armour. Can you not remember?"

Thomas did not know what Mike was talking about, and they stood in silence for a moment, but suddenly Mike clapped a hand to his head and shouted, causing Thomas to jump, "Michael, that's him. The Archangel Michael. He looks after the likes of us. I'd say you have done a good bit of work up here and they are happy with what you've done. I think they must be happy with what I did myself. Well, to go back to Michael now, he's the one who goes through your book of life and finds the good you did, because he hates to lose anyone, and I heard it said, he gets you in here even if he has to squeeze you through a keyhole. I hear he comes down with the big angels now and again to escort us up there, of course, that might just be talk," he pointed upwards towards the glittering gates.

Mike went on, "I always used to think it was St Peter who let us in but no, it's the big fella in the armour. I saw him a few times going before a group of the big fella's. He might come for ones like you and me. The hard-won ones. Anyway, I'm off now. I'm going into me little house."

He ambled across the grass towards his little white house. Thomas watched and saw Mike was actually able to open the door. He'd try when he got back from his stroll.

****

Chapter 9

Thomas walked on for a long time, looking around, listening to the sound of bird song and came across a narrow path. He would follow it and see where it led. There was quite a lot of shrubbery here, in every shade of green. There were roses too of every colour from deep purple to palest pink. The scent was wonderful. He plucked a rosebud and tucked it into a tiny buttonhole in the lapel of his suit and walked the path smiling. Then he came to where it ended with a high gate. This one was different, not a bit like the heavy gate through which he had come in.

Thomas stood and looked at the gate. Where could it lead? Could it possibly lead to the outside? There was a high hedge running alongside it. He stood and listened but there was no sound from the other side. It might be a garden. He touched it. It was narrow, made of something that looked like wickerwork and had a big pull ring made of straw. He caught the ring and gave it a gentle tug. Nothing. No movement. Did it lead to the outside? Could he leave now and find the road? But then, would it be the right road? What would happen if he managed to open it and get out? Would they come and drag him back? Others must have found this gate before him. It was not guarded. The thought struck him. Nothing here was. The only place guarded was the great gate away in the distance. So that meant nobody was able to get out. Did they want to? There was a rustling somewhere close by. He looked around quickly, but could see nothing. Did he want to leave?

He had been much more at peace most of the time now in the gathering place. So that meant everybody in here was happy and did not want to leave, did it? And yet. And yet! Something rustled again. That was here, inside. What was it? Then he heard another sound. A voice calling from a distance. There was a small movement as if the gate was being pushed from the other side.

A voice called, "Is there anyone in there. I need to call someone. I had an accident."

Thomas wondered what to do. It was not a situation he had come across, but should he, or could he, open the gate? No. Should he speak? Yes. No. He made up his mind. "I think you have to push the gate," he called, "I have to call somebody," the voice called back, "but I can't get a signal on my mobile."

Thomas grinned, "I bet you can't, you are not exactly in line with a signal here." He chuckled to himself.

The voice sounded young. Then the gate began to open slowly. Thomas could see a black leather clad arm and leg as it was pushed. The opening widened. He was able to see the road now and it was not the one he expected. Cars sped along opposite directions on eight lanes.

A young man in motorcycle leathers came hesitantly through the gateway. His held his helmet in one hand and a mobile phone in the other. His face was pale and large blue eyes gazed around in surprise. Thomas glanced behind him and saw the motor-cycle lying on the grass verge. Then he saw the snow piled up in heaps and the ice shining on the road. That was a puzzle. As far as he could remember it was probably early Summer. He could also see the body of the young man lying face down beneath the bike.

A car pulled on to the hard shoulder with a screech of brakes and two men got out, hurrying towards the scene of the accident, one of them pulling out a mobile phone as he went. They seemed not to notice the open gate then Thomas realised they could not see it. Suddenly the gate began to close of its own accord and stopped just short of shutting completely. The young man he felt, must still have a spark of life left. He thought he'd seen a hand move. His spirit was here but there must still be something left outside the gate. This was probably why it was still ajar. "I came off my bike. My head hurts," the young man said.

Thomas felt a deep sympathy for him. He looked about eighteen. He held out a hand, could at least offer a sign of friendship. The boy might die, his life cut off before he had done or seen anything very much, before he married or had children of his own. Another young life finished almost before it had begun. A waste? Maybe, maybe not, still he could at least be kind to him. Thomas remembered how afraid he had been before the gatherers found him. "My name is Thomas," he said, "You are welcome," but then stopped, feeling the young man might not be staying.

The young man smiled showing a big gap in his front teeth and came towards Thomas, "I'm really pleased to see you. I was getting really scared out there. It's so cold it makes you feel sick, but it is warm in here." he paused, "That's odd.

Why is it warm in this garden, when it is so cold outside?" He glanced outside as the gate opened a little way and drew in a deep breath, "Is that me out there on the ground with those men?"

Thomas nodded, "Yes, it is you."

"Am I dead?"

"I don't think so. I think there is life still in you."

The young man stood uncertainly in the gateway, "What is this place?"

Thomas wondered what to say to him. There must be someone along soon to help the boy. He looked all around and saw an elderly man and woman hurrying along the path. The man wore the white suit and the woman a long white robe. At last, someone to help him. "Liam," the elderly man called, "What are you doing here?"

"Liam darling you shouldn't be here yet," the woman said, "How did you find your way in? I suppose you have been racing that motorbike of yours along the roads."

She was a very pretty old woman with the same large blue eyes and pale skin as Liam. Thomas wondered if they were his parents but no, they were too old. Probably his grandparents. "Gran, Granddad," Liam called, "What are you doing here. I thought you were dead. Is my dad here too?"

"We have passed over, but you should not be here, you must go back," the old man said, "You cannot stay."

Liam seemed to fade a bit. He looked worried, holding out his hands to his grandparents "Am I dead then?" he asked wonderingly and began to fade again, but he was soon back, "I came off my bike. Did I get hurt bad?"

His spirit form faded and returned several times as they watched. "You have to go back. Go back to your mother. It is not your time. You are just like your father, driving too fast. Go live a life my darling, a long and decent life and return to us when it is your time," the woman said.

Two of the Gatherers arrived fussing gently about it not being his time. He must leave. Then a man who looked just like an older version of Liam came hurrying up. "They said you were here son, but you can't stay. I mean, it's lovely to see you, but you have to go back. It's not your time. You got to stop driving at speed son. It will hurt to go back but only for a while. You don't belong here yet. Tell your mum I love her. I love you too."

The young man stepped backwards towards the gate, which opened wide of its own accord.

Thomas could see an ambulance now and two paramedics working on the body of the young man. A police car had arrived. One of the officers seemed to look towards the gate frowning. Thomas thought he might sense something. Liam walked backwards looking at his father and grandparents. "I love you," he said, "I'll tell Mum I've seen you. Goodbye."

Thomas looked towards Liam's father, who smiled and said, "His mother will not believe him you know. She'll say he got a crack on the head."

Then Liam was gone through the gate. The last Thomas saw was the young man waving and then his shape disappeared back into the body on the ground, which moaned and then cried out as if in pain.

A paramedic said, "All right son, we've got you back now. Stay with us. What's your name? Talk to me."

The body on the ground mumbled something.

The paramedic spoke soothingly, "OK. You're going to be fine. It hurts now but we're going to give you gas and air to help you breathe and something for the pain, then get you to hospital."

The gate began slowly to close and gradually faded away.

Thomas turned to look at the Gatherers who smiled and walked away. The man who was Liam's father and his grandparents smiled at Thomas. They too walked off.

He wanted to call out to them to ask how they knew the young man had come here but realised it did not matter. It was his job to be there when the boy came through. If he was to go back then it simply had to be. There was no need of explanation. Thomas smiled wryly. Nobody was going to explain anyway. He was learning that in this place explanations were not always given, nor thanks.

Thomas looked thoughtfully to where the gate had been. The world was so close to this gathering place. Could a soul go back to the earth, one who was truly dead? He heard of ghosts when he was alive but as far as he knew had never seen anything remotely ghostly. Although often when he was a child sleeping in the back bedroom of his parents' house had felt there was someone else in his room in the dark of the night. As he grew older Thomas forgot all about it and in teenage would not have woken if the house came tumbling down around him. As his mother used to say, when the angel Gabriel blew its trumpet on the last day, he would sleep through it.

Thomas walked the pathways enjoying the sights and sounds. He could hear a dog barking and birds singing but they were never seen. He wondered; would it be possible for him to go back?

Maybe he could, just to see if everything was all right. The next time he saw Mike he would ask him if he was allowed to return, maybe as a privilege or something. If he had done well up here. Thomas thought of himself as being up somewhere. He could see the great gates and they were above this place. You had to look upwards to see them. He walked back in the direction of the little houses. It might be the time to try and get inside his own.

As he turned a corner Thomas saw a large group of people. Two were soldiers in uniform, not English soldiers though, but deeply suntanned men wearing dark glasses. Behind straggled a group, some of whom were wearing long robes and headdresses. There were also several young people who looked like students. Thomas was not sure about the soldiers or the people in robes. The children were a mixture of modern dress and vaguely Arabic clothes. "Why are you here?" he asked a teenager standing watching.

The boy turned his head, he was a handsome suntanned young man with dark eyes, "We were on a bus," he said, "It exploded and it was terrible, people were torn in pieces by the blast. I lived a while, but not long. The pain was so bad, but then suddenly darkness came over my eyes and then the light came again and the terrible pain was gone. I found I was in the desert with the people from the bus. They said they had to find the gateway to Allah. Are we all dead?"

"I'm sorry to say that yes, you are." Thomas felt sad for the boy who looked about seventeen.

He realised something then. They spoke the same language. "You speak good English," he told the boy who looked puzzled. "I am Israeli. I only speak a little English," the boy said, "I have not yet studied it much. I speak Hebrew and Arabic. You speak Israeli like me."

'So that's it,' Thomas thought. Language has no barrier here. We all speak the same language.

The boy looked around. He smiled, "I was afraid at first but now I don't mind. It looks beautiful here. We just thought we should all stay together, because one of the old men said we were on a journey and he hoped there would not be danger, but in case there was, we should stay together. Stay close. We walked for a while in the desert, until we came to the great arches. We saw fearsome dark shapes but they did not come close, just watched, then went away." he looked around, "We saw the gate and tried to pass through in but it would not open. The old man said there was another land inside the gate, he knew of it from when he was a child and was badly hurt, and got inside, but they sent him back It had writing on it. It was beautiful, all decorated with peacock feathers etched on it. We tried hard to enter. Then two men dressed in white came to the gate. They said we were welcome. They brought us inside to here, then they had to go for somebody else. Did you come in by the peacock gate? Did you see how beautiful it was?"

"No. I came in through another gate," Thomas said.

He was beginning to realise many things, one being that there was more than just one gate and more than one Portal. It was an interesting concept. There must be gates and Portals in every country in the world. In fact, there could be gates in every town and county in England. Gates everywhere in fact. You could probably walk down any street or alleyway in any town or country and never know there was a gate waiting to open. Amazing.

There was a sudden flurry of wings and a big group of angels arrived, some of the people were taken on and some in other directions. The young Israeli lifted a hand and waved to Thomas who then walked slowly away from the group. Two huge angels came and took small children straight up. Thomas watched feeling sad. So young.

Back at the house Mike was sitting smoking his everlasting pipe on the veranda. "Been off on yer travels then?" he asked, "Did you find anyone?"

Thomas nodded, "I found a young man who had come off his motorbike but they sent him back, said it was not his time. I found a group but they were already inside. Then there are those gates. They seem to be everywhere."

Mike nodded and puffed on his pipe, which sent clouds of fragrant tobacco smoke around his head. "They do that a fair bit here you know, send them back I mean. A lot are accidents. A great many seem to have a spark of life left in them when they arrive. I often wonder how they manage to make it here, but they do. They always send them back if there is the merest glimmer of life left in them. As for the gates, well, there do seem to be an awful lot of them. It makes sense to have them all over the place, otherwise how would some fella in the outback of Australia get here, or for that matter a chap from the Hindukush?"

Thomas nodded thoughtfully. It certainly made sense. He had something else on his mind though. "I was wondering too about these little houses." Thomas said, "How come I can't get inside?"

Mike nodded, "Oh that, well now, you can get in but you have to make a start on yer life. You know, like I said, up here you have to work things out, finish them. They don't make it easy and no reason why they should. When you get your book cleaned up a bit, then they let you in."

Thomas looked puzzled. "Look, come in here and I'll show you." Mike opened the door to his little house.

All he could see inside the little house was a table, a chair and bare walls, except that the walls glowed with pinkish light. Mike pointed at the walls, "It's a funny thing that, how them walls seem to be made of light, and they're soft too. I never managed to work out how they do it at all. Now, look at this." he pointed to the table, "That book was put on the table. That book of life business they talk about. An odd-looking thing it is too, far longer than it is wide. It was rotten with dirt when they showed it to me for the first time, but look at it now."

Both men stared at the book. It was shining gold. the cover was filigree work with what looked like diamonds and pearls embedded in it. "You see them little stones." Mike said, "I think they are real jewels. Some of them suddenly began to glitter yesterday. I think that when they give you the book it is all filled with the rubbish and stuff we accumulate, isn't that a nice word, accumulate, anyway, in our life time. You see. I think, I only think mind you, that we have to clean it up, because it was that mucky and now it is looking much cleaner. There you are now, and you see these walls. They are all soft, like clouds, not a bit like wood. Touch it. Go on. You can't even feel the walls. There is no wood at all. It just looks like it but it's all softness. I think that when the book is cleaned up, we have done the job. I still have a fair way to go through to get all these little gems cleaned."

Thomas was bemused, "Yes, but how do you clean it up?"

"I dunno," Mike scratched his head, "The chap who was here before you told me that contemplation was a good way to do it. You sit at the table and there's nobody here to break your concentration, like out there on the veranda, with people coming from every direction and angels flying in and out and them blasted annoying Gatherers. Them fellas is always late. They are like the bloody white rabbit in Alice in Wonderland, rushing all over the place muttering. Still, they have a job to do. Anyway, I come in here and contemplate. Sometimes I say a little prayer too."

"Nobody tells you anything here, we have to find it all out for ourselves." Thomas was cross, "So, what do you contemplate on, if you see what I mean?"

Mike frowned, "I see what you mean, but it's like I say, they don't tell you. Listen, the thing is this as I see it. You contemplate on your life and how you lived it, good bad or indifferent, and you think how you could have changed it, made it better for yourself and others, and you have to be sincere in that. Like, well you are sorry if you hurt others, in any way like. If you did good, it counts. If you were wrong, well, then say, I was wrong and I'm sorry. Talk it all out with yerself. Sometimes I say I'm very… sorry for acting like a clown most of me life, which I did. It's simple. There is a bit more than that but I'll let you find it out for yerself."

Thomas made a face. "Aye. You can make all the faces you like," Mike grinned, "You have to work for your own salvation here. They don't hand it to you on a plate you know. What did you expect? Them little cherubim waiting on you hand and foot? Not likely, they're only interested in playing music and watching everyone by the gate's, and the Seraphim would give you short shrift if you expected them to run around after you. It does not work like that here Tommy me boy. We all help each other find our way in here. But you see we can only do it up to a point. You can pass on the word the same way I pass it on to you. But you have to ask before it can be given in return. Never be too proud to ask. Pride does not work here. Humility is the thing you see."

Mike puffed away on his everlasting pipe. The pipe sometimes annoyed Thomas and he wished he could grab it and throw it in the little waterfall.

Mike went on, "You have to begin to understand how they work here. They gave us free choice all our lives. They give you that here, up to a point. You see that is the thing. They help you up to a point only. The rest is for you to do. The choice is simple. Work and leave here as soon as possible. The other choice is." Mike laughed, "Don't work and stay here for eternity. Well, I am going to do a bit of contemplation now. I've been here in this place long enough. I want to be on my way up to the big Gate. Go on, have a look inside your own house my friend. That should tell you how you're getting on. Off you go and open the little door. I'm sure by now you will be able to open it and get inside."

****

Chapter 10

Thomas stepped out and crossed the patch of garden to his own little house. He knew what would be in there. His room too, would be filled with the light which came from nowhere, a table a chair and three bare walls at which to stare, and an odd shaped book that could do with a good cleaning. Thomas knew the Lord's prayer. It was funny how most people seemed to remember it even if they left religion behind them a very long time ago. Should he say that a few times. It wouldn't hurt.

Thomas remembered the day he and James made their confirmation. Robert was not Catholic and was there as a guest. He thought it was hilarious when the Bishop came with his robes, staff and mitre and asked all the children a question, or if they could recite a certain prayer. The tall man in his robes made the children nervous and James was terrified. He forgot everything he ever learned. He kept whispering: "Please God, don't let me get The Magnificat prayer for my test. I can't remember it."

Poor James. He was asked by the Bishop to recite the prayer. His face went paler still and he stumbled his way through it sweating profusely and almost fainting back on to his seat. Afterwards, Robert had roared with laughter. He thought the whole business was a scream. He had been confirmed by a bishop of the Church of England who was a friend of his father. He said that someday his own father would be a bishop too. James jeered at that and they punched at each other half-heartedly. Thomas had got the Credo and knew it off by heart. He could not remember it now.

He sat thinking. Praying was not something he found easy to do even as a child. He would start off well enough but then his thoughts wandered, in fact from the age of fourteen had not said one single prayer that he could recall. He could say those he did know.

Something told him, he had to mean these prayers, believe the words. Could he do that? "I will try my very best and if I can't do that, I will talk what I feel."

Did that make sense, he wondered. It was all he could do. As his voice said, he was only one tiny speck in the universe. Would he be heard? Thomas looked at the odd, elongated book lying on the table all brown and scruffy looking "I will do the very best I can do," Thomas promised. He was not altogether sure to whom he made this promise, but it was heartfelt. Just for a second he thought he caught a flash of light from the book.

Thomas stayed in the little house a long time. He bowed his head down into his hands and put his heart and mind to what he must do. After what seemed a long time, he lifted his head and looked at the book. It looked less dark and dirty. He reached a finger to touch it and was shocked to hear a voice say, "Do not place a hand upon this book. It is not yet time." he looked around. There was nobody there.

Later, as he sat and watched a large group of children arrived, some appeared to be African and a couple were small Asian children, he wondered what had brought them to this. Little lives finished almost before they began. A tiny infant carried by an angel made him wonder where it had waited to be found, of course, it had. Perhaps it was just picked straight up. Then a young woman came running up to the Angel and he handed her the infant. Minutes later the Great Angels came for them both. He wondered if the mother had passed on first, then the infant and she was waiting for it. Probably.

He wandered around his little garden. The flowers were becoming really lush. New blooms and shrubs were appearing rapidly in every corner. Tiny flowers like pearls grew, from the wood work of the little veranda, although when he touched the wood, it was soft, not like wood at all. He laughed. What an amazing place. Mike's little garden was almost full of flowers. Was that another indication of how they were progressing?

There were four of these little houses together. The other two were behind, their verandas facing in the other direction, so he had never seen the occupants. He walked around to have a look. One of the little gardens was a blaze of flowers, the other beginning to flourish, like his own. Thomas had never seen anything like it on the earth. This brought back that other thought. Would he be able to go back? Just for a short while. Just to see how things were, how his daughter Kate was and, well, anybody really.

If he was honest, it was to see if they missed him, because somehow, that would be the hardest thing to take, if nobody missed him, or nobody cared. What if nobody cared? Was there no good memory of him left behind? Thomas felt a terrible sadness wash over him. It was just possible nobody gave a damn one way or the other.

A small group of children played now on the grass outside his garden. One looked through the gate at him. He waved and the child waved back. Thomas wondered if there would ever be any grandchildren of his on the earth. Of course, if the boys had children, they would not be related to him. If Kate got married there would be grandchildren, but then they would never know him.

Then he heard the beating of wings and three of the great angels arrived holding out their hands to the children who were laughing and dancing around. They lifted them in their arms and all soared high up towards the gates. He felt sad. Deep regret, a sense of loss, even a little fear. But above all a huge desire to move forward, and yet. There was always that word. Yet. He wanted to go back, but back to what? "Hello Thomas." A familiar gentle voice spoke just behind him.

He turned to see the angel Cadamiel standing on the veranda smiling, long slender hand joined. Once again, he was stopped in his tracks by the beauty of these, what? Were they he or she or it? It was hard to know. What was spirit anyway? "Come. Sit here and ask, what it is you want to know?" Cadamiel was smiling.

How did it know he wanted to ask a question? Thomas stared hard at the angel. The last time he saw it Thomas had not looked very hard at it. He had of course, seen the overall effect but now he stared at the face. The face was smooth, incredibly beautiful, unlined, the hands the same. The eyes were kind and gentle, a pale shining silvery blue. Great beauty. Glorious beauty, almost indescribable. "Please sit, Thomas," Cadamiel gestured towards the rocking chair.

Thomas sat down on his chair, but then asked if the angel might like to sit instead.

The angel said: "Thank you Thomas, I do not sit. I am here to watch over you to guide and help you. I do not rest in the sense that you do. My rest is in deep contemplation and adoration of him who is and always will be, and who's will is my will."

"Do you not get tired? I mean standing around all the time you could get aches and pains."

The angel laughed softly: "Ah Thomas, do you not remember that I am spirit. I have no body to feel aches and pains. You see me in a bodily form because you need to. You also need to be able to make sense of it all. Is that not so."

Thomas nodded and Cadamiel continued, "You see me in a similar sense as you saw me first as a child and in a picture, with wings and a long white robe. You can even see me with a halo of light around my head if you choose and memory serves. That is how you see all of us here. I am spirit Thomas, as you will fully be in time. Others who enter here will see me as they wish me to be.

"They see us very often as they themselves are. I may appear to them as one of their countrymen. All see us differently. As to spirit, let me tell you simply. I have no body. I was created by the Almighty to serve and support and I rejoice in that service. Think of us here as being of the mind and the heart and the soul, not the body, although I am clothed as if I were body. Do you understand that?"

It was difficult to take in, as was this whole place, but Thomas was beginning to understand. "It is difficult." Cadamiel agreed, seeming to read Thomas's thought, "Yet, the time will come when you do understand, even the great mysteries of the universe and of life, and the mysteries of faith you will understand. The time will come when you understand everything."

The man watched the angel. Now was the time to ask the question. "I want to ask something." Thomas said, then lost the courage to ask and changed the question, "I was wondering, have you always been with me?"

"No. I have known you though," the angel said, "You had your own angel guardian and yes. I have been there at many points in your life, even before your birth Thomas. I saw your anguish at many points in your life. We tried to help, but you refused our help. You refused to acknowledge or accept anything." Cadamiel held out pale hands, "You know Thomas, that is our biggest problem, because you are all given a free will. Trying to guide. To prevent you harming yourselves is difficult. We here, we saw the damage you did, not just to yourself but to others."

The angel was silent for a while, "We too saw the things you did that were good when you would rather have punished the children for their father. We saw the punishment of the woman to whom you were joined, also that great thing you did that nobody else ever knew of, the thing which opened the Portal to you. I felt a joy which was great when you came here to this place instead of that other, and remember one thing: you are not free of that other place yet. Beware that place. The temptation of it will come to you even here. Remember what I say, do not dismiss my words. Be heedful of them. They cannot take you, but you can go to them. That is where the danger lies. Remember that."

79

Thomas nodded quickly and went straight into the question he really wanted to ask because if he had not asked at that moment, he would not have asked at all. "Can I go back?" he said, "Please. Can I go back to see if they are all right? Can I go back to see if they are happy? I want to see if anybody cared? I would like to know if anybody misses me even just a little bit."

"Is that the only reason you would wish to return to the earth," Cadamiel asked. "The only reason?" Thomas frowned, "I think so, but I am not sure. I just need to go back. I think there are things to be completed."

"I will make your request known." Cadamiel said and was gone.

Thomas could have wept as he waited and waited. How long would this take? He sat watching but the angel did not come back. He waited for what seemed like days and still no messenger came to answer the question.

As he sat waiting hopefully on the veranda Mike walked past to his own little garden and waved. Thomas called to him and he stopped: "Can I ask you a question?"

"You can ask all the questions you want," Mike grinned, "but there's no guarantee of a sensible answer."

"All I want to ask is this," Thomas said, "Did you ever go back, did they let you, you know, go back to when, well back to when you were alive?"

Mike sighed, "Aye, fool that I am. I asked to go back like many of us do and they let me. Some they do, some they don't. One thing I will tell you is this, it can be a big mistake. When you go out there, out there among the living, the things you see they have done when you are gone, you have to take it on the chin, but it's hard. Things change out there. They change radically and quickly. You might not be able to take the fact that the world does not stop turning because you are no longer in it, or that time moves at such speed. It's terrible hard."

Mike walked away but stopped and turned, looking sad, "I wasn't able to take it you see. That's why I've been here so long." He stopped at his own gate, "If you are thinking about going back my answer to that would be, don't. It's not worth the pain. Just get on with what you have to do here If you have a grain of sense you will stay here and work out your salvation. You can do terrible damage when you're away from the close protection they give you in here. I created havoc out there with my father who still lived. They warned me to leave him alone, said he was frail and not in his right mind. I tortured him. I did. Revenge you see. It's a terrible thing. He didn't know it was his dead son, invisible and tearing his home to pieces with anger. I gave him the heart attack that killed him. He was an old sick man and I killed him."

Mike looked grief stricken, "The big angels hurled me into a dark place for a long time and I tell you, that dark place is worse than anything I ever knew. I had to climb that great mountain of pain."

"That is why I'm here so long a time. I'm lucky they let me back in," He paused, "But I tell you this now, and my friend, heed me, please. No matter what anyone tells you, if they say yes, you will go. You will not be able to resist it. Life has a terrible pull on us in even here, but it is not worth it."

He went into his little house and closed the door. Thomas stared at the closed door. He only wanted to go back and have a look. What would be so painful about that? Yet there was now in his mind a seed of doubt. The little seed drowned quickly in a sea of self-delusion. He would be different.

Because he was so impatient for an answer time dragged before the angel Cadamiel returned. Thomas had been sitting with his eyes closed. The only sign of the return was a gentle breeze wafting across his face. The angel stood on the veranda with wings folded back and hands inside the long flowing sleeves of its gown. The other smaller angel was just behind. Fariel.

The usually serene face of Cadamiel seemed troubled, "Thomas, I have asked for and been given guidance. It was thought at first you should not go. It might be difficult for you."

"Why?" Thomas wondered. "Because," the angel told him, "You made life very difficult for yourself and possibly would still find it so. The other possibility is that it could be difficult for those left behind. Some of them see and feel things, are aware there might be a soul among them without a body. This sometimes frightens those upon the earth. There is however, something else. Do you truly not remember how you were upon the earth? Do you not remember your anger when you did not like how your life had become, or if people displeased you? Did you forgive and forget that which you should? If there were changes, how would you feel?"

"I've done all that forgiving and forgetting. None of it matters now," Thomas said earnestly.

The angel nodded, "I see. Yet will you still feel like that when you have seen what you want to see, I wonder? If you do go back, will you look and see what has happened in the interim with calm eyes and a peaceful mind and soul? Will you then return in peace to work out the rest of your salvation when you have seen all this? Will you Thomas?"

Thomas nodded vigorously, "Yes–"

Cadamiel nodded, "You are being trusted Thomas. You have been given permission to return."

Thomas leapt up delighted and danced around the little lawn. Cadamiel waited until he stopped whirling. He smiled his gentle smile. The angel Fariel did not smile, just watched its great amber eyes thoughtful. "Can I go now? How do I get out of here, do I go out by the gate?" Thomas was excited. "I will show you the way but, not until you have heard the instructions," the angel said.

Thomas was so impatient he almost shouted: "OK tell me the rules."

Cadamiel nodded, "Thomas. listen to me. You may go but only when you have listened to the instruction and advice from above."

Thomas jerked his head up and down impatiently and moved from one foot to the other. "It would be wise if you were to listen with patience to the angel Cadamiel," the soft voice of Fariel said, "Listen and understand or you may find you lose your way outside. That would be dangerous."

Thomas looked at the smaller angel. It stared hard at him; amber eyes wide. Oh oh, he thought, this is a tough one. No meek and mild little angel this. He took a deep breath and calmed himself right down. "Sorry," he said, "I am just impatient to go."

Feriel gave a slight nod but the look in the amber eyes said he should listen. Thomas felt that if that angel had its way, he would not put a foot outside the gate.

Cadamiel continued then, "You may leave the gathering place when I have finished speaking and you have agreed to do as you are asked. You will be allowed to return to life for a period of twenty-four earth hours. You may wander at will through that place and seek out all those you wish to see. The time may seem short, but it is long enough, since you move faster without a body. However, remember this instruction and remember it well. You will not cause fear or distress to any, especially those who were close to you in life. Particularly, you may not cause distress or pain to the woman to whom you were joined. They who live now have the rest of their lives to work through. They are no longer your responsibility. They are no longer yours to chide or praise. Is that clearly understood?"

Thomas nodded. Come on, he thought, get this over with and let me go.

Cadamiel continued, "You have earned the privilege of returning. Now. Heed well what I say. If you cause any fear or pain, you will lose everything you have gained here. Remember this also. There will be a harsh punishment if you do not accept the decision from above, of that there is no doubt. Do you still wish to return?"

"Yes, yes." Thomas was impatient, barely listening. "Very well," Cadamiel told him, "If all is well, I will come for you at the end of your allotted period of time. If all is not well Thomas, the Seraphim will come. They will not be mocked. Remember that. Is all that understood."

Thomas nodded.

The angel took his hand and led him out through the little garden gate and along a pathway Thomas had not seen previously. Fariel followed. Thomas looked around. This place had so many strange ways. They walked swiftly for what seemed like ages and suddenly there it was, the plain wooden gate banded with copper through which he had entered. The angel Fariel touched the gate and it opened on to the world he had left and to which he was now returning. "You may leave now," Cadamiel said, "Remember the warning. You are no longer of the earth. You own nothing there. Nothing. As I have said, there may be a few who can see you, who will know you for what you are. One final thing. Beware the Scavengers. Once you have left The Gathering Place, they will have greater access to you. If you need us, call upon us."

Thomas walked through the gate on to the grass verge, then looked back apprehensively but the angels were no longer visible. He could still go back. The gate was still open. No. He walked out with more confidence than he felt on to the grass verge and found himself on the bend in the road where he had died.

He looked around. It seemed to be winter here. He must have been away longer than he thought. It had been April when the car crash happened. He looked for the broken bricks on the wall where he crashed. It had been rebuilt. He looked for the fallen tree where he'd sat, cold and afraid and where those two faceless beings came and mocked him. He shuddered. They had terrified him. The old tree was still there. and a new wire fence ran the length of the field. Looking across the field to where Col Blacks daughters trained their ponies, he was surprised to see two blond haired young women riding a pair of hunters around and taking them over jumps.

Col must have sold the paddock. It was a pity the girls had gone. He had a moment of fear and panic. This was all too much. It was not big change but it

83

was sudden. He was going back to, what? He did not know After all he'd only been gone a matter of months. So, what else had changed in such a short time? No, he was going back to his little house. It was safer in there.

Thomas turned and almost ran back to where the entrance gate to the gathering place had been.

There was not even a sign it had ever been there. How was he going to get back inside? He calmed down. The angel Cadamiel had said they would come for him, so it did not matter that there was no gate there now. They would come. He was here, yes, and would see it through, no matter what changes had taken place. He'd now make his way along the road back towards Barton Trinity, but the graveyard at the church would be the first port of call, there was something he needed to see.

****

Chapter 11

Thomas walked along the road toward the village of Barton Trinity, stopping occasionally to look at the cottages. He knew some of the people who lived here, but mostly they were acquaintances. He knew a few better than others. He was not a man who made close friends. Surprisingly some of the cottages were added to now, a room here, a conservatory there, others had a new roof or windows. The trees were bare of leaves apart from a few evergreen shrubs and the holly trees were rich with berries, bringing a little relief and colour into the starkness of the winter scene.

He looked at Cassie Chasen's cottage. It looked different. Cassie, the daughter of his mother's best friend Rebecca. The chunky solid Cassie was someone he could trust. She had been the one person, apart from his daughter Kate, with whom he felt at ease, to whom he told anything. He ambled up the short drive to look through a window. Nobody home that he could see. The room was full of modern furniture. Odd that she should change everything. She was what was termed, old-fashioned.

Further along the road, he heard the sound of horses hooves behind, then noticed a strange woman coming towards him. He forgot for a moment and was about to say good morning when the woman called out, "Good morning, and how are our Miss Blacks this morning?"

Thomas turned to look for the girls but it was the two young women who'd been riding the hunters. There must be another family of Blacks around but looking at them closely, the pair seemed familiar. "How are your mother and father," the woman asked. "Col is much better now, he's got over his flu," the smaller girl smiled, "May is trying to get him to have a holiday in the sun."

Thomas frowned. Col's daughters had always called their parents by their first name, but surely these were not his daughters. They were only about twelve and fourteen. He shrugged. It was not important There were many more important things to do and only twenty-four hours in which to do them. He could see in the distance the spire of the church in which he and Valerie had married. The place Thomas wanted was the graveyard which was on the other side of the church. Coming closer to the village he saw new houses. Town houses on three floors. There must be twenty or so.

Almost all looked lived in. There were two in the middle empty. The gardens were quite mature considering they had only been built since he left. How long ago was that? If it was winter now, it could only have been about eight months at most.

There were Christmas trees in the windows of some of the houses. Was it before or after Christmas? Probably before, he mused, walking through the big black iron gates and across what seemed like half an acre of yellow and grey flagstones. Private houses then. Thomas looked through the window of a house and saw a minimally furnished room with a glittering black Christmas tree in the corner waiting to be decorated. A pile of red bows lay on the floor. Very modern. Not to his taste. He preferred traditional. Not that it mattered now. "Hello man," a young voice made him whirl around, "Do you want to talk to my Daddy? Lots of people like to talk to my Daddy but he's gone away to work. He says he has to make money to pay for this place. Mummy and Granny are here. Do you want to speak to them?"

A small boy with two large golden Labrador dogs stood behind him. The dogs were big, even for Labradors. They stood quietly with lolling tongues and wagging tails. The child was well wrapped in jeans and padded jacket with a blue knitted hat pulled down over his ears and blue gloves. A little blue boy, Thomas thought amused. The boy's bright intelligent blue eyes sparkled. He had a few chicken pox scabs showing on his pink cheeks. Thomas thought that would account for his being here. What worried him was that the child could see him. Yet, what was it Cadamiel said? There may be a few who will see you and know you for what you are. Would the child know him for what he was? Thomas looked at the dogs. They too could see him. The boy was way ahead of him. "The dogs won't hurt you," he said, "Cos they know, you won't hurt me. But you can't hurt me, can you? Cos you're not a real person. If you did want to hurt me and you was a real person, they would bite your legs off. I would tell them to do it."

The dogs wagged their tails approvingly. "No." Thomas smiled, "I just wanted to know if it is Christmas yet."

"You are funny," the boy said, "Don't you know when Christmas is? It's a week and three more days, silly. Daddy will be home then and Father Christmas is going to bring me lots of presents, cos I have been really good and didn't scratch my spots. I have chicken pops so I can't go to school. I don't mind not going to school cos it finishes in two days."

"Don't you like school?" Thomas smiled at the boy.

The boy shook his head, "I like school, but it's not the school. It's Shane Warwick. He's nasty and he hurts me. He gives me a Chinese burn. He twists boy's arms too if they don't give him their crisps. I don't get crisps but he still twists my arm. We have to give him our pocket money. I think I might be going to another school soon. Mummy thinks it might be best."

"Who are you talking to Peter?" She stood at the open front doorway looking around, a slender blonde woman in slacks and sweater. An older version of her stood slightly behind, "Not one of your invisible friends again?"

"He's not invisible. I can see him and Sam and Ben can see him. They like him. He's a nice man and he wants to know when it is Christmas. That is silly because everybody knows when it's Christmas."

The older woman spoke softly, "Not if he is lost. Ask him if he is lost Peter. Ask him if he needs to find the light."

The boy Peter turned to look at Thomas who said, "Tell her I am not lost, just on a journey to find the truth. I have found the light already."

Thomas watched the older woman as her grandson relayed the reply. She nodded and said, "Whoever you are I hope you find what it is you need."

The younger woman turned sharply to her mother, "Please Mother. I don't like it when you do that. I don't want Peter to do it either."

"Whether you like it or not," the older woman said, "Peter sees, and hears them and there is nothing you can do about it. Say goodbye to your friend, Peter, and come inside. He has a journey to make and you have been out long enough, It's getting very cold."

The young woman looked back nervously just before she closed the door behind them.

Thomas walked slowly back to the gates feeling a touch of sadness and stepped through them, then looked back. The boy and the older woman watched from the window. He waved and they both waved back. The woman could indeed see him. He smiled and waved again and left. "I have caused no problem here," he said aloud, worried in case anyone was watching and listening.

I bet they are he thought. Sneaky bunch. Thomas thought he heard a chuckle. They were listening.

He had reached the graveyard. This was what he wanted to see. He passed through the railings and went in to look. His eyes searched the graves, looking for the inscriptions on the marble headstones. The older ones he did not bother about. He searched for the newer headstones. He could not see his name anywhere. One caught his eye. Cassandra Chasen? Cassie too had gone. He looked at the date. Surely not. Had he been gone so long? That could not be right. It was a mistake, wasn't it? He could not see a headstone for himself.

Thomas climbed to the top of a huge stone Celtic cross and sat for a while looking around. He could see across the whole place and then his eye was caught by what seemed to be a newer area recently opened up. He jumped down and walked around to it, then suddenly there it was. A black marble headstone with gold lettering. There were small shrubs on many of the other graves but on his, nothing. Just a plain concrete surround filled with marble chippings. Thomas looked again. There was a small withered plant in a ceramic pot in the centre of the chippings. He stared at the inscription on the headstone. Thomas James Beck aged 70 years. R.I.P.

That was it then. Nothing more. He scowled, felt sudden surge of anger. Not husband & father then. Just his name, age, a few words. What did they mean? Nothing. Was that all he amounted to in life? Was that all she thought of him? He was gone and forgotten. But then, did he deserve to have a better inscription? Perhaps not. A small sound like a sigh came from behind but there was nobody there, and yet it seemed as if a voice inside his mind said. 'Take heed, remember my warning. Do not take umbrage at what you think is due to you but is not written there. You no longer have a place here, apart from that small patch. Understand that there is nothing owed to you here.'

He left the graveyard quickly. That was probably true. That small patch was all that was left of him. Nothing was owed him. He owed nothing either. Or did he? Thomas shook his head. Liar. You lie to yourself man, you owe a great deal. Someone said once that if we do not pay for our wrongdoing in this world, we pay for it in the hereafter. He had laughed then. He was not laughing now. There was a hereafter and he was right in it. Some lessons were learned too late.

Thomas stood and looked all around. Every cliché in the world could be used but it made no difference if you did not follow some kind of rule, did not apply those rules to what you did and said. Because applying the rules to everybody else and not yourself was stupid. Delusional. You conned yourself and it all came back to haunt you. You made the rules for yourself therefore you could bend, twist, and justify everything. Thomas sighed deeply. Payment had to be made and he owed so much.

He was determined not to return to the house in which he had lived. Yet the thought was there. Why should I not go back he thought mutinously? It is mine. "It is not yours," a soft voice whispered. Fariel?

A cold harsher voice said, "If you do not return how can you ever make good those things? Go back. Ignore them. What do they know?"

He shut out the voices. He would not return to the house. Thomas moved on and away from the graveyard.

The clock on the spire told him it was still early. It was amazing how little time counted in the Gathering Place. Nobody asked the time or cared. Yet here he was back on the earth, in his own village and one of the first things he thought about was time. Thomas stepped off the road and on to the village green, past several men putting up a Christmas tree in the centre. He stood a while and watched. There had been a tree on the green for many years at Christmastime. The old landlord of the inn had started it. There had been lanterns on the tree then. It was always switched on by some minor celebrity, like the seventeen-year-old Carnival Queen of Great Barton who looked at all the men from under her long lashes and giggled her way through the proceedings. Thomas remembered all the young men loved it. So too had the older ones.

Valerie used to bring the children and when they left home, went alone to the switching on ceremony. That last year she had gone alone and came home flushed and happy to tell him about the church choir singing carols and the hot sausage rolls and the adults drinking mulled wine. He had held the paper before his face, pretending to ignore her. She had stopped mid-sentence and gone into the kitchen. He heard her fill the kettle but he also heard her softly crying, and to his shame now remembered how he had enjoyed her pain and loneliness.

The tree was decorated with flower lights now, but were not yet lit up. One of the men, who knelt on the ground doing something with cables stood up. It was Jim Pacey the young landlord of The Inn on the Green. The man seemed to have aged suddenly, had lost some of his hair. That was quick. There was too, he could see, a new covered area with outdoor heaters attached to the side of the inn. So many changes in such a short timer, and yet, was it such a short time.

Col Black stood there holding a big star. He too seemed a lot thinner and greyer. He must be on one of those diets. There were people Thomas did not know. Still, that was not surprising, he had always tended to keep to himself, had not known a great many in the village. Then there were the new houses. That was not the most important thing however. He looked around and across the green in the direction of his daughter's cottage. The hedge seemed to have sprouted unbelievably, and was a right mess. It needed cutting back. He shook his head.

Thomas needed to find Kate. It was she who had lightened the darkness in his mind when things were dreadful. She lived on the other side of the green just behind the big messy hedge. He walked away from the men working on the Christmas tree and in behind the hedge. There it was. He had given her the deposit for her cottage. Surprisingly there were no curtains. It looked bare. The cottage was empty with a for sale notice attached to the front gate. Where had Kate gone? He stood and stared around, then slipped inside. The place was indeed empty. No furniture. The kitchen, which was once very small and poky was now huge where an extension had been added on to the back of the cottage, with two extra rooms and a shower room. What was going on? But then there had been that odd date on Cassie's headstone and people seemed older.

It seemed as if the village had been re-built in a matter of months too. Maybe it was a little longer. Thomas would have to return if he could not find Kate. How, though was he going to find her. He had been told not to go back to his old home but he might have to disregard that. There might be a clue there as to where she had gone. Maybe she had moved back in with her mother. He needed to find her, needed to be sure she was well and happy. He'd not been able to say goodbye to her.

He wandered out. The green was empty now of people and the tree was lit up, like a coloured beacon. Thomas stood at the end of the avenue and stared along the surprising length of it. It had been less than half this size when he left. Where had all these houses sprung from. They could surely not have been built so quickly, and the gardens looked as if they had been there for years. He was coming to the conclusion he had been dead a lot longer than he thought.

An unfamiliar woman walked down the avenue with a little Jack Russell terrier. It pulled and tugged on its extending lead, diving across from one side of the pavement to the other. It was either badly trained or just plain aggressive. Probably both. "Stop it, Storm," the woman snapped as the dog almost tripped her up. "Storm," Thomas laughed, "You are not a storm. More like a little squall."

The dog stopped and stared, its eyes glinting, teeth stripped. It did not like what it saw and this was something to get its teeth into at last. The small dog

90

snarled and growled. He realised the animal could see him and ran at it knowing the little thing could not bite or hurt. The dog, surprised by what it saw as an attack, ran behind its mistress who pulled hard on the lead and staggered a bit, then told the little animal off in no uncertain terms. Thomas hoisted himself up to sit on the high wall of the corner house, laughing. This wall too was new. The woman and dog walked on, the little animal bouncing around and turning its head to watch Thomas.

A cat prowling across the Virginia Creeper stopped and arched its back, hissed then slipped back down to the ground. He heard the sound of sirens and watched an ambulance drive around the corner, sirens wailing and stop at a house he knew along the avenue. The paramedics went inside with their emergency kits, but as they did, he saw an elderly woman step through the wall of the house. She wore a long-sleeved nightdress and no slippers. Her thick white hair flowed down to her waist. The woman was smiling and he recognised her as the wife of the red-faced butcher, Reg Kane. She too had aged a lot. Mind you she had never seemed young. She waved to him. "Hello Thomas Beck," she called, "It is nice to see you again. You been gone a fair old-time haven't you? It's my turn now and I must say I don't mind one little bit. It's been a painful old life. They're in there pummelling what is left of me, trying to bring me back, and sticking an oxygen mask on my face, but there's no way I'm going back to all that. No, I'm out of it and I intend to stay out. So, what happens now? You left us a fair old time ago so you must know. I must say, it's great to be able to walk again. I feel light as a feather." She beamed at him. "Your husband will miss you," Thomas said. "Reg? Not him," Sue grinned, "He has his eye on someone to take my place." She giggled, "Good luck to her. She'll need it."

Thomas suddenly thought she might know what had happened to Kate and asked if Susie knew. "Your Kate? Oh yes. I heard from the District Nurse your Kate moved out of the cottage some time back. She let it for a while, but it's up for sale I hear. She's moved in next to your Val, where old Mel and his Mum used to live. His Mum passed on you know and he sold up. Kate is living there with Jack and the kiddies."

He stared. Who on earth were Jack and the kiddies and was about to ask when he saw the pair in the white suits turn the corner? Just when he was getting a few answers along they came like a bad smell and now they were taking the one person who could answer his questions.

He shouted, "Hang on. Give us a minute. I want to ask Sue something. How long have I been gone Sue?"

She did not hear him, was running toward the white suited pair as if she knew them well. They did not stop. She went off with them chatting merrily, delighted with herself. He sighed. They disappeared then, into a patch of mist a short way along the avenue and did not emerge. Thomas could not blame her. Susie had spent many years trying to get around on a pair of walking sticks while her husband drove around in that big car. He sniffed and stared crossly at the patch of mist from which the trio had not emerged. "Another gate. There are as many gates as there are gatherers." Thomas muttered crossly. So, what was he to do now? He would have to go back towards his old home, but if Kate was living next door, he had little choice but to see it at least. Anyway, there was no reason to go inside, he would just pass by, not even glance in its direction. Just go and see if Kate was happy. If all was well with her then he'd go and have a look at the twins to see if they were all right. He owed them that. Thomas leapt off the wall and saw another pair of Gatherers walking towards him. They had better not be coming for him. "I don't have to go back yet, do I?" he said, crossing the street towards them. "We are not here for you," one said, "You have been gathered in. We are here to find a girl. She is lost and we need to find her soon. If we do not find her, she may be lost for a long time. She is young, and could be frightened. Have you seen a girl?"

He shook his head, "Sorry, An old lady but not a girl."

They smiled and walked on and he drew a deep breath.

Thomas walked along the avenue. He became aware of a figure walking slowly towards him. A young girl dressed in jeans and a cropped sweater who watched him carefully, looking as if she was about to run away but seeming to gather courage as he smiled. The girl appeared to make up her mind then and came toward him, moving slowly watching him warily. She was barefoot, her hands were held tightly against her chest, as if holding her thin body together. Some of her fingernails were broken and dirty Long black hair fell around the pale face and there was grass and twigs stuck in it. He felt pity for the girl. Her face was almost blue white. A drug addict? He stared at the pale worried young face. Then Thomas realised she was like him as he had been, a lost soul searching. Was this the one the gatherers looked for?

The girl looked straight at him, "Can you help me please. I'm not a drug addict or anything. I'm not into that stuff if that's what you think. I got hurt.

Three men came in to the roadhouse where I work, yeah. They were taking the p..." she stopped, then began again, "I got them out in the end. Jack, he's the boss, he weren't there. I was late leaving, had to clean up sick. Like some divvy got sick. I missed the bus, yeah. He usually waits for me, but he didn't this time, too long a wait you see. The three blokes, they must have waited too."

"What happened?" he asked.

She looked around, "People can't see us, cos you and me, we're dead, yeah, but them dark shadows, they can see us, yeah. I had to hide from them."

Thomas glanced swiftly around but could not see any Scavengers. "Them blokes. They were laughing like." the girl said, "I said no and they called me names, like a tart and stuff and I got scared and ran across the car park to the field. I ran on to the back road but they caught me up. The car hit me in the back. They killed me. I never saw them before and they killed me. Why? Why would they do that to me? Like, why would they murder me? One of them got out of the car. He was crying. He told them I was dead. He was like, a kid. He looked down at me on the ground. I heard the others laugh, but he cried." She nodded, "Yeah, they laughed. But I forgive him. Not the others. I never seen them before. Why? I don't understand why would they do that to me, to somebody they didn't know. I did nothin' to them."

She stood looking at him from under thick black eyelashes and he thought she was very beautiful even in her messed-up state. He had no answer for her. "I know I'm dead," the girl said, "I know, 'cause I got up after they hit me and I could see myself lying on the ground all twisted. I lost my shoes. There wasn't any blood though. I was real scared then but I'm not now. I feel good. Funny, yeah?" She paused then said again, "You and me, we are dead. Yeah?" She needed to know for sure.

He nodded, "I got killed. A car accident. I drove my sports car into the wall."

"Wow, you and me, yeah. We are so cool," she laughed, not afraid anymore, "I never thought about going this young. Funny innit. I'm glad I found you."

He liked this girl, even her funny way of talking, but felt a deep sadness that those men felt the girl was there for them to hurt and as it seemed now, had killed her. "So, where do I go?" she asked, "I mean, like what happens now. Like I know something happens. Yeah. Mum always believed in what she said was a greater being and a lovely place. I need to find it, this place. Mums been there for a long time. I mean, she went there when I was seven. I need to find mum. I know she'll be in a good place. Can you help me?"

Thomas smiled, "Yes, there is a place, a very good place and I'm sure your mother is there but I think they are searching for you. I met two of them and they said they were looking for a lost girl. They are good people, so don't be afraid. They need to find you soon. Have you been on the road a long time?" She nodded, "Yeah. Like, I think I've been on it for days and nights. I tried to go home but I seem to be stuck here in a short bit of this road. I thought Dad might be home. I think he might be worried." She bit her lip, "Nah, he won't be. He's got this girlfriend now. She's called Paula. She's a tart. My step-mum won't care either. There ain't anybody to care." The girl smiled, "So, can you show me where to go please?"

Thomas stared across the road. The patch of mist was still there. Sue had gone into it and not come out, so it had be a gate. The Gatherers he had seen looking for a girl must be around still. He would have to find them. They said there was not much time left, although he did not understand what that was all about. It would probably be better to take her to the gate. She might be able to push her way in. "What's your name?" Thomas asked. "Lily Bowler. Stupid name," she grinned, "My nan was called Lily, so that's what they called me. I don't remember her, I think she died young."

Thomas looked hard at her. There had been a Ray Bowler he knew vaguely from the Inn on the Green, a mouthy bloke, but his girl was much younger, about eight years old at that time. Bowler was always going on about how clever the girl was, yet he never went home to look after her. He'd heard a lot of her but not seen her. This girl was about seventeen, maybe older. Yet the way things were going, but no, she was too old. Then again, Thomas thought, he could not be sure of anything right now, besides this girl needed to be found. "Come on," he said, "There is a gate over here."

"I can't see a gate," Lily said, surprised. "It's in the mist," he said, then asked, "Have you not heard a voice talking to you telling you where to go? You know, a sort of little voice in the back of your mind."

She shook her head at first, but then said, "Oh. Is that what it is? I could hear it but it seemed really far away. I thought it was the smack from the car making me hear voices in my head."

He took her arm and they crossed the Avenue, walking towards the patch of mist. They had almost reached it when somebody called. Turning, they saw the two men in white. They held out hands to her. She smiled at Thomas, "Is this them then?"

Thomas nodded. The two men came almost at a run, "We must get inside the gate with you. There is little time left."

"Thank you." Lily Bowler said. She smiled broadly at Thomas, then called back, "You are cool man." and walked away with the Gatherers.

Thomas smiled as he watched them walk away and reasoned that they must have only a certain amount of time to find people. That must be it. At least she had been found in time, but then, he wondered, where would they go if they were not found. Would they just wander the earth for a long time? He shrugged his shoulders. What did he know anyway? He stood on the empty avenue; shoulders slumped and felt very sad, then walked slowly on thinking.

It was astonishing, he thought, what came out of the depth of really thinking without prejudice. It was amazing what he could dredge up from the past. He had heard of lost souls and remembered being told by a priest in school days they should pray for lost souls. So, if they were not gathered in, were they then left to wander around the earth until somebody took pity on them and prayed for them, or sent them on? He guessed that was what they meant and was pleased Lily had come his way, and that he was able to send her in the right direction.

Thomas felt that at least he had done something good. That poor young murdered girl, even if they had not intended to kill her, they were up to no good. The driver must have thought about what he was doing before he put his foot on the accelerator. Was it manslaughter? No, it was murder. He had driven at her deliberately.

He wondered what would happen to the men who did this. They had taken an innocent life. Would they be taken to that other place when it was their turn? Suppose they had not meant to kill her? Did it matter what they meant? They had other things in mind for Lily. There must be a punishment for them. The girl was found and was now safe for all time. He wondered too, if those three men felt any pity for someone so young? It seemed one of them might have. Would they go about their lives and work and not even think about her? One of them surely did, the one who cried. Would he have the guts to do something about it, go to the Police? Thomas hoped he would.

Where was her body now? Thomas stared along the avenue. She mentioned the roadhouse. He knew of it. Lily said she had run across the field on to the back road. Had her body been found? I should look for her, he told himself. There might be nothing he could do, but maybe somehow, if the girl was not found, he might somehow be able to send somebody in that direction. He would find her.

He could move fast without a body and it should not take long to get from one place to another. There would be enough time to find his own daughter afterwards.

A few minutes later Thomas saw them. A line of villagers in the next field with a group of police officers showed him they were looking for something. He saw Colin Black and a few others he recognised. He heard a whimper and walked up on the narrow grass verge and looked over the hedge. A black and white border collie was looking at something in a damp hollow, turning its head from side to side. Lily's body lay there face down, her arms flung above her head, one leg twisted beneath her. Thomas looked across at the men. They were moving off in the opposite direction.

Thomas called to the dog. It looked at him, could obviously see him, "Go find" he waved an arm in the direction of the group but the dog simply turned to look and then turned back to watch the dead girl. Thomas became impatient, there must be something he could do to get the stupid animal to, to do what? Yes, that was it. He pretended to throw something at the dog who barked loudly at him. Thomas kept pretending to throw and the dog became frantic. He looked up as a young officer came running. He stopped, waved his arms and called. The men came running. Ray Bowler ran past the officer, who tried to stop him. He was the first to reach the body of his daughter. He roared and howled out his grief. Thomas shook his head and thought, maybe if you took better care of her... he stopped the thought. Do not judge others. He left then, had done all he could.

****

Chapter 12

Thomas walked down along the avenue, but kept his eyes on the ground. The house where Mel and his mother had lived was next door to his own and now Kate was living there, with a man and children. He wanted to know what it was all about. In front of the house he stopped. Mel was about Valerie's age, younger than Thomas. The garden was a little overgrown now, even though it was winter.

Someone had built a brick wall about four feet high in front of the house and there were black enamelled gates set in posts. He looked towards his own house and saw the same. Where there had been an open gravelled drive there was now a paved front garden. It had not taken her long to change that. Thomas stepped towards the place he still considered his home but stopped and turned away quickly, then went towards Mel's house, where he understood Kate now lived. Where had Mel moved to, he wondered? Thomas stepped in through the wall.

The house was empty of people. He moved through the hall. Two rooms had been opened out into one to make a large living-room and there were children's toys scattered about. A huge plasma screen took up part of the end wall and beside it a music centre and piles of children's DVD's He let his eyes rove around the room taking in the big leather sofas, the rugs on the bare polished wood floors. There were photographs in frames on the deep window sills.

He saw then a picture of Valerie which had been taken at a wedding, and knew this must be Kate's place. So, it was all true. There was another, larger picture of a wedding group and he looked closely. Kate dressed in a white lace dress and veil holding a bouquet of flowers. Beside her stood a tall thin young man, somebody he vaguely remembered, but who had not then been a boyfriend. Two bridesmaids, unknown to him and a couple of young men. A small girl dressed like Bo Peep stood in front of the group. Then he saw his own photograph on a small table, taken as a much younger man. When had she married? There had been no mention of marriage before he crashed the car and left. There was another picture of twin boys in school uniform much too big and another of a baby girl with one of those silly bow things on her head. He grinned, no hair and a big bow.

Several things hit Thomas all at once. He had been dead for quite a lot longer than he thought. In fact, it must be at least five years, maybe even longer since he left. Kate was married and he had not been there to walk her up the aisle. He looked again at the photo of the glowing bride who was his only and dearly loved daughter. She had children, at least three. His grandchildren. Twin boys, like Valerie. Twin boys? There had been no twins in his family that he knew of, but here was Kate with twins also and a little girl too. That could just be a coincidence.

He heard a car drive up and sound of voices and two fair haired boys about five years old hurtled into the room pushing each other out of the way in their eagerness to get to the screen. A little girl about two, wearing jeans and a hooded jacket, toddled in and to his astonishment smiled at him, said 'Hello man', then struggled her way on to the sofa to watch television. She could see him, Thomas thought, but after the first look and smile the little girl ignored him.

He heard Kate's voice calling them to come to the kitchen for milk and biscuits. Then she was standing in the doorway. His Kate, a little older but, still pretty much the same as she had always been. Tall and slim, her dark hair long now and tied back in a ponytail. His beautiful Kate. The boys got up reluctantly and walked backwards trying to watch the programme on the television. "Can we have our milk and biscuits and watch telly?" one of the twin boys asked. "No, you can come and sit at the kitchen table. I have no intention of mopping up crumbs and spilt milk because of you two fighting over what's on the TV," Kate said. "Man comes too," the little girl stood looking at Thomas.

She was a sturdy little thing with a beautiful face topped with shining blonde curls and large grey eyes. Thomas frowned. She reminded him of someone "What man," her mother asked, not really paying much attention, "There is no man darling,"

"That man," the child insisted and pointed with a chubby finger to Thomas and then to the photograph on the table.

Kate looked at her daughter and then in the direction she was pointing and shook her head and smiled, "No sweetheart," she said, but she frowned slightly bit her lip. "The man comes too," The little girl insisted then walked across to the picture of Thomas and pointed towards him again.

Kate picked up her daughter, "You mean Granddad Tom," she bit her lip again as Thomas watched, would she understand. "Ganda," the child said and pointed a chubby finger at a spot between the windows.

Kate stared at the spot, then picked up the child and took her to the kitchen, sitting her in her high chair, told them to eat and drink then went back to the living room. She looked around and seemed to listen for a while. She sniffed as if to catch some remembered scent. Then she nodded. He stood in front of his daughter and looked at her. There were tears in her eyes. "Are you here Dad," Kate whispered, "I can't see you, but if you are here, then I'm glad. Have you seen your grandchildren? Are you happy now Dad? I hope you are happy and at peace. I missed you so much after you died. It was so sudden, so awful. Mum, she was so ill after you died. She was in the hospital more than a month. She had a breakdown. She said you'd never forgiven her. She wanted that more than anything. It was like waiting for you to forgive her gave her a reason to live. After you went, she had no reason. It took her a long time to get better."

Kate stood in the centre of the room listening and waiting for something, anything, then said, "If you are here, and I think you are, just remember, I love you so much. I still miss you. You were a great Dad to me. The boys, they loved you too. They appreciate how much you did for them. David thought it was because you could not show love. They are very successful because of you."

Thomas frowned, successful because of him? That was something he did not understand. He had meant it to be the other way around. Good grief, they had achieved *because* of him. How could that be? "Thank you for everything Dad."

Kate broke off at the sound of a key in the lock and a man's voice called out, "Hello all."

"It's your son-in-law," she whispered and smiled broadly, "He does not believe in ghosts."

Thomas watched as she threw her arms around her fair-haired grey-eyed husband and whatever tiny suspicion he had that Kate also might also have been Roberts child was gone. Because the thought had been there. He wondered what he could do to let her know he'd really been there and loved her so much, that he was not a figment of her child's imagination, or of hers. "You may give her a sign," He heard the voice of Cadamiel say, "Touch the picture."

Kate released her husband and he grinned at her, shouted "Hi kids" and walked upstairs. She went back to look at the photo of her father. He touched the photograph and hoping he could do it, concentrated hard and slowly it moved across the table. He watched his daughter.

Her eyes widened. She touched it and moved it back. He moved it forward again. "You are here," she whispered, "I love you Dad. I love you so much."

He watched as she picked up the photograph and kissed it holding it in her arms, close against her heart. She was happy. It was time to go. He slipped through the wall. Thomas looked back at the house.

She was fine. The boys he had brought up as his own were fine. There was nothing else. He would return to the Gathering Place. There was no need to stay longer. He had been there quite a while and darkness was coming on but there was no sign of his escort or a gateway through which he could go. Yet they had given him twenty-four hours and the time was not up.

He sat on the wall outside his daughter's home, watching people on their way back from work, some on foot, a few cyclists, one or two without lights or florescent patches and barely seen in the gathering darkness. A fox, sleek and well fed glanced at him, stopped and watched, then moved slowly towards a grey shape in the darkness, another fox.

A people-carrier slid in to the kerb just alongside where he sat. A very attractive young woman sat beside the driver. The man reached for the girl and kissed her on the lips. She got out and stood watching him with a little smile, but to Thomas it did not look as if it reached her eyes. To his astonishment the man did a swift turn across the road into the driveway of the house opposite. He got out slamming the door. He shouted "Hello darlings," as he opened the front door. A woman and two children came out of a room, then the front door closed.

Thomas watched the young woman. Are you wondering if he will leave her for you? Are you wondering if you will be a mistress forever, never his wife? Or, if you would be the cheated and not the cheater. Strangely he got the answer from the young woman herself. She stood biting her full bottom lip, shaking her head and he heard her mutter: "What am I doing? What am I getting from this? A lift to work and the odd lunch and a drink," She shook her head, "You're never going to tell her, are you?" She turned to look back at the house, "Next time Mike Sammes asks me out, I will go and if he doesn't, then I'll ask him. I'm going to get myself a life."

The young woman smiled happily and trotted on her high heels along the avenue to one of the houses further along. Thomas applauded her.

Thomas sat on a low wall and waited for whatever would happen next, but all was quiet again on the Avenue. No cats dogs or birds. No people; Empty world. The silence after the evening rush-hour from work to home. He stood and began to wander slowly along the avenue looking at the new houses. They looked pretty much like the others. Everything looked as if it should be there. Some had lights in all the rooms, others just one light. Some doors had security lights others completely dark. The last house which was close to where the back road began, was lit up.

Through the open blinds Thomas saw children sitting on a sofa watching television and eating from plates on their laps. A light snapped on in an upstairs bedroom and he saw a woman clambering up on something to get a big box from the top of a wardrobe. He looked back into the lower room. A bare Christmas tree stood in a corner. Then the woman came in and dropped the box on the floor where decorations spilled out and the children put their plates down on the floor and jumped up to help her. "What do you think you are doing?" A loud voice snapped behind him.

He turned swiftly to see a huge dark shape in a long cloak with a fur hat pulled down over the forehead. He stared. A very tall elderly woman stood holding what looked like a shepherd's crook in one hand and a torch in the other. The torch was not lit but held up over his head in a threatening attitude. "I said, what do you think you are doing? We don't like peeping toms around here. Or are you looking to see what is available to steal." The tall heavily built woman moved closer, "Speak, or do I have to knock the answer out of you."

She moved closer when Thomas did not reply. He was too shocked to answer anyway. She shone the torch on him. Then she gasped and stepped back. "Oh my God, you're one of them. What do you want here at this house? Have you not taken away enough when your kind took a good husband and father and left a widow and orphan children. Go away, leave them in peace. I command you."

Thomas found his voice, "I can't go," he said plaintively, "I have to wait until they come to take me back. I can't take anybody with me. I don't have the authority. I only came to find something."

"Have you found it?" The woman was less aggressive but still held the crook threateningly. "Not yet, and you can put that thing down," he told her, "You can't hit me. It would go right through me. I wouldn't feel a thing."

The woman looked at the torch and the long wooden staff and lowered both arms smiling ruefully. "I suppose not," she said.

The window just behind Thomas opened suddenly and a woman called: "What are you up to now Marjorie, are you doing your neighbourhood watch bit?"

Thomas walked quickly away, chuckling to himself, "Try telling her you've seen a ghost," he muttered.

A short while later he stood still. He wanted to get back to The Gathering Place. There was nothing he really needed to see. He'd been allowed to return, had seen there was nothing he needed to do. Sure, it was not all as he would have liked but what did that matter? He was moving onwards. They were all living their lives here. It was the best it could be. Thomas looked around then. Where was he? Then he realised he was directly outside his own house and stared hard at the windows, the lights were on in the sitting room they had rarely used. There were two cars in the drive. He wondered if? No. He was not going inside, had been instructed not to cause problems.

He wanted to call Cadamiel, but found he could not even think the words, much less speak them. He hesitated. Something whispered, "Go on." He turned away. The voice whispered again, "You know you want to go in. Go and see what you want to see," the voice insisted, "It is your home. Yours. You have a right to go in. You own it."

"I own nothing," he called to some dark place in his head.

The darkness came back at him: "Fool; they only tell you that to keep you from seeing that which is your right to see. They are making a fool of you Thomas. You own it. What right does she have to it all now?"

"I own nothing." Who was whispering to him, tempting him? "Go away," he called, "Whoever you are, go away."

It came back at him, insistent, "Step inside Thomas. Step inside and see what you want to see. You know you want to see what she has done. She is there. With him. Go in." The voice in his head trailed off in a hiss.

Him? Thomas stood uncertainly outside the black enamelled gates. It might not be a bad idea just to go in, and make sure she was all right, then leave. It would be the end of things. It would be like the last sentence in the book, would prove once and for all there was no pain or anger left. Maybe it would be a good thing. Then he could return to the Gathering Place in peace. In his heart he knew he was lying. Who was this him?

Thomas chewed on the inside of his lip. The question remained. Why were there two cars in the drive? Who else lived there? Him. It might be just a visitor.

What visitor? Robert was long dead. Was it a friend? What friend? As far as Thomas was concerned Valerie had very few friends, he'd made sure of that and so far, as he knew, none of them drove a Renault. A thought, sharp and suspicious whipped into his mind: Mel had a Renault. Thomas Beck's eyebrows drew down in a frown. Could it be he was the visitor? He had, it appeared sold his house to Kate and her husband. So, where did he live now? Inside? In my house? Mine. What right does he have to be there?

His mind shouted the words. Anger was rising in him. The car looked new but he did not look at the number plate. If he had Thomas might have left everything and gone to wait for the two angels, would have been certain change was inevitable, because too many years had passed. But Thomas Beck never could leave well alone. He had to do this.

Turning he looked at the front door. It was white, had been painted. She'd changed the colour. He had always liked to have a black door. Classier. White was cheap. The curtains too were gone and there were slatted white wooden blinds on the window. Aggression stirred. What right had she to change all this? Common sense gone now, Thomas stepped through the front door and into the hall. The lights were on. He stared at the bright creamy colour of the walls. Why had she painted them such a bright colour? Valerie knew he liked muted colours like beige and coffee cream.

He walked along the hall towards the kitchen. The lights were on here too. Wasting electricity. His eyes opened wide. The kitchen dazzled. It was all black and white. Black marble surfaces and white cupboards. He looked around. Silver grey washing machine, tumble drier and dishwasher stood in a line and a big American fridge freezer hummed softly beside them. This was not his house. His house was warm, comfortable. Not this clinical cold room that looked like an operating theatre. "This place is not yours. Leave now." the words came sharply from somewhere behind him. "*This* is my house, I will not leave," he snapped back.

Something else was here, inside the house, something big, but Thomas had lost all sense of propriety. The new voice was loud. He did not care. "Leave now. You own nothing here, Thomas Beck. You are long gone from this place. Do not heed the lies, the tempting voice. You are placing yourself in a position from which you will find it hard to extricate yourself. Go." The voice was very loud.

This is my home. Mine. The words thundered through his own head. She has destroyed it. Then he stopped. No. He must not lose it. Hold on to reason. Yet he could not resist looking around.

His eyes took in the big new conservatory where the French doors to the back garden used to be. Another door led to a shower room. He came out into the hall and stared upwards. He took the stairs two at a time. The room in which he and Valerie slept in their single beds now held a huge king-sized bed and she had broken through the wall into the bathroom, which was now en-suite. His head felt tight, someone had tied a band around it. He felt angry again, extremely so. Who had done this? She, or was it someone else? For that matter, who was living here with her?

There was no doubt in his mind that she lived here, Sue had said, "The house next to your Valerie's."

It had to be him. Mel. Mel who took her hand and smiled at her. She had to have a man, but not him, not her husband. Someone else, always someone else. He went back downstairs, slipped into the kitchen, walked towards the door leading into the sitting room and slipped through. They sat on the sofa holding hands, watching a programme on the television. Valerie and Mel, an elderly couple. Thomas felt rage rise like a tidal wave. He stared around wondering what he could do to shatter this illusion of happiness.

His eye caught the big coloured photograph of a bride and groom with their guests. His eyes bored into it as if he would set fire to it. Valerie dressed in a cream suit with a huge picture hat, gloves, with a bouquet of tiny cream and pink roses. She was smiling happily. The man beside her was Mel. The old fool too was dressed in a cream suit. He beamed, his arm around Valerie. So, she had remarried, could not wait to get rid of him. "Do not do this thing." a voice told him, "You and you alone made the decision which brought all things to this moment," a warning voice told him. "Go away," he snapped. "Then, be warned. On your head be it Thomas Beck." The voice called.

He walked towards the couple. She looked pretty much the same. Mel looked greyer. How long had they been married? "It's suddenly become a little chilly darling," Valerie said.

Mel put an arm around her, "It's beginning to freeze over outside," He pulled her close and kissed her cheek. "I think I'll turn up the thermostat," Valerie said getting up from the sofa.

Thomas followed her out into the hall with its hated bright colours and watched as she opened the white box on the wall, stared at the thermostat then turned it up a few degrees higher. He waited until she went back then turned it right down to zero. I knew I could do that Thomas smirked, then waited.

Ten minutes later Valerie came back to the panel under the stairs, frowned and turned it up again. This time he did not wait but as she watched, forced it back down again. She turned it up, he turned it down. Turn it up all you want he thought, I will make sure it freezes in here. She called Mel who came and said it must be slipping and would get someone in to look at it tomorrow.

Thomas left them and walked back into the now empty sitting room. He looked at the desk in the corner. There were invitation cards scattered about, some written, some in envelopes waiting to be stamped and posted. He looked closely. Anniversary invitations; Meredith and Valerie Drew. Anniversary dinner at the Belmont Hotel. He stared at the date on the desk calendar. He was gone over ten years and she married again so quickly. Rage roared through him. He stared hard as they came back into the room, stared at the diamond encrusted rings on both their left hands. They hardly had the decency to wait more than a few months. He wanted to tear this house down. How could she. Then there was Mel or as the invitations said, Meredith. He'd not know the man was called by such a stupid name. Meredith Drew.

He was dead over ten long years and they had seemed only a matter of weeks. He stared at Mel. "You could not wait either, could you," he shouted at the unheeding, unseeing Mel.

The couple now sat staring at the screen in the corner. Thomas wanted to hit out. Then his eye caught sight of the photograph of his wife and her husband on their wedding day, with all the family and a group of friends. He hurled himself at the picture and somehow, he did not know how, managed to knock it off the wall and hurl it across the room with such a force it crashed against the far wall. The frame and glass shattered. He stared in fury at the TV screen. It shattered, sparks flying out.

Valerie screamed and Mel jumped up staring, shocked. Thomas hurled himself through the walls creating an icy wind, slammed the cupboard open and tripped the switches. He heard the scream and shout from the sitting room as all the lights went. He turned them all back again, then off and began to laugh. "I can do this," he roared, "This house is mine. I can do whatever I want."

He slammed doors and shouted with pleasure as he heard the fear and cries of the elderly couple.

Then suddenly, anger spent, he stopped. Oh no, he thought. No. What have I done? He stood terrified by what he'd done and then slid down to his knees on the floor, head in hands.

Something, someone whirled through the house and then threw him so he was lying face down on the floor in the hall. He could not see properly because something brilliant and flaming was before his eyes. Then he was then lifted from the floor and as his eyes slowly cleared, he saw the Great Angel.

It was huge, reaching up nearly to the ceiling, dressed in armour with great wings spread wide and the flaming sword in its hand. "Do not lift your eyes to look upon my face Thomas Beck," the angel thundered, "Leave now, while you are still allowed to leave. Go, before the Scavengers come to take you, and I have a mind to let them do so. Go. Leave these two in peace. They have done nothing to give you cause to put them to such fear. I have much damage to repair because of your stupidity, ignorance and above all your childish disobedience. Go."

He was released and fell to his knees, scrambled up, ran from the house and kept running. He stopped at the end of the avenue and dared to look back towards the house. All was quiet. He looked around. Christmas trees twinkled in some of the windows. Two of the gardens had lanterns on fir trees. It looked, normal. The street was silent. He stood bewildered, ashamed and most of all frightened. Yet there was no Great Angel with flaming sword coming after him. Had he imagined it? Something moved in the shadow of a house. Then he smelled them. Saw the three shadows, faceless, smelling of something long decayed, heard them sniggering at him, "Fool, one hissed," Thomas panicked. Please do not let them take me. They were laughing now, that harsh rasping laugh. He jumped in fear as something rustled beside him. It was Fariel, wings wide, shielding him. "Go swiftly," the angel said, "Go. I will keep them at bay. Run for the Portal. Cadamiel waits to guide you through."

Thomas ran as he had not run since a child, along the road out of the village. He could hear sounds behind and that fuelled his terror. "Don't let me be taken. I am sorry. I am deeply sorry. I will never do anything wrong again."

Then he saw it, the arch of the Portal and the angel Cadamiel waiting wings spread wide. The angel held out its arms, "Come quickly. Enter now."

Thomas ran through the arch. "Walk towards the gate. You will see it eventually, but you may not yet enter the Gathering Place Just wait. One thing, do not turn your head to see what is behind."

Thomas moved swiftly along the road. The night was chill. Nor did he look behind. Had he done so he would have been astonished by the sight of three angels? One huge and in battle armour, shield in one hand and a flaming sword in the other with two smaller angels their wings spread wide, as they fought to keep a group of three dark shapes from passing the Portal.

Thomas walked and walked but there was no sign of the gate. They had lied to him. There was no gate. He was in a sort of limbo with nothing, no one. He was being punished now. He walked until he could pass no further, then turned and walked back. Somewhere in the middle he stopped by a big oak tree. Thomas stared up into it, feeling there might be a measure of safety in being off the ground. He pulled himself up and into the branches. The tree was bare of leaves but the branches were thick and heavy. They hid him, he felt safer up here hidden from the ground.

The whisperings began. Whisperings on the ground, whisperings all around; in the air. Something whispered close by his ear and he jerked his head around. Nobody there, but he could hear the words, "You had a right of entry to the Kingdom; a great gift. You were allowed to pass through but you threw back the gift. Did you not answer?"

Thomas turned his head from left to right. Nobody, only a hard whisper, "Answer."

This time it was louder, more insistent. "No. I was foolish. I behaved like an angry child," he cried. "Foolish old man. Not a child. You never learn Thomas Beck. The gift should have been accepted with the utmost humility. Could you not have done that one thing? Did you never in all your life or death learn one lesson? Did you ever listen to any thought except that which emanated from your own foolish angry little mind?"

"I'm sorry," he groaned. "Sorrow after the deed. Little thought before. No true repentance. When will you learn?"

The whisperer whispered no more and the silence following was long. He sat among the branches hugging himself against the wind and waited, not knowing what would happen. Terrified. "Where are you Cadamiel, where are you Fariel? Come back. You said you would come and help me. Where are you," Thomas wailed as he dropped from the tree to land on hands and knees.

Then he saw them. Three huge angels with shields and flaming swords held aloft, standing away from him. All three fixed fierce eyes on him. "Stand before us Thomas Beck" came the command.

They seemed to grow bigger as he stared. Terror stricken he scrambled to his feet to stand before them feeling very small. In a voice cold as ice the Angel in the centre of the three called out: "You cry that you do not understand. Why should you understand? It is not for you to question our ways. It is for you to follow in our ways. You were given a great privilege, and were trusted. You betrayed the trust placed in you. Yet, we are merciful to you. We have not sent you out into darkness. You are still in the Portal space."

He watched the three angels warily. "I need an answer, a reason," he called, "I need to understand."

The eyes of all three Angels seemed to burn through him, "Do you not hear what is said, Thomas Beck?" The Angel in the centre spoke again, "You do not have the right to an answer. What need do you have to understand yet? It is not your time. You do not demand answers of us. Accept this. Accept that you are one of ours now and should follow our ways. You still have the right to stay in the Gathering Place for as long as you wish. You have the right to privileges, but you do not have the right to abuse them. We, the Seraphim do not have to give you reasons. We owe you nothing. All debt is yours to pay. Yours alone. Foolish one, do you still not understand this? The gate will open soon and you may enter. You will wait there just inside. Learn from your foolishness."

They left him then, and he stood staring after them until their light faded away. But being Thomas Beck, he was not finished yet. He threw a tantrum. Like a small child he shouted, screamed and kicked at the gate, stamped his feet and cried tears of rage. Then he stopped and sat on the ground.

A small golden head popped up from the shrubbery. A little cherubim smiled. "Have you stopped behaving badly?" it queried politely, "You have? Good. There are two Seraphim waiting. Turn to face them."

He turned, heart-sick, to see more of the Great Angels. Both wore breastplates and carried the flaming swords and shield. Two more of them. What now? This pair looked even fiercer. "Obey the command. Enter here." The faces of both were impassive. One pointed to a small gate further along the path. He slid past them into a place which seemed strangely dark now, feeling the heat of the flame from the swords. Up this close they were even more frightening. No gentle angels these. God's Warriors.

The second spoke: "You will now pay the price for the fear you created upon earth. You are no longer of earth. You were instructed to cause no fear or pain. Your covenant for this was with Heaven alone. A trust was placed in you, which you have broken. We have taken away much of their fear from them. You had another twelve earth hours of time left. It is revoked. Enter now through this gate. You will not see or hear us until it is time to return to The Gathering Place. Enter and climb the mountain of repentance."

Thomas stepped forward and found himself alone in the cold grey iciness of the road where he'd found himself over ten years previously.

Chapter 13

It was dark here; the wind blew cold. It worked its way into his heart like shards of ice. The only sound was the wind which whistled and keened. Everything was cold. His fingers had no feeling. In time too, it took over his body. But not his mind. That remained clear. Every thought, every sense was intensified and there was always the numbing cold. He sat on the ground like a beggar, unable to walk. I am a beggar, his mind called. I beg for forgiveness. He stared up at the sky and stars. A full moon shone mistily and coldly. No other sound. Only the wind; Fear returned and with force. Desolation.

The night did not pass. Daylight did not come. There was only the relentless sound of the wind. The scream of a vixen would have been welcome in this awful seemingly permanent night. Thomas had a thought. He would call out to break the silence, then to his horror realised he could not. No sound came from his throat. His mind screamed.

He began to hallucinate. He could see a snow-covered mountain in the distance and a bright yellow sun shone right on the top. What had Mike said about climbing his mountain? If he could climb up there, out of the dark night of this place and up to the top, into the light, maybe he would find relief from the cold. He would stand in the golden glow of that glorious sun and be warm again.

In his mind, Thomas began to climb, fingers scrabbling into the icy hard-packed snow. His body felt the freezing cold. Almost at the top now, almost there. His breath blew in a mist. His fingers reached for that last lump of snow. Now. The snow crumbled in his hands and he slid all the way back down. He cried. Time and time again he tried to climb, but each time the snow crumbled in his hands and he slid down. He believed he was really climbing the mountain. It was real. He could not reach the top. In despair his mind cried out: "How long? How long must I stay here? Must I stay for all time? This is the worst yet."

Out there in the night someone, something, laughed, a mocking, jeering laugh.

When he felt, he could bear it no longer and begged for mercy, crying out for pity, there was a change. He felt it almost immediately. He discovered he could move his numbed legs and got to his feet. It was warmer. Not much, but it was something. The darkness lightened a little.

He heard them and got their smell before he saw them, and ran behind a tree to hide, but their mocking jeering laughter came ever closer. Terror shot through him like a blade. Then they were beside him. The faceless woman was closest. "Do you want to stay here forever?" she whispered, "See, we have given you a taste of what you can have. Feel the warmth." he felt it, "There is more, so much more. Let us give you more."

He shuddered as she came closer to him. He thought, I can smell the grave, and death and there is no face. God help me, he thought. "Come with us. We have taken away some of the cold as a gesture of good faith." She and the other dark shapes began to laugh. "A gesture of faith," he said.

The female scavenger said, "If you come with us there will be great warmth. Join us. You can have anything you want. Anything your heart desires. You can have everything. Reach out and take my hand."

For one moment Thomas thought he would do it. They stood before him, hands reaching but not touching. He kept his hands tightly under his arms, he must not reach out. "Go away," he called, "Leave me alone. I will pay my dues. I will pay what I owe to Heaven and not to, to your place." He was unable to speak the word, "I will pay for what I have done."

"Fool," the woman shouted, "you could have had it all. Now you have nothing, Feel the ice of the wind. Feel it forever,"

Then they were gone, their mocking laughter fading into the distance. The silence came again and with it, the numbing cold. However, Thomas could still move and realised it was not they, the Scavengers who were doing this. The eternal night was gone too. That gave him hope. Daylight had returned. He was able to walk and speak. Still wretched, he waited. The nights when the wind became sharper and colder were the worst. There was always the fear of the Scavengers. Sometimes they walked past him saying nothing, but sending a waft of heat towards him. He tried to breathe it in. They laughed and went away. The temptation of warmth was frightening.

Then a huge fireplace appeared before him with great logs blazing and he felt the glorious warmth, curving his body toward it. They let him have it for a minute and he revelled in the joy of it. Then they took it away. His desire for warmth was the one thing which might let him take that step into their hands. Yet there was always the smell to hold him back. That smell which was dark, secret, deep, and filled with evil.

They were relentless now, bringing their heat with them. When he least expected it, a blazing fire appeared before him, each time the warmth lasting longer. He almost gave in. That was where his weakness lay and they knew it. They always went away mocking and laughing. How long could he hold out against them?

Even in his freezing state, Thomas wondered: What was the answer? He had to accept things as they were. He had to change things for himself. Was that it? Accept and comply. It was hard to obey the rules when a body did not know what they were. But that was not true. He knew the rules. The more he thought about it the more the answer came back and each time it was the same. Learn Thomas. Learn and obey. Throw away your bitterness and anger. Forgive. So, they went on, the grey days and the cold endless nights, broken by the Scavengers who delighted in tormenting him, trying to break down his resolve. He knew now how the homeless felt in the icy coldness of winter and wished he had stopped to help those whose eyes looked pleadingly at him from the doorways of shops. They too must feel the fear of the unknown, especially the young. "I could have helped. I wish with all my heart I had. I am so sorry I did not." Thomas whispered through chattering teeth.

When he thought he could bear no more, Thomas saw a shooting star trail across the sky and suddenly it seemed as if the wind was less fierce and the air warmed a little around him, and he saw coming toward him the figure, misty and ethereal. He thought it might be Cadamiel, but the voice when it spoke was that of another, "Soon Thomas; It will end soon. A little more time and it will be over." Then the misty shape was gone. There was a change then. It grew less cold. He grew less frightened. There was hope.

Then, another soul came in through the Portal. He stared at the youngster who looked about sixteen years old. There was something familiar about him. Thomas thought he looked similar to the young man who slept at night in the doorway of the hardware shop in Great Barton. Too many years had passed and the boy would have become a man, was probably off the streets or maybe even dead a long time ago. As he drew nearer Thomas realised it was, but how could that be. "Scuse me for talkin' to ya. I been searchin' like." The ragged youngster stopped speaking and the big haunted eyes bored into Thomas, "I bin tryin' to find a place. In me mind, I know there is a place I 'ave to find."

When Thomas did not reply he stared around, sniffed and his mouth twisted to one side. He rubbed his filthy hands together. "Cold innit." He snuffled and wiped his nose on a torn sleeve. He looked at Thomas from red rimmed eyes. "You don afta talk to me if you don't wanna. Nobody ever talked much to me back there. See, I just wanna know where I 'ave to go. I bin lost since that bloke gimme the Charlie. It killed me. It was bad gear. I bin all over the place since. Then I met a bloke in a white dress. He said I should come in 'ere, that I was a lost soul and I needed to be found, but then I got lost again."

He snuffled again and looked around, "Wot is this place anyway. Please mister, I only wants know if I'm goin' the right way. He said it was warm if I go the right way. I never bin warm that I can ever remember."

Thomas was unable to answer because of his terrible feeling of sadness, but he nodded his head and reached out a hand. The boy stared at it as if it was an alien thing then slowly reached his filthy nail bitten fingers towards the clean slender hand the man held out to him.

Thomas managed to speak at last, "I will try and find a place for you. I'm trying to find my own way back to where it is warm." He closed his hand over the boys, "Can I give you a bit of advice? Never ask them to let you go back into the world. I made the mistake of going back and I messed the whole thing up. If we wait here a while, they will let us in."

The boy grinned, "I wouldn't wanna go back there mate. I was always cold and hungry, even when me mam was alive. I might be cold here but I ain't ever bin hungry since I died. This has been the best time of my life. An I ain't got no pain neiver. Great, innit?' He laughed showing black broken teeth. 'I know it 'ain't life mate, but you know wot I mean. I wanna get out of 'ere. Them fings wivout the faces is around all the time. They promised I would get warm, but I don't like them; scary. Tell you wot though, I told 'em it was worse bein' alive and I wasn't goin' back, they didn't understand that an they went off some place."

Thomas looked at the boy, the only attractive thing about him was the huge eyes and he thought, this poor scrap of humanity managed to out think the Scavengers; amazing. They sat and waited a long time and then it seemed as if the air around them became warmer.

The boy felt it too. The greyness lifted suddenly and it was brighter. The gate appeared. Thomas kept staring at it, willing it to open. Then in the distance he saw them. Two men in white suits hurrying towards them. He tightened his grip on the boy's hand and they began to run towards the Gatherers. "Thank you, Thomas," the first one spoke, "he has been missing a very long time."

"You too are coming home Thomas." The second smiled. "Welcome back." They spoke in unison, then gestured to the gate, "Enter now."

The gate slowly opened. The boy was grinning hugely and Thomas noticed his teeth were no longer black and broken and his hands no longer filthy. He looked like an altogether new person. He was clean and laughing happily. They walked hand in hand into the warm sunshine of the Gathering Place together. Two angels came towards them and Thomas saw one was Cadamiel. The other one took the boy by the hand and led him off. The boy looked back; his smile wide then went off into the distance with the angel. "Welcome back Thomas," Cadamiel said in his gentle voice, "It is nice to see you again."

Thomas looked away across the plain towards his little house, feeling a deep sense of embarrassment. "I have made a dreadful mess of things. I let you down. I know that. I suppose I have to start all over again, do I?"

Cadamiel nodded, "You do indeed have to start again. You have learned a harsh lesson and you realise of course; you will never again be able to return to life. Any unfinished business will have to be dealt with here, and will take, what is for you, a long time."

Thomas turned to look at the angel. It smiled its gentle smile. There was no feeling that he was being told off. Everything Cadamiel said was matter of fact. "I deserve a right telling off," he said. "Ah Thomas, surely you know us by now. I am not one of the Great Angels. I do not tell you off, as you say. We are not here to do that. We guide, give you the rules, but not in any way other than as a directive." The angel smiled, as if amused, "The Great Angels do not have our patience, since they have much work to do. All of us here are a part of this." The angels arm swept around in an arc, "The book of your life had indicated you were deserving of a place here. Few are turned away. What is sad to us here is that some turn away of their own volition. So now you must start again. You will be given other work now, helping the helpless. One thing you should know, the Seraphim asked for a longer period of isolation. It was not granted. I would be wary of them Thomas. You have caused them much trouble."

Thomas stared at the angel as it moved away and thought, I have made enemies. How stupid have I been?

The angel Cadamiel smiled to itself and it was almost a mischievous smile. The Seraphim had indeed asked for a longer period of isolation. That was true and if Thomas chose to believe he had made enemies, well then, did it matter. The angel's smile grew: That should keep you out of mischief Thomas Beck. Then it was gone leaving behind a mere whisper of itself.

Thomas looked out across the plain. He thought, I have really made a dreadful mess of everything. He walked slowly gazing around as he walked, feeling a great sense of relief and peace. He had been stupid, had forgotten where and what he was and had gone back to believing life was his once more.

Valerie did not deserve the pain he caused her to suffer. Yet she had stayed with him, never given up on him. He felt shame. Those boys, Robert's children. It was not their fault, and yet Kate said they believed he was the cause of their success in life. How had he done that? Yes, he gave them a good education, fed and clothed them, but what else? Valerie was the real carer, loving and being a good mother to her boys, not he. She had given all the nurturing, the love, the direction and he sat and glowered. All he ever thought back then was of how she betrayed him, never of how he was punishing her and the boys. He blamed the children too. They had no part in it at all.

Thomas lifted his hands impatiently not wanting to think the thought. It came anyway. How did he manage in that instant of knowing they were not his, how did he manage to stop loving them and her? The truth of course, was that he did not. That was why he wanted to keep them all with him. He loved the boys. He loved Valerie. Yet he had lost them. Driven that wedge deep. He lost them because of what he let himself become. He always had to justify everything. He'd justified nothing, fool that he was.

Then there was Robert. He always thought of him as being confident, successful, but the reality was he'd lost out. He lost out on Valerie and his sons, had only seen them for short periods of time and had died alone in the remote house in Norfolk. Poor Robert. Thomas stopped short. Yes, it was poor Robert. He had suffered but in a different way. There was every reason to pity the man who had lost everything. We were both the instigators of our own misfortune. Valerie would have told me. She would have stayed with me, not gone to Robert. I created my own monster inside my own sad unforgiving soul, nobody else. I did it all myself. I must destroy that monster now and forever. He sighed deeply and came to a resolution. I understand now. I have to let it go. I did it all myself.

A huge weight seemed to fall from his mind and body. Thomas felt curiously light, felt new, as if he'd been reborn. He had things to do now.

Thomas walked towards his own small patch and opened the wicker gate. There was no sign of Mike. He wanted to tell him about his return visit to the earth and the mistakes he'd made. How right had Mike been about all that. But then he too, had said he messed it all up and he also, must have had to pay. Mike too had to climb the mountain. He looked out across the plain. People were still coming in, some with Gatherers, some alone. In the distance he saw several pairs of the Great Angels coming down; down from the direction of the huge gates behind the mist. Then he saw two outside the gates of the house on the other side of Mike's little house. They entered and in a very short while came out with a man Thomas had never seen. He must have spent all his time inside.

The man's face was glowing. In his arms he carried the book. Light seemed to dance from it. It glittered and gleamed. Thomas caught his breath. Was that what it would look like? The two Great Angels placed a hand beneath each of the man's arms and slowly they rose up into the air. He watched as they grew smaller and the mist before the Great Gate lifted and Thomas saw it was open wide, and saw the light, like a great beacon, shine from it, but there was little else to be seen once the tiny figures passed through and the mist came over it again.

He opened the door and looked inside his house. The Book of life was on the table. It was a mess, but some of the filigree work showed a glint of gold. That was all he had left. Well, there was nothing for it but to start again. He turned, and came out on to the veranda and as he did, saw a man in a white suit watching; a pale man with silver hair that seemed slightly out of place. Something was not quite right. Thomas nodded and the man nodded, seeming about to speak. Thomas swiftly turned and went back inside his little house. He wanted to get on with the business of cleaning up his book, because that was what needed to be done that was obvious. That was much more important than chit-chat. He did not see the man's eyebrows draw down in a frown.

****

Chapter 14

It was the middle of February. This year once again, winter had been bitterly cold, with heavy frosts and thick heavy snow. By now most of it had gone from the fields around Barton Trinity and there was a small amount of thawing brownish grey residue left at the roadsides and along country lanes. The graveyard of the church at Barton Trinity village was shrouded in a cold mist, with a thin drizzle of rain which was starting to defrost and wash away the slush. The red hooded coat of a small girl holding her mother's hand made a bright splash of colour in the dullness of the afternoon.

An elderly man and woman led a small group of people along a pathway. The graveyard could be an odd place the woman thought. In the dull mistiness of the afternoon the gravestones in the older part of the cemetery, which went back centuries, looked like some square primitive headless beings, as the group made their way along the mossy path toward a grave.

Valerie and Mel Drew, together with her twin sons, Jonathan and David, with their children, her daughter Kate and her children, walked towards the grave of Thomas Beck, Valerie's first husband. Kate, tightly grasping the hand of her own small daughter, came slowly along the path. Her husband Jack Duval walked further behind warning his twin sons to behave as they giggled at something silly.

Valerie Drew always had a slight feeling of depression after Christmas, but this thing they had to do kept her occupied. She had been thinking about it for years, but always put it off, waiting for a more suitable time. The time had to be now, because when she thought about it, there was never a suitable time. Just do it, she'd told herself.

They found the grave. It was not far from the path. Valerie had only once visited after her first husband's funeral. That had been on the first anniversary, when the stone had been erected. That time her whole body shook, almost with a fever. Her sons had stood beside her, each holding an arm. That had been after her breakdown.

All these years later she still trembled a little and slipped an arm through Mel's. He pressed it close to his side. The psychiatrist had explained her fear to her: "In layman's language, it is a consequence of years of mental abuse, years of tension and fear. You suffered it for a long time. Then, when it was no longer there, you had nothing to put in its place. Now you have to deal with that." She'd got over it with help, but it surprised her that after all this time she should remember or even care about the man after his treatment of her. It all came back so swiftly it was like a physical pain. Take a few deep breaths she told herself and heard Mel whisper, "Good girl."

"Some girl," she grinned back shakily.

Her first husband had been gone from them over twelve years now. She had no feeling of anger left after the disaster of her long marriage to him. That was over. Yes, it had all been her fault but what was the point now of going over and over all that old ground? She had practically destroyed herself with guilt and desperately tried to make amends. Valerie stood and stared at the gravestone. If only you had heard me out Thomas, all those years ago. Yet what was done could not be undone.

Thomas believed the baby to be his, had revelled in it. There was no denying it. She had not slept with Thomas before their marriage. Robert had laughed when she told him, had loved the idea that she was married to Thomas and carrying *his* child, only as it turned out, it was twins. Robert actually had a deep jealousy of Thomas. The more she thought of it then the more Valerie realised he actually wanted to be Thomas, had always known he loved her, almost before he knew it himself. So, he took, simply because he could and because, she realised now, he was jealous.

Her pregnancy had given him a twisted kind of pleasure. That secret knowledge, his pleasure in it shocked her. He adored the twins though, and after their birth, came to see them whenever possible, eventually moving back to Barton Trinity to be near them. I should have got away from him, but really it was too late. It was pre-destined. It had to happen.

That day; the day when everything fell apart. Her stomach twisted even now at the thought of it. The twins' birthday fell not long after her mother's death. She decided to give them a little party. All they knew was that it was their birthday. They did not really understand her mother dying. That day changed all their lives forever. A new and terrible beginning. She and Thomas started to live separate lives, well, almost, but not quite. He disassociated himself, that was the only way to describe it. Isolated her too, from her friends and his colleagues. If it had not been for the boys, they needed a settled home, she could have ended it all, gone far away and begun again. Not with Robert though. She was certain of that.

When the dust settled, yet, did it ever really settle, she had started taking the twins to visit Robert, sometimes going up to town with them just to have lunch with him. He adored his sons and they had to know who he was. She became devious. Holidays, because Thomas did not want to be with them, were spent with Robert. He had a place in Norfolk, where the boys lived like wild creatures and loved it. They learned quickly not to mention what they did when they came home. What had she done to them? Then, there was period then when Thomas became affectionate, kindly even, but only up to a point.

Life changed for the better, became peaceful again during her pregnancy with Kate, but once the little girl was born it all started up again. She lost hope for a bit then, almost did something terrible. She almost cracked up but the thought of two defenceless boys alone with him did not bear thinking about. Then too, there was her little infant. Who would love her, care for her, tell her everything she needed to know, watch her as she grew and guard her against the pitfalls? She battled and won with the help of her doctor. Thomas never knew, would not have cared. Valerie still did not understand why she stayed. Then she left it too late, and there was no going back.

The children grew. Robert began to feel unwell, yet he did not say what was wrong. Valerie was not there when he died. She wanted to be but dare not, spending whatever time she could with the dying man. She had not mentioned to her husband that Robert was dead, keeping it all to herself. The boys were at University, knew he was their father. They were with her at his funeral. Robert did one good thing; he had worked hard for his sons. He left them wealthy young men. Thomas did not know that either. Not then.

It amazed her now how she had separated their lives. When they graduated, they did not return to Barton Trinity, except for the odd visit. Thomas never even asked about them. Well, it was to be expected since he never asked anything. She had lived two lives and managed to keep them separate. No wonder she had another breakdown. That one was mild. She had come out of it quickly. This now was the third and final part of her life. The part which helped blot out the dark years and the pain. "I was a mess." Valerie said and was startled to realise she had spoken aloud. "What did you say Mum?" Jonathan asked, smiling down at his tiny mother. "Just thinking aloud." she said.

But it was true. She had managed to separate her life so completely it was surprising that she stayed sane. Anyway, what was sanity? For her it was just having peace.

I did love Thomas in a way, Valerie thought. Perhaps it was more caring than loving. We were together a long time. There was happiness in the beginning. But Robert, he was different. Dangerous. What was it I felt for Robert? Not love. Passion? I don't know, but I don't want to think about that now. This is more important.

It was over, all past and gone. Yet her mind refused to let it go. Valerie remembered the fear at discovering she was pregnant, but that was just after her wedding. There was the worrying knowledge that it could not be her husband's child. She had truly not known on her wedding day. Not lied and cheated then. There had been no morning sickness.

She tried to tell him the day he asked her to marry him that although she was fond of him, she did not love him in the way he loved her. Thomas refused to hear the words. Would not listen. She had gone off with Robert when he crooked his finger. They went away for that last fling to Paris, and she lied to Thomas, said she had to have a dress fitting, and got away with it; temporarily. That must have been when it happened, and then with all the preparations she'd not even thought about her missed period. Valerie prepared to settle down after the wedding, to live the best life she could and maybe someday, even love him as he loved her. She had not suffered in pregnancy as many women did. Nor did it show much later on. In a way, that helped preserve the lie.

His mother did not like her, had been suspicious, but she kept calm, thought she had got away with it. No, that was not what she meant. What did she mean? It had been in a way, simply hoping to hold it all together. But that had not happened, well, it had for a few years, then came the years of misery for them both. They had both clung on to failure like limpets. But why? There really was no answer to that. It was all so complicated; it would take a psychiatrist years to work it out. Her second marriage to her lovely Mel had given peace and love and a life of quiet contentment. That peace was balm to her soul and Mel was so happy. "Waiting for you was worth every second of my life," he told her so many times.

Now, as they all stood in silence at the graveside of her first husband, the three younger grandchildren edged away silently to play in and around the gravestones, the two boys trying to hide from their small sister. The older teenage children of David and Jonathan Beck, two boys and two girls stood quietly watching, not quite sure what to do, knowing that standing silently made sense, and it would soon be over.

The younger ones did not want the grown-ups to notice they were playing hide and seek, and played silently, running across graves, peeking around gravestones, the boys poking their tongues at their little sister. Nana Valerie had spoken to the children in the car on the way. She said that coming here was almost like going to church. They had to be quiet she said, had to have respect for all the people who rested here.

The youngest of Valerie's grandchildren, the little girl Sara, kept an eye across the cemetery to the big headstone where the two men in white suits sat watching. Sara Duval sniffed and wiped the back of a plump little hand across her nose, before sneaking a glance at her mother. That was not allowed. She fished in her little bag among the beads, bracelets and a couple of dolls shoes for tissue and sniffed again, could not be bothered searching and wiped her turned-up nose again on her sleeve. She turned to look at the men, had seen them lots of times.

This was Kate's daughter. Small round, fair and serious, the little girl watched them carefully. She was just gone four-and-a-half years old now. Sara knew the men were not real people. Those people who sat for a long time waiting or sometimes rushing around like Mum when she was in a hurry, they were not real. The child knew they were just people who came and looked and sometimes went away all in a flash, some even spoke but at the age of four and a bit the child did not really want to talk to them or even properly understand what it was all about. She would look at them and smile and go back to playing with her dolls or watching her television programme.

The men dressed in white were a part of her life. Sometimes they just peeped in the door as if they had lost something, smiling and waving. They looked along roads, behind bushes and around the corners of buildings. Sometimes she watched, but by now, had become so used to them she scarcely glanced their way. Today they made her cross, so she kept an eye on them, "Go away you," she whispered, lip stuck out petulantly.

Valerie watched the children and Sara could see her watching. She was much nicer than Granny Duval, who hated children to touch her or her clothes, or for that matter anything belonging to her. She lived in France and only came for holidays. Valerie watched now as the children moved swiftly and silently through the gravestones. As long as they did not make too much noise and be disrespectful of this place of rest, she would say nothing. She very much aware they got bored at times like this.

Just after Christmas Valerie had gathered her family about her and they decided it was time to do something about Thomas Beck's gravestone. It really was a bit bare. The whole business had been done when she had not been very well after his death. The boys decided that leaving it until she was well again before completing the wording would be best, but of course, like many things it had been left on the long finger. Now however, it was necessary to complete the memorial. It was done at last. That time before Christmas two years ago when she was sure he was in the house, well, it made her think. The gravestone needed to be properly sorted, the wording completed. Nothing flowery, just simple.

Valerie glanced around at Mel, her husband. He had put on a little weight since their marriage and it suited him. She adored him and he her. He'd been worn to a shadow running around after his elderly mother who had died three months after Thomas. They comforted each other and she had grown to love him. He was an easy man to love. So kind and generous. He said, he had loved her for years. She was astonished. Who could love her? As for wanting to marry her, well, who would want a pathetic person like her?

But she learned. They had been married now for over twelve years and confidence had grown and made her a truly different person. She could love without fear now. These last years had been wonderful. Apart from the first few years of her marriage to Thomas, life had been stressful and most times wretched. Then he had been killed in that stupid accident. Nothing could have been done to stop it. Valerie blamed herself for the accident then, but Mel and the psychiatrist made her see it was not her fault. Thomas lived by his own rules. Thomas decided. Thomas did. That was it.

Yet, in all honesty there was a small part of her that asked, if it had not been for you, would it not have been different? That question was always there. Now she no longer allowed herself to think very much about it. She had found a way of locking such things away in the depths of her mind, though admittedly it did occasionally come to the fore. This now should be the final task. No more self-blame. People did what they wanted to do. You could not stop them. If only you could. Mel had got her to see otherwise. Made her stop thinking 'if only'. As he said so many times, Thomas made his own rules.

She had thought long and hard and made the decision about the wording on the gravestone. It really needed changing. It might even be a good idea to put up a new headstone, particularly since that business too with her granddaughter Sara before Christmas a couple of years ago, when the child had pointed to the photograph and told her mother Kate that he was in their sitting room.

On Christmas Day she had again pointed to the photograph and told them: "That man is not coming any more. That man is gone away. You know, the grandpa man."

When she thought he had been in the house Mel said, "He can no longer hurt you, or me for that matter. Only the living can do that and he is not alive. Suppose he was here just for a short time. What does it matter? It is you and I now. It is our life together. He made you wretched when he lived and I know you cannot simply forget he existed but we have our lives to live."

Now she was no longer bothered by the thought that Thomas might have come back. There had been nothing since. Valerie spoke to the Vicar who told her it might be that Thomas needed prayers. Souls did get a little lost sometimes. He would do that over the Christmas period, pray for him. Maybe there was something her husband had left undone. She should think about that. She might be able to complete it?

Valerie felt there was only one thing the man left undone in his lifetime. He had never forgiven her for her betrayal. Maybe that was why he came back. Had he forgiven her? No, not Thomas. He was unforgiving. It was very hard to know. Yet in life, Thomas had never asked for anything; demanded yes. Asked? No. Later on, Valerie remembered the gravestone. It should be completed. She would speak to the boys. It was time to deal with it now.

They all agreed on a new gravestone. She felt surprisingly peaceful and happy having made the decision. She went to the stonemasons. The wording would be changed, added to and she would forget him for all time, assuming of course she could, and she would damn well try. So, there it was, standing tall, the new headstone. Gleaming black marble and gold lettering, a circular plaque at the top with the small figure of an angel. Mel took her arm under his and squeezed it, smiling. She felt humbled that this truly good and kind man had chosen her to love and care for.

Did it matter what was written on the gravestone? Probably not, but they had to do the thing properly. The boys had obviously forgiven him. Maybe even forgotten his harshness in the lives they now lived. Kate loved him. The man was long gone and life was good now. She and Mel had been talking of selling the house and moving from the cold wet English winters to the warmer climate of Spain. Kate and her husband and family might join them. The rest of their lives would be far from Barton Trinity. The boys were settled in London with their families. The decision had not yet been made.

Valerie looked around. But I love Barton Trinity, she thought. I have lived most of my life here, good and bad. Maybe to go away from all this and lead another life in another country was not a good idea at their age. Things were not so great abroad either. The warmer weather of course was a lovely thought, but spring and summer would come again, and again. What was most important was that they close that particular book on the past now. A new beginning.

She looked back at the gravestone. The round plaque at the top with the image of the angel seemed to glow in a sudden shaft of winter sunlight. The gold lettering on the black marble stood out and the words which Thomas Beck would love to see were there, even if they were not strictly true.

Valerie had a moment of absolute clarity.

I was the one who caused all this. I was the guilty one, not Thomas. She felt as if a bolt of electricity had shot through her body. I only thought about myself, always saw myself as the unforgiven, yet it was my action which began all this. My forgiveness does not need to come from Thomas alone. It has to come from beyond that. I created all this. I must live with the guilt. She felt suddenly drained. "It was all my fault," she said and looked around swiftly. Nobody heard except the men in white. Whatever turns my life may take now Valerie thought, I will have to live with this. She nodded, turned and looked at her husband. This is mine, my guilt. I will not share it.

The two men smiled and nodded their approval. They walked past the group of adults and children, smiling at Sara. The child watched as they walked along the pathway to the gate, turned, waved to her and then they were no longer there. The small girl turned back to her mother. "The men are going back to that place. The Heaven place," she told her.

Kate shook her head lovingly at her little daughter. Where had she got this idea of men coming from heaven and going back again? "I did saw the men going back to heaven. They are not coming back for a long time," the child said, "I did saw them."

Kate shook her head again and hugged Sara. "Yes." Sara said, nodding her golden head, "The men is gone back heaven. I saw them. I know."

Kate took the hand of her small child. She was always saying odd things. Sara was, what was it Mum used to call it? Fey, that was it. A little elfin. She was probably right, Kate thought. Yet things had happened, so maybe Sara knew something the rest did not know? She put her arm around the child's shoulders and pulled her into her side. Sara looked up at her mother, snuffled loudly and said, "I love you Mummy."

Her mother took a tissue to the child's tiny nose and said, "I love you too darling, but I wish you would not snuffle. It's not very ladylike. Blow."

The child giggled and her mother pulled her close again.

The family now walked together slowly along the path between the grave stones. Jonathan and David with their wives and children. Then they were kissing Valerie goodbye and shaking hands with Mel. She gazed fondly after them as they all climbed into their respective cars and drove away. Her sons were tall like their father, like Robert. They and their children were all fair haired like him. She noticed her son's hairlines were now receding. Valerie smiled. Her son-in-law Jack called to them to hurry. It was getting really cold. They all climbed into the people carrier.

That which needed to be done, Valerie thought, has been done. She thought for a second that there was a movement in the mist to the left of them, and glanced swiftly in that direction. There was nothing. Well, people came in here all the time to tidy and place flowers. It did not necessarily have to be something other-worldly. My imagination is working overtime again Valerie thought and pushed her hand into the hand of her husband. He held it tightly.

Mel glanced at her seeing her nervous look. She still worried about that odd day in the week before Christmas a couple of years ago. He knew something strange happened that day, and yes, for all that he did not seem bothered by it, it had happened and it had been worrying at that time. Otherwise, why were they all here now trying to settle something they were barely aware of? He smiled down at his wife, "Everything is fine," he said reassuringly, "everything is just fine."

****

Chapter 15

Thomas sat in his rocking chair, in the little garden, watching people come and go. A girl in a wide brimmed hat, decorated with ribbon, wearing a long brown dress patterned with yellow flowers and wearing lace gloves stood looking around. She caught his eye and smiled. Another girl about twenty with long black hair streaked with vivid blue and threaded with red ribbons sat on the grass, watching. She wore knee length black boots and the shortest of mini-skirts. A young Asian man walked by wearing a white robe. These looked as if they had come in on their own. He was puzzled by this. He had been met on the road, but by a small voice only, had been lost for a time but then found by the men. Why then did some come in on their own? He smiled wryly. He was still questioning their ways.

He heard the familiar gentle rustling sound and looked up to see Cadamiel moving towards him seeming to float rather than walk. Today the angel's robes had taken on a different hue. Sometimes they were a dazzling white, sometimes mixed hues. Today, however, its colours were a pale blue. "Hail Thomas," the angel smiled, "You are asking questions again. Some I can answer for you, in fact I can answer many things, but it is not always necessary that you should know. In time all will be revealed, but not here."

"It's just that some people come on their own, like those three," Thomas was now used to the angel knowing his thoughts and pointed at the girls and the young man.

The angel looked at the young people and nodded, "Souls do find their own way in you know. People differ, they have differing beliefs, some seem to have none but most who enter here have, somewhere deep in the depths of their being, a belief, even if it is very small, that there is another life, a better one. Many deny it, yet they hope. Some do not believe, but are truly good people, and have done much for their brethren. Some come swiftly, like the girl with coloured hair. She had no recognisable faith, had tried many, yet found none which gave her any

126

hope, but she had a belief in a better life, so strong it was for her a living thing. She came alone, from a life filled with pain, determined never to go elsewhere. Some Thomas, are born filled with goodness, some lose it on the way, others, like you, subscribe to an earthly sophistication. A feeling they do not need to listen to their own hearts, or anything else. They say they do not really believe, but all Thomas, are souls worth having, worth the fight. Human life is diverse but it can also be perverse. So, we here fight for them, to give them true life."

The angel Cadamiel looked at the girl with the coloured hair. "Some come so swiftly and yes, unexpectedly, as she did, so it is often hard for the Gatherers to keep up. All mankind has an allotted span of life, but life sometimes has other ideas. Everything moves at such a pace. Mankind is frail. It was not made for this, for the swiftness of life as it is now. Life has become destructive to many. Sadly, this is how it is."

Cadamiel turned beautiful gentle eyes on Thomas. "Now Thomas, you were given, and you carried through to the end a severe punishment. You have learned much and it has all been noted. You may think you have not learned, but those who see these things are pleased. The Seraphim are pleased."

Thomas looked sceptically at the angel, "They did not seem very pleased the last time we met and to be honest if I don't see them again for a long time I will be quite happy."

Cadamiel seemed amused. A tiny smile twitched around the angel's mouth. "I see. Well. It might not seem to you that they were pleased. Yet, since you have learned much it has therefore been decided you will work for your salvation in another way. You will walk the pathways to find those who make their own way here alone. There are many doorways, gates, call them what you will, which lead to us here in this place. As I have said, so many come in unexpectedly. It is not always meant that they should come at that time, but they do. So, we need to be ready to hold them. There are others who would do that also. Life can be hard on those who are fragile of mind and body and their minds sometimes suffer, their thoughts lost to what is real, but we watch out for them Thomas, because, for all that mankind thinks of itself, somehow immortal, the day always comes when they realise they are not. Life is fragile. The Angel paused."

"We want to gather all in to us, to give them what they should have had in life, but could not. Down through the ages of time, life has changed and not always for the better. People in their own time change too. Some grow to greatness, some otherwise, Greatness too, can be a cause for evil, or a cause for great good. Humanity is also frail. A cruel seed can grow and be allowed to flourish. As I think you well know, that seed can become a monstrous thing, a malignancy."

The angel watched Thomas for a while as he sat head down, listening and a peace surrounded them, then it spoke again. "It is an arduous thing you must do now Thomas. It means watching and waiting. Patience also. When I tell you that you have done good work, be encouraged by this. I will now take you to the beginning of the pathway and from then on you will work to guide those who enter unexpectedly. Everyone is expected to arrive eventually. The reasons that some come too soon does not matter to you. You are not allowed to judge or comment on their lives. You are there simply to help. You may also meet evil on your journey. Be aware at all times. This is most important for you and whoever you may find and bring to us. There will be temptation, but you will be protected. We are a call away."

Thomas nodded accepting what would be and stood up.

The angel said, "Come, I will take you now to the pathways and you will find the gates appear before you. Then, your work begins. If they who enter wish to talk to you, you may speak with them in return but of course, you must not be tempted to send them back because they are young, or, for any other reason. They will be returned to life if a single thread within them holds them to that life and if it is a right and proper thing to do. If this is not so, they will continue on into this the gathering place You may not make that decision on their behalf. You do understand Thomas?"

"I do," he said.

Thomas had no intention of a making dreadful mess as he had done before, and said so. "You may not intend to make a mess Thomas." Cadamiel said, "But you will find temptation will come your way. The danger is that you may not recognise it. Be aware. Now, another thing. The Cherubim have passed to us word that your family from your previous life have prepared a memorial to you at that place where your earthly remains lies. Let me show you. It was the decision of your whole earthly family and a fitting memorial."

The angel held out a hand and pointed. Thomas glanced in the direction it pointed and saw the churchyard with the headstone. A shining oblong of black marble with gold lettering, with a plaque on the top portion which had an angel carved with wings unfolded and hands joined. They had changed it. He read the gold lettering, saw the words. It told him he was held in loving memory, that he was a beloved husband and father, the date of his birth and death. It asked that his soul rest in peace.

Thomas Beck smiled. A peace crept over him. They had changed the stone and the wording. He was indeed remembered and it seemed with affection and for some it was with love. The memorial was there for all to read. The vision then faded and Cadamiel guided him towards the pathways. "Are you now satisfied Thomas?" the angel asked, "It has been done as you have wished?"

Thomas nodded, he could not speak and deep in his heart something welled up and spilled over, warmth, a love he had not felt for a very long time. He smiled and nodded again. "I leave you then to watch over the gates." the angel said, "You may return at times to reflect and rest from your labours since there will be others sent out, as you are. You will know when to do this. You are here at the beginning of your labour now."

The Angel paused and pointed in the direction he should go, "See, the gate awaits. Remember what I have told you. Do not be tempted to take anything upon yourself. This is an instruction to you, heed it well. Be aware at all times that evil too enters here. Should it come, call out to us. Now, goodbye Thomas. Remember the instruction. It comes to you from above. We will meet soon."

The angel Cadamiel drifted back along the pathway to where Fariel waited with another angel, Haramiel. "It is done?" Fariel asked, "Thomas is gone to his duties?"

"He is." Cadamiel turned to look after the man walking away along the path, "Yet, he is as a child. A watch must be kept. Haramiel, set a cherub to watch over him and report back."

The angel nodded and floated away to seek out one of the little ones.

Thomas turned to face green shrubs. There was no sign of anything remotely resembling a gate. His eyes roamed along the green hedge. Then he laughed. It was a very small gate, barely half a metre-high set in the base of the high hedge. He stared at it. What was this all about? Who was small enough to come in here? He stepped forward to the gate and bent down putting an ear close to what looked like a tiny lock. There was no sound. He touched it and snatched his hand back again. It was a very odd feeling. It vibrated with an intensity which seemed to go right through him. Was there someone coming in? He stood for an age staring at it.

He watched and waited, yet nobody came He should remember, of course, that time meant nothing here. Maybe he should go and look for another gate? No soul was coming in through this one. This was boring, but then, he thought, this is my work. It has been given to me to do. I have to do this. He sat on the ground, then lay down, hands clasped behind his head, then he stood up and hummed a remembered tune looking at the tall hedge. Nothing: Oh well, he must wait.

A while later Thomas heard soft footsteps and turned expecting to see an angel but saw a man in a white suit walk towards him head down. The man looked up; it was the man with the silver hair. As he saw Thomas, he raised a hand in greeting but turned and went swiftly back the way he had come. That was the man who walked past my gate he thought. There was a familiarity about him. Who is he? Thomas turned back toward the little gate in time to see the head of a cherub, as he now knew them to be, disappear behind a large shrub, and thought he heard it say, "It is all right now, it has gone away,"

It, Thomas wondered, why do they call the man it?

Time went on and Thomas began to feel annoyed. He was supposed to be helping people but the feeling that he was being punished was gradually creeping over him.

A voice spoke, so close to him, he jumped, "Hello, are you waiting here to bring people inside?"

Thomas swung around quickly. A thin dark man smiling pleasantly, dressed in a dark suit, stood on the pathway behind him. The skin around his eyes was dark and the eyes themselves so hooded as to be almost invisible. His hands which were folded at his waist were dark and covered with heavy gold rings. "Who are you?" Thomas felt a tremor of fear.

The dark man smiled, "I am Sebastian. I am here to help. I arrived some time ago. I have been working out my life, and they gave me the privilege of helping with souls coming in. I was told I should help you. You are Thomas, are you not? They said I should look for you by the smallest gate. Oh, and if you are wondering why I have no white suit, it is because I have yet to earn it."

He smiled and the smile was open, pleasant. Thomas relaxed. Probably another one like himself. Then he had a glimpse of the little cherub peeping through the shrubbery just behind the man Sebastian, then it disappeared again just as quickly. Thomas thought he heard a whispered, "Another one,"

Sebastian said, "So, what do we do with them when they come in. Do we take them to the other door and send them on?"

Thomas looked sharply at the man who gave him a timid little smile and a questioning look. "What door? There is no door to go through. They come in and go either to the angels or the Gatherers. There is definitely *no* door."

"Ah." the other said softly with a knowing smile, "There is you know. I have seen it. I found it. There is a door out of here. They do not always tell you the truth, keep the best for themselves and I have knowledge they have not, especially about the door."

Thomas listened, he was not sure of this, but he asked: "Why would they not tell me about it?"

The man Sebastian smiled his knowing smile, "Because, some who enter here are not yet ready, not completely without life. They like to hold on to them. You were not without life when you arrived at the Portal. They kept you there until all life was gone. They did this with me, but I discovered the secret of the door back to the world outside. I cannot go myself now, it is too late, but I try to send as many as I can find back through it. They do not help as they should when you arrive, make you wait a long time to find your way. It is frustrating and frightening, as you well know. We would not want another soul to suffer as have you and I, Thomas."

Thomas nodded. This was true. He was drawn to the timid gentle Sebastian, to his understanding and warmth, his caring for others. He almost believed the man. Yet what had Cadamiel said? He must be aware, there was danger. Why too had they not given Sebastian a white suit?

Sebastian watched Thomas, then said, "A woman is coming through, so I have been told, by my angel. She is not yet ready. You need my help to send her through the door. You and I will send her in the right direction. We will do this for her. She deserves this. Yes?"

Thomas stared at Sebastian. The man seemed more timid than ever, his voice low, yet the words were insistent. There was something wrong here. There was no door. They were called gates here. Had Cadamiel mentioned a door? No. That was not right There was a Portal and gates. Nothing was ever said of a soul leaving by a door, certainly not leaving without permission. He racked his brain. No doors, there were no doors. Thomas asked his voice croaking nervously. "Are you sure about this. Where is it anyway?"

Sebastian seemed to grow more confident, "Come with me. I will show you the way. It is to a beautiful and friendly place. Come, give me your hand."

Thomas stopped, "This is a friendly and beautiful place here, don't you think?"

The other smiled, "It may seem so, but I have grave doubts. Listen Thomas, the door through which I take you will give you your heart's desire. Let me take you there and I will come back for the woman who is to come. You do not need to wait. I can do this alone. Let me do it."

He turned suddenly to lead the way and Thomas saw to his horror that the hands Sebastian reached out to him had become claw like, the man turned and came back towards him and he saw a change in the others appearance and got the first faint smell of the Scavengers.

He shouted, "What are you? Go away."

Sebastian reached to Thomas but gave a harsh cry as with a flurry of wings two of the huge Great Angels appeared and filled the space between Thomas and the man, both holding a shield and flaming sword. They drove at the man with their swords and one called. "Go from this place Scavenger and do not return." Their voices echoed all around "Leave, this is a command. Obey. You have no rights here."

The man Sebastian shouted at them in some unintelligible language. He screamed and hissed as they moved closer, then tried to get to Thomas calling, "Take my hand Thomas. We can leave this place together. Take my hand."

"Heed not his false words. Touch not his hand." One of the Angels came back to Thomas its great wings shielding him from the man. Thomas did not see what happened then but there was a scream and all was silent.

Thomas was released from the protection of the wings and the second angel returned.

He said, "You were wise not to trust his words. You are safe now. We leave you to your work."

They were gone and he was frightened. He whispered, "Don't leave me." and heard the words float back, "You are safe now."

Time passed and he became calm again. It was quiet now. Yet maybe too quiet. He peered around shrubbery in case the man was hidden. There was nothing, nobody. He realised now the full importance of not touching them voluntarily. They wanted you to take their hand. That was it. They wanted you to reach out to them. If you reached out a hand and took their hand, you were lost. He must never touch them. He walked around still worried. But then he became aware there was a noise behind him. Not that, not the return of the man.

He turned at the sound of a click, like a key turning in a lock and saw movement of the small door deep in the side of the shrubbery. Bending down to look he saw a pair of white hands, fingers adorned with glittering rings, long fingernails gleaming scarlet, pushing their way through, then a pair of arms followed by a large black hat, with a red rose attached to the wide brim. He chuckled. There was a lot of grunting, gasping and small yelps of frustration. Eventually after what seemed to be a real struggle a pair of shoulders clad in glittering black appeared and a woman crawled through on hands and knees. "Made it," she said breathlessly, "I made it. Ha ha. It was a bit of a tight squeeze but I made it."

She stood up, gave him a wide smile, dusted her hands off, and picked at bits of twigs on her dress throwing then across the path, "They said, I would never make but I did." Her smile faded as he said nothing.

She watched him warily, eyes roaming over the white suit and shoes, gave a hesitant little smile, eyebrows raised questioningly. "Is this the right place? Am I in the right place? Yes or no? Who are you?"

"Depends on what you mean by the right place," he said still uneasy, "This woman could be another of them, and I am Thomas."

She bit her lip, "I just want to know, did I make it to Heaven or is it the other place?" then she went on, not waiting for an answer, "It doesn't look like a bad place. Is it Heaven?"

"It's not Heaven." he said.

She suddenly looked desperately sad and turned away, but not before he saw tears in her eyes. "Look," he said quickly, "It's not a bad place. I am Thomas, here to help you," he said, "and this is called The Gathering Place. It's where they collect souls who are not ready to go onward yet."

"To Heaven you mean?" she questioned insistently. "Oh yes, absolutely," he said. "Just tell me one thing," the woman said, "Is this a good place or a bad place? Sorry to be so demanding. I just need to be sure I'm not on the wrong road."

"It's a very good place." Thomas smiled.

The woman sighed deeply and seemed relieved, pulled her wide brimmed hat off and a thick mane of black hair fell down her back. She smiled then, a wide smile showing dazzling white teeth. "My mother always said I would never make it into Heaven." She nodded her head, "I bet she didn't makes it, rotten old woman. She was wrong. I'm getting there. Mind you she said I would never make old bones, she was right about that, but my Granny always said I should say a Hail Mary every day to the Virgin Mary and ask her to keep me safe, because my lifestyle was a bit suspect. She said if I did that the Virgin would open a window for me when they shut the gates of Heaven against me. So, I think she did open the window. I had to crawl in on my hands and knees through a tunnel to get through that little window."

"It's a gate. Though it looks a bit like a trapdoor standing on its side." Thomas said. "It might be a gate from where you're standing," the woman grinned cheekily, "but from the other side it's a couple of metal bars at the end of a tunnel. It really was a tight squeeze. Anyway, I am in. I am. Yes?"

Thomas smiled and nodded.

The woman chattered on, all the while looking around: "My Granny was a real good woman you see, she came from a religious family in Ireland, went to church every day. I was always called a bad girl but I know she prayed for me a lot. She loved me. My mother said I was like my dad, rotten to the core. She had no room to talk either. She was worse than me or my dad. You see, I had this mad thing inside me. Couldn't stop myself doing stupid things. Always making the same mistakes. So stupid, never learned from my mistakes." She grinned, "I always went for the same kind of bloke. Every single time, the wrong ones."

She spun around her long hair flying, black skirt swirling and sparkling in the light. "Well, I've done it now, something right I mean. Feels good. Come on, let's go." she danced along the path, "Where do we go from here?"

He followed her. She was a really beautiful woman, in her thirties maybe. He was curious about her. She still chattered on, "I never could go for a decent bloke you know," she said, "They were boring. A bloke always had to have the smell of danger about him before I was attracted. Trouble was, I always did love the smell of danger. Do you know it, that scent, the feeling that comes with it? It's like a high, an adrenaline shot. It's exciting, isn't it?" She did not wait for his answer, "It's like a flame to a moth. You just can't leave it alone. You know you are going in head first but you can't stop it. It would be like trying to stop a volcano blowing. That was me. I used to get into trouble and then I'd feel guilty and promise I would be good. Hard to be good isn't it? Being bad is much more fun." She laughed then stood still and looked around.

He was about to tell her they had to be on their way into the Gathering Place when the woman walked off again along the path, then stopped and looked around. "Have you seen her?"

134

"Who?" he asked puzzled. "The Virgin Mary, who else" She looked around, "Is she here? I always wanted to see her, like those kids at Lourdes. That would have blown my mind."

Thomas laughed, "Not as far as I know. I've not seen her."

"You been here a long time?" she queried looking disappointed.

He nodded, "A long time, at least I think I have. Time doesn't have much meaning here."

"She's probably somewhere sitting on a throne or something," the woman said, "She was special being the mother of Jesus and all that."

Thomas smiled at the innocence of the woman but thought that he would not have known, what the Virgin Mary looked like. There had seen a statue years ago which belonged to his mother, of a young gentle-faced woman dressed in a white dress and veil with a blue sash around her waist and roses at her feet. But that was a statue. Hard to tell from a plaster statue.

He looked at the woman again. About thirty, very tall and slim, with beautiful slender hands and feet, which were bare? She had lost her shoes somewhere. She was quite beautiful in a dark exotic way, reminding him of an actress he adored in his youth.

The woman eyed him quizzically then asked: "What's up? Have I got dirt on my face?"

"No," he said, "It's just that you remind me of an actress I liked when I was young."

"Yeah," she grinned, "My mother said it wouldn't do the likes of me much good looking like a film star."

He felt now that there had been enough of this chat and he should find a couple of Gatherers or even an angel. "Now," he said, "My name as you know is Thomas and I have been put here to help people who find their way in through the gates on their own. I have to take you onwards to meet either the Gatherers or the angels, whichever we meet first."

The woman was delighted, "Gosh. This is exciting. My name is Dorothy, Dory for short by the way."

He wondered if she would find it so exciting when she had to sit down and work out how she was going to find her way into one of the little houses, or how go on towards the big gates. Still, she seemed very bright, and could probably work it out more quickly than he had. Yet she did not ask him any questions about the place, seeming to accept what he said. She just chattered on as they walked back along the pathway.

Dory stopped him in his tracks then, "I got murdered you know," she said in a matter of fact way, "It was sad I suppose, but it doesn't matter now. It was supposed to be an accident. I watched them after I died and they were saying to the police that they didn't know who I was. I couldn't believe it. They said I stepped off the kerb and under the truck. Tony pushed me. He was my bloke. I knew too much about his dealings. Should have kept my mouth shut." She looked at Thomas, "Don't say much, do you?"

Thomas smiled at her: "I'm not supposed to ask questions if that's what you mean. I have been sent to find people who get lost on the way and need directing. That is my work, my way of making up, well partly, for some of the things I did on the earth."

Dory stared at him, "Oh, you're not an angel then? I mean you wear this white suit and shoes and look a bit like an angel, except you have no wings."

He smiled: "I am not an angel, just another soul who has been gathered in and is trying to work out his own salvation. That is what you have to do now. Once you meet your own angel it will tell you what you have to do, well, up to a point. You have to work out a lot of things for yourself. You see, I was not supposed to be able to come in here but it seems I did something good in my life and it changed everything. It seems like a lot of us come in in different ways. Anyway, you will be told what to do."

She said slowly, "Do you ever get a chance to go back, like they say a ghost does. You know, can you haunt somebody? I'd love to go back to haunt Tony. Do they let you go back?" Dory giggled like a little girl. He looked at her and shook his head, "Take a bit of advice from someone who made the mistake of asking to go back." Thomas stopped walking and spoke very seriously, "Don't do it. It's not worth the heartache and you can make a terrible mess of things, especially if you take revenge on those who… Look, it's not worth it."

Derry scratched her head, grinning. She smiled a lot but he liked that, "You mean it's not worth the kick in the teeth you get when you see how little they care.? Is that it?"

"Something like that." he said.

The had reached a turn in the path and the plain came into view. Dory began to laugh like a child and clapped her hands in delight. "It's beautiful. This is just so beautiful. I feel like I've just come home. I never felt so good in my life."

She looked over his shoulder and her eyes widened as an angel came towards them. "A real angel," she said wonderingly, "It's a real angel."

"You are welcome here Dory," the angel said, "Thank you, Thomas. I will take care of her now. You will want to return to your duties." The angel looked at the woman, "I am Gabriel. I am your angel guide. Come with me now Dory."

"You know my name," she said wonderingly, "How do you know my name?"

"I have known you and your name all your life," the angel told her and they walked away together.

She looked back at Thomas and called, "Bye Thomas. Thanks for finding me."

Thomas smiled and nodded. Ah well, it was time to go back to finding and helping. Back to the day job as that man used to say on the radio.

****

Chapter 16

The girl Ushta ran terrified, from the block of flats. Her breath came in gasps. Her chest burned as she ran, but the seventeen-year-old did not dare stop. She and her father were refugees and the fear was always there, that the men who would kill her father might find them again. Now they had come and so swiftly. She dare not stop, but what of her father?

Ushta never went out alone, always had someone with her, a cousin, if her father Aarash was not well. He was often not well, had much pain and it was hard to walk. Now the men were in the flat, their faces uncovered. She had seen their faces, which meant that she also would die. The terrified girl had not time to put on the hijab or an outer garment and her waist length dark hair streaked out behind as she ran.

It was cold but the girl barely noticed as she kept running, heart racing and occasionally missing beats. There was pain in her heart now. Winter in this country was harsh compared to her own country. She only had the soft silky robe, the ababa she'd had put on this morning.

It eventually dawned on the running girl that nobody followed her. She had to stop because she was unable to catch her breath. She was deep in among the huge blocks of flats. Ushta stopped and stared around. No people. No sound of footsteps running behind. There must be somewhere to shelter? The girl crept around the corner of a building. Then she saw the vents with steam coming through and slipped in behind the huge garbage collection bins.

It was much warmer in there even if there was the slight smell of garbage and she could get her breath back and think. She needed to drink, her throat was very dry but it was Ramadan and still daylight and no food or drink would pass her lips until after sunset. She was ill and did not have to fast but her Father too was ill and he fasted. They did this together. Her heart still pounded and did that horrible thing it sometimes did. It seemed to stop beating and there was a stab of pain, but it passed. She had not taken her medicine with her when she ran. In her

138

terror she had not even thought of what she called her puff machine, which she carried everywhere.

She needed the medicine because her heart was not good. She went to the hospital every few months since they came to this country. Ushta had a heart condition, so running like this and the fear were not good. Her mother had the same affliction but had died from it. She did not want to see the dark Angel of Death look into her own face. She was only young.

Ushta began to take slow deep breaths and eventually her heart slowed to a normal beat and the strange thing it did stopped and so did the trembling in her limbs. What had gone wrong? They had been told nobody knew where they were. It was a safe place. They were told they would be safe from assassins here. Who had found out? What had become of her father? He had shouted at her to run when the lock of the door shattered and the men burst in. Then he raised his hands to protect himself and one of the men lifted a knife. "Run Ushta. Run." Her father had called. She heard the words but she had stood for a few seconds unsure of what to do. She ran around the table towards the door, then glanced back. Omar. What was he doing here?

Aarash been unable to rise from his chair. His legs were weak and very painful. He tried to reach for the metal crutches given by the hospital. The last thing she saw was the knife going down in an arc toward his body. Tears spilled from the young woman's great liquid dark eyes and down her pale face. They had killed him, she knew this. Now there was nobody to protect her. She dare not go back to the flat. She should go to the police? Her English was good now. Yet she was afraid to go into the open.

Ushta was being taught the language by Fatima the woman she called Auntie Ji the wife of Omar. Fatima came to England as a twelve-year-old and was now twenty-eight. She had been educated here. Relief spread through the young woman. She would go to Fatima, tell her the men had come. Three of them. Yet, would that put Fatima in danger? She did not know. No. It would be all right. She would wait until dark then go there. It was not far from the blocks of flats. Yet, what was Uncle Omar doing with the men? Was he too an assassin? No, it was not possible. She was so confused.

She sat on the cold concrete looking around. There was a bundle of newspaper in the corner. The girl crept over and pulled the pile of paper back to the vents to sit on. There was some steam but not much. It was not enough to make her clothes damp or hot enough to burn. It was warmer here. Her mind

139

flitted around like a tiny bird. Who were the men? Why had they come? Who had told where they were? Was it Omar? Did he do it for money. A betrayal.

Father was always watchful but he did not tell her the reason, although she was aware, they had been in danger in their home country which was the reason for their leaving, and making their way over many months across the Continent, eventually arriving as refugees in the U.K. The girl was tired now, very tired. Her heart made her tired. She lay down on the pile of newspapers.

Ushta slept. She woke to the sharp wind blowing around the bins. It was night and time to go. She stood up, then she slipped back down again, feeling dizzy and her heart did something odd and a sharp pain shot between her breasts. The girl gasped but stayed sitting, breathing as deeply as she could. After a while she stood up slowly. She might have to find her way to the Hospital to get help. She took a few steps. No, she was fine. Ushta walked across the silent quadrangle. The ground was cold on her stockinged feet. Lights were on in the blocks of flats, but there were no people. It must be later than she thought. Should she go home? See what had happened to her father? She decided it might be safe now.

The block in which the girl lived with her father was the end block of ten. To the other side was a place she knew to be a sports ground where games were played. As Ushta came around the corner of the building she saw the flashing blue lights. She might be able to slip inside the doors, but no, there was tape tied to the bollards outside the heavy glass front doors.

Ushta watched as an ambulance came screaming in. There were police cars with their blue lights blocking the entrance also. Policemen and policewomen and men with camera's stood outside. She was glad to see the two women in uniform and moved towards them.

Someone shouted: "Look, there's the old man's kid."

Ushta stopped, startled. Then she saw them. Three men. Two, for certain had forced their way into the flat. Which way to run? To Fatima and Omar or who? Then she saw Omar behind the men. He said something to one of them. Oh no, he really was with them. The betrayer. There was only one way left.

She ran towards the two policewomen, but her chest began to hurt. She gasped in a breath of air, her legs suddenly like lead, but something happened as she ran. It seemed as if she leaped from her own body. The girl felt so light she felt she could fly. Then she stopped, no longer afraid. She would denounce these evil men.

Ushta turned bravely, finger pointing towards the men, mouth open to call the denunciation, but nobody was looking at her. They were all staring at the ground. She turned her eyes to where she could see the slim shape lying on the ground wearing a black embroidered ababa, long dark hair flowing across the concrete. In her mind's eye she saw it. The Angel of Death. Azra'il. He had come as she ran. She was dead! She was free.

She walked back towards the group who had moved slowly forward, closer to the form on the ground. It was she, Ushta. Then for a second the girl glimpsed a tall dark winged shape. A dark Angel. She bowed her head in respect and acceptance. The angel bowed its head to the girl. "Oh," she breathed, "It is I. Ushta. You have truly come to take me, Azra'il, dark Angel?"

The dark angel gestured with a long slender hand away from the crowd, bowed its head again, stepped back and was gone.

The people were crowding closer and the policewomen were trying to move them back. The girl Ushta looked around. Where had Azra'il gestured? This was where she lived, but what now? What should she do? That was when she saw the gate. A tall gate she had never seen when she lived and it seemed to beckon to her. It was by the sports ground and it was wide open. Inside the girl could see it was as daylight and there were two people just inside the gate looking in her direction.

She smiled, it was dark cold winter night out here and yet the sun shone inside that place. A figure stood to one side of the gate in the darkness of earth night. One of the figures inside the gate seemed familiar, but it could not be. He was straight, not crippled and bent. His body was not bent. Father?

The girl took a couple of steps, staring at him, "Abbun. Father," she called uncertainly. He stepped into the light shining out from the inside. He smiled, held out his hand to her. His face was no longer lined with pain or fearful. He looked young, as Ushta remembered him when a small girl. She ran to him, and saw inside the gate the woman she had last seen when she was five-years-old. Her mother, "Ommy," the girl called. The beautiful woman held out her hands to her child.

Then the figure, which had stood outside the gate, followed her inside. A man dressed in white stood there, hands clasped. He nodded to her, smiling, she looked at her Father and he beckoned, "Come Ushta, we have awaited your coming, see; your mother too waits for us. This man has spoken. We are safe for all time."

She ran towards her parents laughing, feeling well, as she never had in life and no longer felt afraid.

The man waiting inside the gateway spoke as they entered, "Welcome to The Gathering Place," he said, "I am Thomas. I am here to help you."

He then took the man, with Ushta his daughter and her mother along the pathway and on to the open plain to hand them over to the angels. They looked at him. He nodded. The girl said nothing just bowed her head to him. The man and woman also bowed. Then they were gone.

The gate closed and he walked back along the path behind them. There would be another gate waiting to open somewhere and more souls to meet. Thomas moved on.

****

Chapter 17

Thomas walked slowly back along the pathway, but then it branched off in a direction he had not noticed previously. He seemed suddenly to be lost and looked around to see if there was a sign to help find his direction. There was nothing. The path turned away towards thick shrubbery. There was a break in the shrubbery and he could see something move in there. Perhaps he should not go into that place. A little warning bell rang inside his head, yet it did not look like a bad place. Why would he think it was a bad place?

He peered in. No, it was just a beautiful place, filled with trees, and a woodland scent reminding him of childhood friends and games. Thomas stared into the trees where sunlight streamed down into a little clearing filled with purple and yellow flowers. The scent wafted towards him. It would be lovely to walk in this place. Peaceful. A part of his mind told him to go on, to find the way to the gates. This place was not for him. Yet, the more he looked the more he wanted to go in there. It was so beautiful, and seemed to be drawing him in. He breathed the clean, clear freshness of spring and of a life lived a long time ago. The trees gently whispered. He heard the soft whisperings in his head. "Come, walk amongst us. The air is clean and fresh. Remember springtime, the scent of violets in your grandmother's garden. Remember? Come. You know how you always loved springtime. You know how you loved the freshness of the air. It is all here Thomas. Come."

He was still unsure, he had never really loved spring except as a child, and as an adult always felt it a disquieting time for the earth. Odd that, when others loved the coming of spring. Well, he might just have a look. Mind made up now Thomas took a step forward and saw the path leading away from the trees. He could now see the direction towards which he should walk, but some stubborn root made him stumble and sent him another way. He decided to walk along this way instead of the path chosen for him. What difference did it make whether he went by this pathway or took a short cut through this lovely wooded place. It was not an excuse. No. It was safe. It was a different world; besides, he was still in the Gathering Place.

The path was edged with great clumps of pink flowers now and their scent was literally heavenly, reminding him of the scent of carnations. He grinned to himself. Heavenly indeed, then he took a deep breath of the clean fresh air and stepped off onto the soft springy turf. He moved slowly forward gazing around in delight. There were trees everywhere but what trees were these? It was a huge orchard except that each tree seemed to carry a different fruit.

He thought, these are not ordinary trees. These were magnificent, almost as if carved from a solid piece of wood and heavily laden with fruit. He touched the bark of one and found it to be smooth and cool, not at all rough, as though carved by the hand of a great sculptor.

Thomas wondered what was the point of all this when you never wanted or felt the need to eat. He wandered through the trees, looking around, could hear childish laughter and a dog barking. There was a flash of small figures running through the trees. There were children in here. A small dog with a lolling tongue and friendly eyes came out of the trees and barked at him, tail wagging happily, then turned and ran back toward the sounds of the children's voices.

He followed it for a few minutes, then stood looking around. The dog was out of sight suddenly and there was no longer the sound of children's laughter, nor was there any sign of the pathway through which he had come. It had disappeared. Everything was different here. There was nothing recognisable. He was lost. He had allowed himself to become lost and stopped to listen for sounds.

He heard the sound of water then, and following the sound, soon came into a small clearing where a dancing bubbling stream of crystal-clear water wended its way through the trees and out of sight. That was when he noticed the tree. It was right in the centre of the little clearing and was different from all the other trees in what he now thought of as the orchard. It seeming to be gleaming, a dull gold colour. Thomas walked closer staring at it. It was laden down with what looked like gold coloured figs and if there was one thing Thomas Beck loved it was a fresh fig. Yet figs so large and such a colour as these he'd never seen. He could taste them, smell them, had to have one. He raised a hand to touch one of the golden fruits but the fruit seemed to shiver and he dropped his hand just before touching it. He knew without doubt that this was not right. Something was wrong. What?

Something he once heard touched his mind. The tree of life. Was this it? Should he reach out and touch it? There was a desperate longing inside Thomas Beck to reach out to the tree and touch it, slide his hands over the golden bark. No, he should leave now. There was no hunger in this place. Beware Thomas, he heard the warning inside his head. The thought came into his mind that this might be a temptation, and yet it was hard to resist the magnificent figs. "How do I know that? How do I know this is temptation? It might not be. This might be a privilege," he murmured, stepping back to look up along the trunk.

Something moved in its branches. Something dark, shapeless, a thing. He shuddered. What was that? I should leave now, he thought, and yet! "How do I know I should not touch you, not eat from you?" he said aloud and feeling a sense of loss.

This was ridiculous. He should not feel like this. There was no desire for food or drink here. Thomas was very much aware now that he'd been here many years and had not previously had the slightest desire for either. Nobody in this place ever ate or drank. The children sometimes had those huge lollipops, but then they were children. Surely this place would not take everything from a child.

He had to get out of here. He was lost though. Was it them again, the faceless ones? The strange Sebastian man or the shadowy dark things who managed to find their way in. Where were the Great Angels now with the shields and swords? If he screamed, would they come? Thomas was becoming frightened and opened his mouth to shout for them to come and tell him what to do. But then, there was the feeling and it was very strong, that he should not be here. He would be in trouble, be punished. The Great Angels would punish him. He knew this without a doubt. Something was whispering the words inside his head. Eat of this fruit and you will be punished. He turned to leave. "You are a silly one, Thomas Beck," said a soft female voice in an accent that sounded Cornish. Thomas had always loved the softness, the allure of a Cornish accent, "Come over here, you silly one. What are you afraid of, a few figs?" the voice paused for a few seconds, then asked softly, seductively "Or me." Those two words were a whisper. There came the sound of a woman's soft laughter from somewhere behind the tree.

The woman who stepped out from behind the tree was the most beautiful he had ever seen, astonishingly beautiful, her lovely figure was draped in white silk. He stared hard at this gorgeous being, had never seen anyone like her. She shimmered from head to toe, yet, if anybody had asked Thomas afterwards to describe her, he would not be able to do so, but knew she was dressed in white, her gleaming golden hair hung down past her waist and that she was incredibly beautiful. "You came," she said softly and his eyes closed as if she had wrapped herself about him, "I have been waiting for you and now you have come," the woman said, her voice caressing his mind, "Funny you know, but when I saw you walk smartly on with your head up, I thought you would walk straight past and then you stopped, and I wondered if you would like to come and speak with me. I thought, it would be so nice to speak with you. You looked so handsome in your white suit." She paused, "It can be lonely here looking after the fruit orchard. Not a great many come this way."

"Who are you?" he asked breathlessly. "Oh, I am just Salema, who loves and looks after the garden." she said, "It is my duty to offer refreshment to any who may pass this way. As I said, not many come, apart from the Great Angels. They do not speak much and can be a bit harsh to a poor female like me. But I would love the chance to speak with you."

"Do you, I mean, are you a gardener here?" he mumbled, not at all sure of what he said.

She laughed: "Goodness no, Thomas. The gardeners do all that. Do these hands look as if they do that kind of thing?" She held out perfect white hands towards him. He shook his head. "I am, I suppose you could say, the caretaker of the garden. Well maybe I should say I am the controller."

She reached out one of those long slender white hands and plucked a fig from the tree, holding it out to Thomas.

He shook his head, "I don't need food," he muttered, "I don't need drink. I have been here many years and have never eaten or drunk."

She laughed softly: "Oh my dear, dear Thomas. You may eat or drink of anything you wish. It is all here for you. All these wonderful fruits are here to be eaten and many have done so. The Great Angels eat of this fruit. Let me tell you a secret. It is what makes them great, gives them their power. Why do you think they can fly?" her beautiful dark eyes slanted at him and she smiled seductively, whispering, "You know that you too could have that power? Think of it, they have all this up there beyond the Great Gates. It is their food from the tree of life. It is their life; it means eternal life. It would do that for you too, make you great and powerful, as it has for me. Make you one of them, one of us. It can make one beautiful. You could return to your earthly life and live forever if you chose. You can have great riches and power beyond your wildest dreams. All you want Thomas, can be yours. All." her voice was hypnotic, "You only have to eat. Here lies the secret of life. They, up there, beyond the Great Gates, they do not want you to have it. They are jealous, they have favourites."

Thomas stared hard at her. He could not remember telling her his name, but she spoke as if she knew him. From somewhere in the distant past came a memory. God has no favourites. God's love does not change. God loves all mankind equally, the good, the bad, the indifferent. How strange, she should say that, but then again, when was it other than strange in this Gathering Place. Nothing was ever straightforward here. Why would the woman Salema not know his name? She held out the fruit once more and he could smell it. That smell, it was drawing him to the hand which held the fruit.

In his mind a voice whispered, do not reach out. Do not. Yet, more than anything he wanted that fruit to eat. Again, it came, the whisper, sharply. Do not reach out. The fruit began to drip a golden juice almost like the golden syrup he used to eat from a tin with a spoon. He could feel it slide down his throat and swallowed. He heard her seductive laugh. Do not reach out your hand to them, the words echoed in his mind. His hand reached out but then it dropped. This was all wrong.

Thomas could not remember figs dripping golden syrup-like juice. Not like this. He put his hands behind his back and stepped away from the woman, who smiled at him and lifted the fruit slowly to her full red lips He stared in fascination as the white teeth bit into the fruit, then she licked her lips, slowly, sensuously. He swallowed hard. No. There was something going on here and it was not right. What was this? Something, a reminder of something in the past. What? He shook his head.

It must be no. It would be wrong to eat that fruit. This woman was doing something wrong. What, he was not sure. This was like the time so long ago when the girl in his office had come after him, determined to seduce him. She had long blonde hair also. Later he remembered hearing they had a bet on it in the office. He had almost fallen into the trap then. He'd been very angry about that. That memory brought him up sharply. Thomas stepped back again. He had to do something, say something. "What did you say your name was?" Thomas swallowed again. "I told you," her voice was a soft purr, "I am Salema, child of Eliam. I am a Queen. I am the Queen of all this place." She took a step towards him and he stepped back. He thought, she said she is caretaker, controller and now she says, a queen. What is she?

Salema laughed softly, "Are you afraid of me? Oh Thomas, why would you be afraid of me. I am a true friend. A friend to the angels. A friend to you. Come closer Thomas. Do not stand so far from me. Come to me. Touch my hand. Look at me, am I not beautiful? Do you not desire me?"

He stood as if hypnotised but then managed to shake his head. "I can make you great, greater than all that." she raised her other hand and pointed in the direction of the Great Gates, "They guard it jealously. They're afraid of others having any of what they see as theirs alone. That is why they keep a veil between us and a great gulf, to keep us out. Yet they do not have a right to it. It is for all. Come, Thomas. Taste and see how great the fruit is, see how great you can become. Greatness and power will be yours. It will give you power over all this and should you wish it, a return to life with wealth beyond belief. I will give you the power and none can take it from you, and I too will be yours for all time."

Her voice had risen. The gentle seductiveness was gone. It rang out, there was harshness in the voice now.

Thomas stared up at the Great Gates. A light seemed to flash up there and he understood everything. This was a temptation and it fell from him like a cloak. No, the gates were waiting for him and were more important still, they were his goal. He was not going to lose that. He turned back to her and saw there was something of the night about her. Above her the leaves of the golden tree seemed to tremble, as something dark moved in its foliage and down the other side of the tree. The thing slipped into the stream and its long dark shape moved sinuously through the water. "No," he shouted, "I know you. You are one of them. You are evil. Go away from me."

She laughed again high and sharp, like a bark almost, all seductiveness gone. She came closer to him. Her eyes were cruel, her hair darkening. The hand she held out claw-like. "No. Do not come close," Thomas turned and ran.

He ran and her harsh laughter followed and suddenly he was on the path again. Thomas stopped and stared around. Cadamiel waited near a big gate. Just behind, like a shadow, stood Fariel. He glared at the pair, the tall silver fair angel and the smaller dark one. "Well done, Thomas," the angel said, "You did this alone. We watched but you did not need us."

"You should not have left me with that, that thing." he cried. "You should not have strayed from the path," came the swift reply, "You were not alone Thomas. Have you not learned? We are always near. We were there should you need help, but you did not need us. You succeeded in fighting that temptation on your own."

"You were testing me," Thomas shouted back, furious now, "Why can't I just work out my own salvation without all this stuff, those terrible people? You shouldn't let them in here. It's not the place for them. They belong in that other place, that place, wherever it is."

Fariel spoke "You were not alone, Thomas. The Great Angels were behind you. You only had to call out. Yet you managed to work it out for yourself. You know you have to work hard. This was indeed a hard testing. It had to be done and you succeeded in it. Is that not a great thing Thomas?"

"Do you not feel you have achieved something? Will your reward not be great indeed?"

"Oh, I dunno," Thomas muttered feeling distressed and bewildered. Had they not tested him when they let him return to the earth, but no, that was all his fault. He felt stupid and miserable. Imagine letting some person like that almost catch him out. He sniffed and marched stiffly, angrily, away from the two angels, toward the gate, muttering to himself. He could have sworn the angels were smiling as they left in a flurry of wings. Huh. Blooming angels. Think they know it all he told himself.

Thomas Beck was very cross. This testing business was not nice, "You can't trust any of them here, not even the angels," he muttered to himself as he walked towards the gate and stared at it, then hunched his shoulders and marched away again banging his feet hard on the ground. Even that was no good. His feet made no sound and he hardly felt it. He muttered angrily under his breath, as he stalked away head down. He'd been doing his very best and they still tested him. Angels. Huh.

Just for a second Thomas was sure he heard someone chuckle and whipped around staring into shrubbery and back at the gate. He was hearing things now. Nobody there at all. There was a sudden pinch of apprehension inside his stomach, as if some living thing fluttered around in there. Could you have a nervous breakdown if you were dead Thomas wondered? Surely not. He'd like to have been able to have a word with his little voice, but it was gone, gone forever. It had somebody else now. It would have been nice just to have a few words.

O.K. He had not been all that nice to it, had been very rude to it at times. He'd been rude to it most times. I've been rude to almost everybody he thought ruefully. What though, would he not give to have a few minutes with the voice now, because it knew practically everything? It was calming. It had been around for over two thousand year according to when it said it had come into being. It would have been able to advise him about those terrible things that frightened him so much. He shuddered involuntarily.

They were one big worry now, those faceless ones. He knew to keep away from them, although Sebastian had a face as had Salema, so there was no way he could rely on things visual any more. How was he going to know who was good and who was bad? Instinct was all he had left and of course, Cadamiel had said the Great Angels were behind him. He looked around. Not a sign of the big guys. Mind you, all he had to do was, give a small scream and they would arrive. So that was a comfort. Yet, suppose in the fraction of a second before they arrived, just suppose, that the things of the darkness managed to grab him? That was terrifying. Should he give a little squeak now to test it?

A voice deep and commanding from somewhere above him said: "I would not do that Thomas. Save the squeaking for a time of need."

He heard two voices chuckling. So, they really were there and even they had a sense of humour. They read his thoughts, "I would not be too sure we have a sense of humour, especially if you waste our time. Do not test us, we have much work to do." another deep voice spoke and to his annoyance they chuckled again, "Remember this Thomas Beck. They are not allowed to touch you, unless you reach for their hand, although it seems you are truly aware of that."

"Well I shouldn't have to work that out for myself. I should have been told." He muttered childishly. He walked away. They were mocking him now. They said nothing more but he heard the rush of great wings and felt a breeze on his face.

Thomas sighed deeply then he sniffed and pulled himself together thinking that thoughts like that might also be a testing, might make him angry and anger was not a good thing. It could make him do things that could send him in the wrong direction. But he had been strong. Salema could not make him eat the fruit. They might not have been figs. That fruit could have been, what? Poison! No, they could not poison him, could they? Besides he was dead and he could not die twice. It had been a struggle though, not to try to eat but he had said no and run.

Thomas cheered up. That had been a good thing, he had achieved something. Do not get, what was the word his daughter Kate used to use? Uptight. That was it. Do not get uptight. Just get on with your work. You have a job to do and the sooner it is done the sooner you will leave this place and there will be no more fear of things unknown, no more faceless ones. No more temptations. He took a deep breath.

Now there was a funny thing, he could still breathe, yet he did not get out of breath as he had if he dashed for a bus in his later years on earth. Oh well, what did it matter. You breathed; you did not breathe. You were no longer alive, yet you lived here in this place. You could not die again.

Thomas smiled. He knew he had been here a long time now, yet if he stayed here a hundred years, he would never understand the place or its ways and certainly not the ways of those big angels. They were, as Mike said, scary.

****

Chapter 18

Thomas took a deep breath and marched, swinging his arms, humming to himself, along the pathways and turned a corner. A huge bronze gate appeared before him. This really was a big one. Enormous. It was higher than a five-story building. He stood before the gate feeling very small. To the side of it, inscribed in gold was a huge sign. Hero's Gate. Dedicated to all those who died for justice and peace and for their Brethren. He stared at it. As far as could be seen the gate was made of some kind of metal. There were etchings all over it. He went closer. These gates were beautifully made of bronze and seemed to be engraved with scenes of soldiers in battle. He moved closer still, trying to see it all, but it was too big.

These were battle scenes. At the base he could see engravings of small men with low foreheads short legs, long hair and forward jutting jaws. They had naked chests and bits of what looked like moss to protect their bodies. Some carried odd looking axes, others wooden clubs. Another group dressed like ancient Egyptians, others like the Inca. Native Americans too on horses and on foot. Roman legions. Men with blue faces. A woman in a chariot. Ancient Britons? There were men in metal helmets and breastplates with bows and arrows and long cloaks, others held staves. He moved along the great length of the gate looking at various battles and styles of battle dress.

There were scenes of battles he did not think he ever heard of. Men in armour. Men in kilts. Men in turbans. Fierce, short, bearded ragged men holding pikes. Some on horses. Wars in countries all over the world. More scenes of what he recognised to be of the first and second world wars. Men in helmets. Women in uniform. He guessed that the next two he looked at were the Vietnam and Korean and the Falkland wars. The groups spread out and upwards over the great bronze gate.

He came to the last group he could properly see. The third from last that he could see had to be the war in Iraq. He knew that one. There was a scene of men in Arabic dress. The last stood alone. He did not know this one. It must have begun after he left. One man to the forefront pointing the way, the rest behind fading into the distance, maybe three hundred but there were many more, the figures so small they looked like pinheads.

Up towards the top was a huge empty space. Yet underneath the sign there was something he could barely see. Angels? Some light and some dark. Great hordes of them in an arc across the gate. He squinted, could not see clearly. He thought, a battle for Angels? Was that, Thomas wondered in a moment of clarity, a battle for good and evil? Were there more battle's to come? Who did this? Who created this huge gate? It depicted brave men and women. He knew what this was. This was a memorial to all who died in wars.

Then he noticed the broad rim of bronze all around the gates. Hundreds of thousands, more, than that, millions of tiny engraved head. He had seen them as tiny circles at first but on closer inspection saw they were the heads of men, women and children. What were they? He stared at it and then he knew. These were the victims. The victims of wars. All human life was there, all victims. Thomas stared at the tiny heads. Millions upon millions of the dead. So many there was no counting them. The victims of war.

Then a small part of the gate near the base slowly opened. There were six of them. Six tall sun-bronzed men in camouflage uniform and desert boots. Their helmets too were camouflaged. They carried guns and looked around worriedly. Then one spoke. This one looked little more than a teenager. Somebody's son, Thomas thought. Are they sending children out to war now, because from what could be seen through the gate, that was a war somewhere in a hot country? Where was that place? Was it Iraq? No, that was gone. He had been a long time dead so it could have been anywhere. No newspapers here to tell us who, what or where. "I think we've had it, Captain. I think they got us sir," the voice was that of the young soldier.

They all stood in the gateway looking back and Thomas could see outside. The shimmering sun baked vista before them was of a strange country and swirling sand. A vehicle of some sort, he could not tell what it was, it was so blackened and burned, lay on its side. Smoke still rose from it.

He heard a deep voice speak and looked around to see who it was. There was nobody visible. "Welcome my children." voice said. He looked around but saw no one. Why were they being welcomed.

Thomas was stunned. What was that place out there. He did not know about it. There were more men in battle dress running towards the blackened smoking mess that might have been a tank. No, it was too small, possibly an armoured car. Several stopped, men diving down into the sand and dirt as bullets started to fly, trying to gain shelter and firing off shots at what looked like a stone compound. He saw an arm move on the ground and one of the soldiers from the little group walked back out quickly towards the burning ruin of what he was now sure was a truck.

There was a moan of pain and the young soldier who had spoken to the captain slipped back through the gate and into his injured body. The medics by then had reached the place where they lay, most of the bodies torn and bleeding. One was burning. Thomas almost wept.

Another soldier rose swiftly from the ground, then went back down on hands and knees and looked around. He saw it had risen from a body. The figure looked around ducking its head as bullets whined and smacked around. A girl soldier? Surely not. She looked at the body of the young soldier beside her, felt for the vein in his neck, then stared at her hand, looking puzzled.

The gate began to close and the Captain turned to look at Thomas. Then he turned and threw his weapon out through the slowly closing gate and the others followed suit. He saluted Thomas. "Captain Gregory Thomas reporting sir," he said. "Please, you don't have to call me sir." Thomas told him, "It is I who should call you sir."

"Does this mean the war is over for us, sir?" an older man asked. "It is indeed," Thomas told him.

The older man seemed worried, "I know what this place is. I don't want to be here. There is too much left behind to do. I was going home on leave in a couple of days. I have a wife and son who need me," suddenly, he was angry, "I want to go back. I do not want to stay here. I have to go back. Do you hear me?" he shouted at Thomas.

Thomas thought sadly. He is like me, angry, frustrated and he will ask to go back. They will let him go and he will do what he should not. He shook his head and said quietly, "I cannot send you back. If there is life in you, you will be sent back. I am simply here to help you find your way through the labyrinth that is The Gathering Place. You are in it now but it is easy to get lost here. It is a very big place and you need a little assistance to find your way to the plain. Please come with me."

The older man opened his mouth to shout but the big gate which had begun to close suddenly opened again and he walked out. He still had life in him. The young soldier came running through it with a big smile on his face. He was followed by the young woman soldier, the girl who tried to take the pulse of the soldier on the ground, not realising she too had passed beyond life. She looked so young. "Sir. I had to come back," the young soldier said, "I woke up for a minute. It was bloody painful sir."

"So, I had no choice. I had to come back. Pacey had to come with me." The gate closed behind them.

The girl said in a strong Liverpool accent: "Sir I had to come with you. Looks like we've all had it then. Me poor dad, he'll be devastated."

"I am not really supposed to ask too many questions, but I left the earth a long time ago. Where were you? What is that place out there?" Thomas asked. "It is Helmund Province in Afghanistan," Captain Thomas told him, "We had been doing very well there cleaning out pockets of resistance Then when we least expected it, the whole business blew up again, and it's been bad again for the last two years."

Thomas nodded. He did not know of Helmund Province. It was all new to him. How very sorry he felt for their families. They were safe from all harm now but the families would be grief stricken.

Thomas nodded, "Thank you. Now I must ask you to follow me."

The soldiers marched behind Thomas and their captain, as disciplined in death as they had been in life. Thomas led them along the path and the plain suddenly appeared. As they came out on to the plain the soldiers looked all around in astonishment. The girl soldier began to laugh A group of Great Angels were waiting. These soldiers are going straight onwards he thought. Was it that they gave their lives for others as the voice had said? He did not know.

Thomas felt a stab of envy, wishing he was on his way there. He watched as the men and the girl were all taken up. What was that saying? No greater love is there, than that of one who gives up his life for his friend. "Or even his enemy," Thomas said, "Someday though, that will be me. Oh, it will."

They were gone and all was silent now. No figures walked the plain or near the little houses. No angels or gatherers moved around. Thomas was alone and felt only the deep silence and peace of the universe, but he felt the need to go into his little house and sit alone. Yes, he should go into his own space and sit awhile. He turned and saw Mike sitting on the veranda smoking his eternal pipe.

He took it from his mouth and waved it at Thomas who waved back. "Have ye been off on yer wanderings, finding the souls that get themselves lost then," he grinned. "I found quite a few today and I met a couple of those dreadful things but they looked normal. They frighten me," Thomas told him. "Them beggars is always hanging around, and they're terrible smarmy," Mike said, "As for the wimmin, them ones is the worst, always sneaking around and offering this and that and telling you that you can live forever. Tryin' to beguile you. All that sort of old guff. You don't want to pay any heed to them. Just walk on. Mind you, you'd wonder now how they manage to get in here, or for that matter, why they let them put a foot over the gates."

Thomas stared at him, "You've met them?"

"Sure, you can't get away from them and they can't seem to keep away from us." Mike puffed on his pipe, "They never give up. Desperate to get their hands on us. All sweetness at first. The time I met yer woman with the figs I thought all me birthdays was coming together. Then I got a bit of sense in me head and told her to be off with herself. There's wimmin like her everywhere you go." He laughed, "In the wilder days of me youth I once met a girl like her on Stephen's Green in Dublin. It didn't take long for her to spend me few pounds and then I was no use to her. I will admit I was a bit nonplussed when I met that one in the orchard but I remembered the Dublin girl and told her to be off and take herself back to where she came from. They all have a terrible tongue on them when they find that you know what they're up to. She screeched curses at me, called me a few choice names and then she turned into one of the faceless things. Hah."

Thomas could not believe what he was hearing and his face obviously showed it.

Mike asked quietly, "Do you think now that you're the only one they try to tempt in here? That lot are all blandishments and come-hither and promises of living forever and having all the treasures, aye, and the pleasures of the earth, because they want to take you. Have you met the one that gives the cocktail parties yet? She's the worst of the lot. Run like a hare if you meet that one. She will be grabbing for your hand, but whatever you do, take nothing from them. If she gets a hold, she won't let go and the big fella's with the wings and the flaming swords will have the devil's own job getting you away from her, if you see what I mean. Wouldn't you think them lot would cop themselves on. They say the same to everybody they meet."

"Are you not afraid of them?" Thomas asked.

Mike blew out his lips and opened his eyes wide, "Course I am. I'm terrified of the beggars, but you have to run from them and keep running. You see, they know that once you are out of here, they no longer have any kind of hold on you. If you see anything you don't like, get out of there like the fella says. Don't be bothered about offending anybody. You know the song that big American fella sings. Yes, like a bat out of hell," he laughed uproariously at his own joke, "Yeah, get out of there like a bat out of hell, Tommy me boy,"

Thomas laughed, waved a hand to Mike and walked into his little house closing the door, then stopped and stared. His book looked cleaner, the filigree cover gleamed in places He laughed in delight and sat down at the table.

Well. Well. Well. It seemed he was getting somewhere at last and went out to tell Mike about it. There was no answer to his knock and he opened the door to be almost blinded by the light. The wall shone with light and on the table, the book glittered, the stones in the filigree work sparkled. There was just a small patch of dullness. Mike was not there. He was most likely out working on getting his last piece of the book shining. Thomas backed out, feeling suddenly humble and intrusive. He had a long way to go. This was no time for bragging and boasting. He would rest a while, then head off for the pathways to see if any others needed help.

He saw the boy Todd he had found on the road with two Great Angels being raised up and as he watched, they lifted him into the air and the boy was gone from the Gathering Place. He had been about to show off over the dirty cover on his book acquiring a clean patch when this boy had eternity. He, Thomas had very little. The boy Todd, had everything.

Thomas, back on his rounds again met the Angel Cadamiel, who greeted him. They walked together in silence for a while then Cadamiel asked: "Are you not pleased with the good work you have done, because it is good and you have done much,"

"I did my best and yes, I was really happy to see I have regained some of my work back. I'm going to do my best to clean the book up." Thomas nodded, "My very best,"

Just then a small group of people dressed in thick padded jackets came towards them along the path. A man wearing snow goggles, two boys and a woman who smiled at him and said ruefully. "We were on the mountain. Skiing. We went off piste and were caught in an avalanche. The snow was supposed to be stable."

"Obviously, it was not," the older man said sharply, glaring at her.

The small boy kept looking around, seemingly worried, "Where are we, Mummy?"

"We're in Heaven darling. Can't you see the angels?" She smiled at them and Cadamiel bowed his head, "Never thought I'd ever make it," she chirruped happily. "You haven't yet," Thomas muttered under his breath, "Silly woman."

"Do not judge them too harshly Thomas." Cadamiel said, "They will soon discover where they are."

They watched as several angels came to greet the family. "One vain foolish thought, a lack of judgement and a whole family enters here. They bring with them a child who, in time would have done much for mankind," Cadamiel sighed, "That small boy was set for great things. Great and good things, because great is not always good. Now another must be found to do his work. This will not be easy. So, I will leave you to yours and you are indeed doing good work. It has been noted by those above and your book of life has been amended. I go to my place of respite for a little time. Goodbye for now Thomas. We will speak again."

The angel floated swiftly away. Where do you go, where is your place of rest? Thomas wondered. Yet it was none of his business. I might be a spirit now but I will never be one of them, he told himself, then wondered if perhaps he might. There was no point in wondering. He would find out when the time came, best to get on with the work that had to be done.

He walked along a new pathway which suddenly appeared as he turned a corner. This was different.

Instead of the usual concrete path this was tiled. Multi-coloured tiles. Garish, he thought. The borders were filled with clumps of tiny yellow Jonquil, groups of alpines and tiny orchids. A huge mix of everything. Then the gate appeared at the end of the pathway. A small wicker gate. Thomas felt now there was no huge significance in these different types of gate. The Hero's gate, now that was different. Did it matter about the rest? Maybe, maybe not. There probably was some significance if he could figure it out. Why was there a Peacock gate all on its own in the desert? But then it was not up to him. This was the Gathering Place and they knew their own business. Probably somebody got bored he thought wryly, and decided to make a change. Maybe they just wanted to confuse the likes of me, or even the Scavengers? Maybe.

As he arrived the gate suddenly opened wide. He could hear the roar of traffic and saw a city street with cars, motorcycles and a few large trucks moving at a slow pace. Thomas looked out. Traffic jam. Surely this was London, could that be Oxford street? In fact, it could be any busy high street really. He looked left and right but there no sign of anybody who looked remotely as if they were coming in. A man dressed in a cream suit walked past shouting into a mobile phone. "I'm lost. I can't find the bloody registry office." he shouted over the traffic noise.

Not him then, unless he walked under a truck. Thomas waited and watched a long time.

People passed by, most of them unheeding and certainly not able to see him. A thin pale girl, piercings along the length of her ear and on her top lip came towards him. She looked at the gate then backed away bumping into a man who told her to look where she was going. The girl said 'sorry' and stared at Thomas. He smiled. She came closer, an old-fashioned hippy looking girl with long straggly hair and studs in her eyebrows too. There was another in her nose. He looked at the ring through her bottom lip and wondered if it had hurt to get that done. She had a rose tattoo on the side of her neck. That must have hurt. "You're one of them," she said sharply, "I know you're one of them. I thought at first you were a display in the store window, now I see what you are. I'm not coming in, if that's what you think," she said, looking worried, "I have a life to live."

Thomas lifted his shoulders and held his hands out palm upwards. He shook his head, "I don't think I'm waiting for you. I think I am waiting for another."

"Oh, that's all right then," she said looking much happier and hurried away.

Well, he thought to himself, what harm would it do to tell her it was not she who was to come in. It might be, but then it might not. Keep the girl happy. He stepped outside the gate, saw the arch of the Portal a little distance away. The wind blew sharply. Oh, it was cold out here. Thomas turned back into the entrance. Newspaper blew past him, a sheet of it hitting the windscreen of a car and blocking the driver's view. Was it him? No, the paper was whipped away. It seemed the girl thought he was a display in a shop window. He stepped out further and looked.

The large window of a store reflected the traffic and to his surprise the gate was right in the centre of the window. He chuckled. He was gazing in the window of what had been a fairly big store but was now a charity shop. He had of course, no reflection but could see the shops on the far side, and thought he saw something else on the other side of the wide street. Shadows. He turned and looked across the street. A pair of dark shapes stood in a doorway. Was it them? He raced back inside, then turned to peer out. It was just a couple with jet black hair and black make-up, in dark clothing waiting for a bus. Goth's. Were they? They looked like it. He waited just inside the gate, musing on why they would put a gate inside a shop window.

It was interesting that the girl with the studs could see him. But a gate in a shop window, whatever next? He stood for what seemed like an age, then came back to the entrance to peer out. That was when he saw the elderly clergyman ambling slowly along. The man was small and round like a little barrel with a brick red face and dressed in a black suit with a dog collar. He seemed to be searching, looking down little side entrances and all around and across the street. Then he saw Thomas, and nodded as if satisfied. He had found what he was searching for and hurried forward. "Hallo there," the clergyman said raising his hat, "Are you by any stretch of the imagination waiting for me?"

"I might be," Thomas told him, "I never know who to expect."

"Oh, I see." The clergyman's accent was Irish and Thomas thought to himself, another one. He and Mike should get on well. But then of course, he'd seen Mike's work and all the incredibly beautiful work on his book of life, so he would probably be going on soon. "Well then, it could be myself, I think." The clergyman spoke quickly, in staccato sentences, "I know I am no longer in the land of the living. I've been rambling round the streets looking for the road to salvation. They tell you all sorts about how you get there you know. When you're a child they frighten the blue blazes out of you, telling you this and that, and that you'd go to hell for scratching your bits, down below I mean, but sure that's all my eye and Molly Bawn. You have to find your own way in the end. You're dressed in white so I take it you're one of the good guys. Are you?"

"I hope so Vicar. I do my best," Thomas could not help smiling at the little man. "Father." said the elderly man shortly. "I beg your pardon?"

"Father. Not Vicar," said the priest, "I'm a priest of the Holy Roman Catholic Church. Parish priest of St Mary's, only of course since I am here, then the parish priest is no more, so to speak. I came on a trip to London from my parish in Devon and on my first night here didn't I overdo the prawns. I love prawns. Didn't I go and have a double helping and it was my greed that got me where I am now. Do they have them in here, prawns I mean?"

160

There won't be much eating here Thomas thought, unless of course, you meet the fig woman. The Priest did not wait for a reply but went on; "Do you know what happened? One or more of them must have been bad or full of histamine, or something I did not get to the hospital in time to have the injection. I should have brought my Epipen. I have a multitude of allergies you see. They shoved needles in me and banged and bashed away at me and forced oxygen into my lungs, but sure they might as well have tried to raise the dead. Ho ho, ha ha," his laugh bellowed out, "Well of course, they were trying to, so to speak. Ha ha ha. Well, there you are and here I am. So, where do we go from here?"

"Please come inside." Thomas shot a quick glance across the street to make sure there was no shadow waiting, then stepped to one side to let the little priest enter.

The man of God stepped cautiously inside the wicker gate but held on to the gatepost. He looked apprehensive, peering around as if not sure what to expect. "Well now, the thing is this," he said slowly, "How do I know I'm in the right place> I mean to say. Well, you know the other world has a lot of devious characters in it and you have to be sure you are putting your feet over the right doorstep, so to speak. I mean, you might not be one of the good guys. You might be in disguise. I have seen them out there. They have been following me. I have been dodging around like a leaf in the wind, so to speak. I've seen those shadows following me. I may only be a simple Parish Priest but I'm not stupid. I know fire and brimstone when I get a whiff of it."

Thomas nodded, "The smell is more like wet rot. Come in quickly," he said, "The gates will close and I will hand you over to whoever comes first, the Gatherers, or the angels."

"Oh." said the little priest, "I know all about the angels but the Gatherers is a new one on me. What do you call the bad guy here?"

"Scavengers." Thomas told him and the priest nodded. "Aha. Now that would be a good name for them," he said.

Thomas watched the gate; it was closing slowly. He was nervous now. If they were following a man of God that was a big worry. He reached for the priest's arm and almost jerked him along the path, then released the arm, worried in case it was the wrong thing. The gate closed just then with a little snap. He took a deep breath. "You are safe, I promise you. No harm will come to you here."

The Priest was now looking over Thomas's shoulder with a huge beatific smile on his ruddy face. Thomas turned to see an angel hurrying towards them.

"Thank you," said the elderly priest, "I am very grateful for your help; may God bless you."

"I hope he does." Thomas muttered. "Incidentally, what does the Almighty look like?" the little priest muttered, "I have heard that even though it is said we are made to the image and likeness, that of course, it is not strictly true, because you cannot look on the face of God and live." the little Priest nodded, "and who'd be bothered looking at me?"

"Haven't a clue," Thomas said, "What the Almighty looks like and I don't seem to be in a hurry to find out."

The Priest nodded as the angel arrived, "Well goodbye then and thanks a multitude for your help."

He and his angel walked off into the distance, "Now tell me." The little priest began firing questions at the angel. Thomas shook his head.

Before Thomas had time to move on, the gate shot open with a bang. A young black teenager in school uniform stood there looking uncertain and very frightened. He saw Thomas and ran towards him. "Can you hide me man. I mean, like they gonna get me. They carrying. I need to hide or they gonna kill me. They say I 'ain't got no respect."

Thomas had a feeling of almost despair. A child. A mere child. A schoolboy. This lad could be not much more than fourteen, if he was even that. Through the open gate he saw a group of teenage boys rush past. "Hide me man, please hide me." The boy pleaded. "They won't find you in here, they cannot see you," Thomas told him. He saw the gate close. "You sure they can't see me man?" The boy was breathing fast, his dark eyes wide with fear. Thomas could have wept. The gate was closed tight. The boy was dead and not even aware of it, "They cannot see you; the gate is closed now. You can stay here awhile."

How did he tell this young boy his life was ended almost before it had begun? Two Gatherers came hurrying up and Thomas, filled with a desperate sadness that the child's life had been ended by a group of his own age, ran as fast as his legs could carry him. I am a coward. I know, I am a coward, but I am so glad I do not have to deal with that he told himself. A young life lost.

Thomas came upon them suddenly. Two people, standing before a closing gate, one a Buddhist priest in a saffron robe, who spoke softly to a silver haired man in a white suit. This was the same man he had seen a few times who gave a brief wave but never spoke. The priest turned smiling eyes to Thomas and gave a little bow and said 'Namaste'. The man turned swiftly, almost guiltily and he

162

wondered why. He stopped, welcomed the priest who bowed again, then Thomas turned to the other. For some reason this man bothered him, but he could not have said why. The man nodded sharply to Thomas, turned to the Buddhist priest, grasped his arm tightly saying. "We must hurry. We need to get inside and keep you safe."

There was indeed something not quite right here. They were inside and there was no more need to rush this gentleman. "There is no longer any need to hurry," Thomas said firmly, he looked at the other man, "He is inside now and safe from harm, that is, if there ever was any harm coming to him. The Gatherers or the angels will come for him. You know that. Surely you have been here long enough to know."

The man scowled and was about to say something when an angel came along the path moving swiftly. The man in white left saying, "You will be safe now. I must be about my work."

The angel greeted the priest, but then turned to look after the man hurrying away. It nodded to Thomas and walked with its charge along the path towards the plain. As it passed some dense shrubbery it lifted a hand and pointed a long forefinger in the direction the man in white had taken.

A small golden head lifted and a cherub peered out its mouth a round O of surprise. The cherub said: "I am very sorry Barbiel. I did not see it arrive,"

The angel Barbiel waggled an admonishing finger at the tiny one, and shook its shining silver head, "Less music, little one. More watching."

I was right, Thomas told himself. I will keep a watchful eye out for that one.

****

Chapter 19

Thomas walked back then towards his little house. He was in a dreamy state. It seemed to take a very long time but it was nice to walk between the trees and listen to the birds. Trees? He pulled up short. More trees? A forest? Where had all these trees come from? The plain was just that: a few small trees here and there and the groups of little frame houses dotted all over. The pathways were lined with thick shrubs and flower beds. So, where had these come from? Surely, he was not lost again and back in those woods where the woman Salema offered figs to the unwary. Yet there was no sign of anybody.

He moved quietly listening and looking. There was no sound, although in his nervous state Thomas imagined there were things rustling in the shrubbery. He stopped; ears attuned. There was no sound. No branch moved on a tree. No movement of any kind.

He stepped slowly realising he walked like a cat stalking a mouse, lifting on foot slowly and placing it gently on the ground. Now he was closer to the group of trees. "Oh well," he said resignedly, "In for a penny, in for a pound."

The trees however, looked like the normal trees that grew on the earth when he was alive. He examined one, touched the bark. That was real, a copper beech. He looked all around. It was not as dense as the place where Salema waited like a spider for her prey. Several kinds of tree grew here. So, what was this all about? More trouble for him, of course.

Sighing deeply Thomas walked on. They were at it again. More testing. Could they never leave well alone? He stopped then and called to whatever Great Angel might be around. "Look, if there are any of you Great Angels hanging around, I just want to let you know I am on to you. OK. I know the way you work. This testing business is getting very, very boring. I'm fed up with it. Right! I just want to be on my way. So, show me the way out of here and I will get back to the gate of my little house."

There was no reply nor was there a sound of bird or animal. He listened carefully for voices. None.

Thomas, needing to find his way out, walked slowly on, apprehension now flooding through him. He was well and truly lost. The trees began to rustle and he felt a raindrop on his nose. He saw it drop on to the path. It was raining. He tutted. What next? It seemed darker too, the light was fading fast and the trees were coming closer together. This was worrying. Night was falling swiftly, too swiftly. Thomas did not relish the thought of being lost here. The darkness was coming down so fast he might end up not having a clue where he was. Well actually, he did not know where he was anyway. How come he'd not seen night fall in here in the actual gathering place since he arrived? Now this was really odd. He bit his lip.

Do not allow yourself to be afraid. Things happen here and they pass and then all is normal again. He blew out a breath. Be calm, be normal? "Am I mad?" he asked himself, "What is normal about this?" Of course, he could call the angels. He did so. There was no answer to his call. Looking around he saw there was a rustic seat built around the base of one of the trees and went over to sit down. He dropped his head into his hands. What now?

It was quite a while before he lifted his head and opened his eyes again. It was pitch dark. There was no light of any kind. Deep, dark night. He lay down on the sear and brought his knees up under his chin, holding his hands over his eyes The Scavengers were always busy at night. Then it began, a hissing, giggling, a scream close by. Through that long and fearful night Thomas lay curled up. No pinprick of light so much as penetrated the darkness.

Then other noises began. Squeals and squeaks and then something slapped at him. Rain hit him in flurries. Suddenly there was the whirring, rushing sound of wings, great wings which brushed his face, then his body. He cowered back. There was silence for a time. Then the shrieking and wild laughter began and there was the smell, always that smell of decay. "Get away from me," he shouted, "I know you. I know what you are. Get away."

They laughed and went on their way. Then the noises stopped. The things in the darkness did not come back. He lay down on the seat curled like an infant, eyes closed waiting for something to happen. Then the darkness began to lift and the light came. He stood up, maybe he would find the way out now. Thomas saw a path and ran along it almost colliding with a group of five children with a grey-haired woman who looked as if she was their teacher. "Ah," the woman said staring at him, "Are you lost too? We are lost in this forest. We came on a field trip and darkness came down so quickly. We sheltered in a shack."

He was relieved. The woman was quite tall, dressed in a grey suit and wearing thick lensed glasses. Her hair was grey, in a tight bun. Her eyes behind the thick lenses seemed to be grey also. A grey lady. Thomas almost giggled, such was his relief, but she looked rather severe so he calmed his feeling of hysteria right down. "I think there is a house near," she told him, "I caught a glimpse of it through the trees. Perhaps we should make our way there. The children, my pupils, are cold and we need directions to get back."

"Back to where?" he asked warily. "The Gathering place of course," she stepped quickly away from him, alarmed, "You're not one of them, are you? Those horrible things. They were out here in the night you know. We heard them. The children were so frightened but they went away after a little while."

"I know," Thomas said, "I assure you madam I am not one of them."

"Oh good." The woman's pale lips stretched into a tight smile, "You look trustworthy. I was so frightened for the children."

Thomas looked then at the children. They wore grey uniform, were small and looked very cold. As he looked at them, they drew away almost fearfully. He smiled to reassure them but the children just stared back. "Where is this house?" Thomas asked their teacher.

He wondered vaguely what exactly they would learn here in this place. "I get so confused here; I wish I had never got behind the wheel of that car." Thomas told the woman. "I wish I had never taken the tablets," she said, pushing the children gently forward and speaking softly to them and oddly it seemed was trying to shield them from view.

Thomas raised his eyebrows in surprise, "Taken the tablets?"

The woman looked quickly over her shoulder, "I was foolish. I took too many, accidentally of course. To sleep. You know."

One of the children bent sideways around the woman and looked at Thomas. She gave a wide, grin, giggled then ducked back again. He could hear them laughing now and was pleased they were no longer afraid. It was wrong to frighten children. Yes, it was very wrong. The children began chattering to each other in a language Thomas did not understand. The teacher said "Shush." and moved them forward. "Come, let us go and find the place I saw. I'm sure it was this way." The grey woman told him.

166

The house appeared before them, suddenly, as if it had been dropped there that very second. It was a mansion. There was a big lawn to the front. Tables with sheltering umbrellas and chairs were dotted over the green lawn. The sun was shining. It had suddenly become very warm.

A group of people sat laughing and drinking. Some played croquet. As Thomas, the teacher and her pupils appeared; they all stopped talking, then waved and beckoned. A tall tanned man with fair hair came forward and offered drinks for the children. A tray carried by a man dressed in white and laden with soft drinks was brought from the house. To Thomas this was unusual and he refused the drink from the waiter. He did not feel the need of it.

The waiter did not look at him. He saw the bowed silver head. There was something about the man, but what was it? Thomas felt a little apprehensive. The children and their teacher drank thirstily. The woman telling the tall fair man what had happened.

The man smiled at Thomas, "You have been out in the night too." It was a statement not a question.

Thomas nodded. 'We stay inside the house when darkness comes down here. It is advisable. I take it this is your first time here. You have not seen night fall in this place? The darkness is impenetrable. It is not safe,' the man said. "How do we get back to the plain and the little houses?" Thomas asked. "You will have to wait until after the next nightfall before the gate opens," the man said easily, "You will have to stay in the house with us until the dawn comes again, for your own safety."

Thomas was suddenly worried. What gate? He stayed inside the Gathering Place at all times. "I don't remember leaving by a gate," he said.

The man laughed easily, "Don't worry, we all slip up now and again. I've done it myself. My name is Haagen by the way, and you are?"

"Thomas. I am Thomas."

The man smiled almost triumphantly; Thomas felt. It was almost as he spoke the words aloud. He could hear them inside his head: "Got you."

Thomas now felt really apprehensive. He was almost certain now. They did not look like scavengers, but he knew they were. Worried and a little afraid Thomas tried to remember what Mike said about the woman with cocktails? No, there were no cocktails, well not from the woman anyway. He wondered if they wanted to keep him and the children, to take them to wherever their place might be. He had to warn the teacher and the children, get them away from here. He

167

must not panic, must not show fear or shout. He managed to thank Haagen and walked towards where he'd left the teacher and children. There was no sign of them.

Thomas looked swiftly around and saw her ushering the last child through the big front door of the mansion. He stopped. Oh no. It was too late for them but he was not taking one step inside that mansion. The woman then turned, throwing her thick lensed spectacles across the grass and loosening her hair. It flowed down her back like spun silver. One of the children danced out of the door and he saw it was not a child at all but a tiny scavenger with a face as old as time itself. It actually had a face. The woman pushed it back inside the house. He turned to run but suddenly she was right beside him a cocktail glass in her hand. Something blue and sparkling filled the glass. "Cocktail time my dear. Drink Thomas," she was laughing and was no longer a grey woman.

This was a beautiful woman and remembering what Mike said about the cocktail woman, knew without any doubt now what they were. Scavengers.

She laughed mockingly, "Come Thomas, you know now who we are, know too what we can do for you. Give in, take the hand of friendship. Follow us. Your time with us will be beyond anything you could ever dream. Haagen, come. Come tell him how wonderful it is here with us in our mansions."

The man was standing behind him, his white teeth gleaming, skin golden tanned, his pale blue eyes watchful. "We want you Thomas. We want you for our friend. You will love being with us. Come to us." The man said, his eyes suddenly went cold, his voice harsh, "You should have been ours. You were ours for the taking. You will be ours. Take him." he told the woman.

Thomas was trembling now from head to toe, "I am not yours. I will never be yours and you cannot take me unless I allow you. I know that. The angels told me and they are right. They know."

"The angels." the woman hissed, "What do they know? We tell you the truth. They lie; deceive, tell you to recant of your evil ways. What is evil? We are not evil. We are great, can make you great too."

"You are evil," he shouted.

She hissed at him, changing before his eyes, darkening becoming faceless and terrifying and the smell was there. It came with her. "Take the cup," she shrieked, "Drink. Take this goblet from my hand, drink it and give me your hand. We are fast losing patience with you."

She reached a hand towards him. He almost brushed it away, remembered in time not to touch. The children all looked strange now, changing, their faces fading also. He knew though, that they were not children. Thomas was almost weeping, they were too close, their smell inside his head.

The man Haagen shouted, "Take him quickly. Our time is almost up. Hurry. There is no time left. Do as I say. Now," he howled the word.

Thomas, remembering the words of the Great Angel, shouted: "Leave now. Go from this place. Go. I command you in the name of all that is good and holy."

The woman reached for Thomas and he stepped back and away from her. He could hear a roaring noise. The children began to wail as if frightened. At first there was nothing to be seen. Then he saw movement in the air behind the group. It was small at first but grew swiftly. A vortex. Swirling in the air behind, black and menacing It opened wider. He stared at it. The wind began to howl and the people standing before it began to be sucked backwards. The small ones shouted, trying to run to the woman. The woman threw the goblet at him and the man reached for him. Thomas moved swiftly aside. The scavengers were being held in place, could not touch him. The howling noise increased until it hurt his ears. The Vortex, its black maw huge and terrifying, opened wide and it moved closer, closing in on them. Screaming and cursing they were all slowly sucked into it, men, women and children, then the house, the grass, tennis courts, the trees until everything was gone. The Vortex enclosed everything within itself and then ceased to be.

He stood in the absolute stillness. Nothing was left of them. No trees or grass. Just the bare scorched earth of a desert. Not so much as a twig lay there. He looked all around, and then ran towards where he could see what looked like an opening. Moments later he found himself back on his own pathway again shaking with fear, but very relieved. The opening closed immediately. Thomas knew also that he was now their mortal enemy, and would have to be very careful of them. They would want to be avenged for this days' work. He must, at all times. be vigilant.

Thomas walked swiftly towards his own little house. It was security, safety and rest. He stepped inside and stared at the table and the book. He sat down on his chair.

The book had changed. He could see it properly. It was shining, not like Mike's but it shone. It took from his mind the terrifying maw of the Vortex. This small cleansing of the book had been hard-earned. Was it worth it though? All that fear, punishment and the work that went into cleaning up the cover of a scruffy old book. "Help me. Help me understand. Help me in this," he whispered, "I do not know if it is worth it all. It has taken me so long to do this, and I am so afraid. How much longer? Help me."

He bowed his head, closed his eyes and waited. Yet there was no reply, but then, did there have to be? He had done, as they would say here, that which was expected of him. He sighed deeply. Then, as he sat, Thomas heard the words inside his head, "That book, the Book of Life, is you, inside and out. All parts must be cleansed. All work must be finished." He understood then.

Chapter 20

Sometime later, Thomas feeling easier, left the little house and when he did any fears or doubts or worries were gone. He sat on the veranda wondering if Mike was still around. There had been no sign of the little man. He saw the priest strolling along, and waved. He too, was now wearing the white suit. "I wonder," Thomas mused thoughtfully, "What is it man a of God does wrong, that gets him stuck in the Gathering Place with us sinners?"

"Tell me," Mike's voice came from the doorway of his own little house, "Do you think a man of God is not human enough to make the same mistakes as the likes of you and me. Like, is a man of God not just that, a man first and then a man of God? Because we are, were, all human."

"Never thought of it like that." Thomas said, "But then, I did not know many men of God."

"Now, I have something to tell you. Do you know, what I just discovered," Mikes face was glowing, "Me book is only glorious. All the little jewels are dancing off the cover. I wonder what happens now. I wonder will the big fella's come now?"

They sat and waited to see what would happen. People came and went across the plain. The two men watched. Neither spoke now. Mike clasped his hands together. Oddly, his pipe was no longer lit. There was an air of expectancy between them. Thomas saw the movement first, high up close to the Great Gates. The figures grew bigger as they came closer.

They came, the Great Angels smiling at Mike, who stepped back almost fearfully into his own little house. They all went inside together. Thomas wondered how these huge angels even got through the doors. Moments later all three came out. Mike holding the glowing glittering book. It looked glorious, like a flame, a dancing glittering flame. Taking Mike's arms the two angels lifted him high. "Goodbye Mike." Thomas called, "Goodbye." Two big tears rolled down his cheeks, "Goodbye."

There was no reply. Mike was on his way and Thomas watched until they were no more than dots. He whispered, with tears in his eyes and hope in his heart. "I will see you soon my friend, I will see you soon."

He wiped the tears from his cheeks. He would miss the little man. Thomas got up then and walked towards the door of his own little house but changed his mind. He'd go to the gates and see who was coming in. As he turned Cadamiel stood waiting for him in the garden. The angel stood in silence, hands inside the sleeves of its robe, head bowed.

Thomas stared balefully at the misty figure. Where were Cadamiel and his sidekick Fariel and the Great Angels when he was in trouble back there in the darkness? For two pins he would walk away. He turned to leave without speaking but curiosity got the better of him, "What now," he growled at the gentle patient angel, "What orders from above? What have I got to do now?"

The angel lifted its head, "You know we do not tell you what to do Thomas. We simply direct you."

"That is the same thing in here." Thomas would not be placated. "Ah Thomas." The angel seemed sad, "You are unhappy?"

"Unhappy? Unhappy? Well you got that just a little bit wrong, didn't you? I am not unhappy at all. I am furious with all of you. Where were you when I needed you?"

"I am sorry if you feel we have let you down Thomas but in truth you did not need us. You truly did not." Cadamiel told him.

Thomas snorted: "What about that great whirling thing. I could have been sucked into that and then where would I have been. I'd have been down in that place with them, hissing and screeching and…" Cadamiel held out his hands, "Thomas. Thomas. Be calm, be at peace. It would not have happened. Have you not learned to trust yet? The convolution was there to take them away, not you, and remember this. You called it up. You spoke the word the Great Angels, the Seraphim, waited to hear and they sent it to you. You commanded them to leave that place, in the name of all that is right and good, did you not? They left at your command."

Thomas would not reply and stared into the distance. He still sulked. The Angel smiled and gestured towards the chair; "Sit and rest my friend."

Thomas sniffed, "So, I'm your friend now, is that right?"

"You were always my friend. Now two things, the first is a warning, although, we feel you are aware of this. The faceless ones will be seeking revenge. You must be aware at all times. Not many have managed to call up the convolution. The second is this. I have to ask something more of you and it is within your capabilities."

"Oh no you don't. I'm not getting myself into any more trouble." Thomas was still angry.

The angel watched him for a short time, then said, "Thomas. Dear friend. It is a task you are capable of completing. We need you to find another, a soul. You know this soul. May I continue?"

Thomas had butted in with a rude, "No way. I've had it with you lot."

Cadamiel gazed thoughtfully at the red-faced angry man, and then asked, "Tell me. Do you wish to stay here for all time? You can do that. But if you do, be warned. You are setting up something you will not like. They will come again and again, those whom you fear, to try persuade you to follow them. They do not give up. Each time they come, they will be more devious, more determined to have you and much more dangerous. Is that what you want? It has been done before, and it makes terrible demands on those who protect this place, the Great Angels. Their struggle, to keep safe within the fold of the Gathering Place all those who wish to go onwards, is hard. It puts all here in danger of the blandishments of the dark ones. Is that what you want Thomas Beck?"

Cadamiel's voice had become loud, even sharp and Thomas looked up startled. The angel suddenly seemed to have grown larger, "We, Thomas protect our own at all cost, even the ungrateful foolish ones who choose not to see beyond the length of their noses, how hard we work for them."

Suddenly apologetic, Thomas Beck held out his hands, "I am sorry. I know how hard they work for us. Forgive me."

Cadamiel became as Thomas had always known him once again and Thomas got the feeling that there was a lot more to this angel than he thought. He wondered, was he too, one of the Great Angels? It was possible.

The angel said, "Very well Thomas. This is what we ask. There is a soul, a woman. She is known to you. Look here, you will see the image of her as she is now. She is lost and must be found. The Gatherers cannot find her. I may not go to seek her. You may know that place where she might be. You have twenty-four hours of earth time to find her. You do know her, she is called Ginette Herbert. This was out last sighting of her. She has managed to hide from us."

An image appeared in front of Thomas. A thin pale woman, elderly and with hair cut straight just below her ears, walked slowly along a city street, dressed in a long skirt and a thin coat, carrying a bag in one hand and a walking stick in the other. The street looked cold. Thomas could see patches of snow in small heaps against the edge of the pavement. She wandered slowly along, appearing to talk to herself, sometimes gesticulating and shouting as people passed by, giving her a wide berth. "That was Ginette in life," the angel told him, "She has now passed beyond life. The reason you are being sent out to find her is that it was in helping her, you gained entry here, and yet she has not come to us. Nor do the Scavengers have her. You know this woman Thomas. She was a part of your childhood. She and her brother. You called her Gina. Do you not remember?"

"I don't remember..." he began but then he had a memory of a young woman in trouble. Gina? Of course, James sister. He had helped her couple of times. That was the only Gina he knew; had not known her true name was Ginette So that was it. That was how he had managed to get in here instead of the other place. He'd helped her, had stopped her taking her own life. Twice, she had tried to end her life. Once when a girl and once as a grown woman. He had found her both times.

Now she was in trouble again. He wondered given the state of her now, if he had done the right thing in stopping her. Poor Gina, a sad difficult child and an uneasy woman. Hard to talk to, although he had helped to take her from the road, she was hell bent on walking, at least for a time. It had been a long time since he left the earth. She was much younger of course than he, but how old now? This woman looked as if in her eighties.

A long time ago Gina tried to cut her wrists when she was fifteen or sixteen. He found her in the woods where they used to play. He had taken the rusty old knife from her and got her to the cottage hospital. The wounds she inflicted on herself became infected. She had been ill for ages. Some years later, in those days before his daughter Kate was born, when he was so desperately hurt and wanted only to be alone, and yet not alone, he called on Gina. It had been for no reason that he could think of now. There had been a vague idea in his head that he would be able to talk to her because she was James sister. The sister of his best friend. James had been gone several years. He had found Gina in the back garden. The recollection of the day was of warm sunshine.

He knocked on the door of the old gate lodge. There had been no reply, but he heard the sound of a radio and gone around to the back, calling out. There was a muffled sound like a sob. She had been lying back on a lounger with a handful of tablets in one hand and the bottle in the other. He took tablets and bottle. That

174

was the second time. Something to do with a married man and a pregnancy that was ended. "She is James sister." he said. Cadamiel nodded. "Can you not send James?" he asked.

The angel shook its silvery head, "James is no longer with us in the Gathering Place, you know that. Had he been here with us it is doubtful he would have gone back to help her. I will say this to you. James was a truly difficult man and an even more difficult soul. It was good when we managed to send him onward. This is why we are asking this of you Thomas. Hurry now. The gate is open. It is being held for you. When you have found her, bring her to us. Remember also you must call on me if you need help. Fariel will be with you also, as will others. You will, of course, be visible to Gina, since we know that she does not still live. Her time to come to us is past. Her time for the Gatherers to collect her, is also past. She has not gone on to that other place. That much is known. She is alone and must be found and soon, otherwise *they* will try to take her and she is so fragile, she might just go with them. Remember if you need me, call on me."

Then Cadamiel was gone. Thomas sometimes became irritated by the speed at which they came and went away and of course, when they asked you to do something, it was not really asking. You were expected to do it.

Now, he stood by an old rusty gate. He sniffed. Thomas was about to step out when he saw what he thought was a child dressed in a little white robe. A child flitting about in here on its own. Then he saw the tiny wings. Ah, One of the cherubim. "Hello," he said.

The little one smiled but did not reply. "What are you doing? And by the way, why are you always here by the gates?"

The voice of the cherubim, as it answered was high and piping, "First answer, I have work to do here. Second answer; I belong here."

"Why are you here alone then? It is not right you should be alone."

"I am not alone, you are here too and there are others, though you cannot see them." The eyes of the cherubim were wise and appraising. Thomas was not sure he liked this cherub child, too sharp with its answers. How old did it look? Five? Maybe six? "What do you do here?"

"I open and close the gates, all the Cherubim do this and we pass on the word that souls have arrived, and of course, we, *The Cherubim* are the eyes and ears of the gathering place. It is important work." The little thing puffed out its chest.

Thomas nodded, "Oh, I see. Can you tell me then, why are there so many different gates?"

"You do not see at all," the cherub told him, "But since it is your desire to know why there are so many different entrances, I will tell you one part of the reason, the other you know. The different gates help to confuse those who are not welcome here. They are the beings of the darkness, who creep in and of this we must be aware at all times. I am hidden, therefore I and my brethren can tell. The Seraphs they are here. The Seraphs are very important you know. We too are important. All of us have our work here. The work of the cherubim is very important; we know how to control the gates. The other part, as you know is that gates are everywhere to facilitate entry from all places. Are you satisfied?" The little cherub stared questioningly at Thomas, "Is there anything more? No? I have opened the gates for you and you must go at once."

It waved its tiny hands at him, "Off you go and do your work."

Thomas thought, "Well now, I have been told and by an infant at that," He stepped to the entrance, and then looked back. The cherub was out of sight. A worrying thought struck Thomas Beck. What was it Cadamiel said about others who would have Gina? His heart sank. They must know here how much he feared those faceless ones. The Scavengers; they would not do that to him, would they? Would the angels send him out alone knowing the dark ones had it in for him after the vortex business? No. He would just go and try to find her and come back in here as quickly as possible.

The gate was wide open. He was reluctant to leave. They were out there. He just knew it. Thomas stepped back away from the gate. No, there must be another way to work out his salvation. Those dark things hated him. Sending them into the vortex must make them want to get him. It was like he had power over them and they would be out for revenge. No way was he going out there. The big angels might be hanging around somewhere but what if they could not get to him in time? "O ye of little faith," a childish voice said.

Then something or somebody he could not see gave him a not too gentle push and Thomas stumbled forward out of the glowing warmth of the Gathering Place to find himself on the road between Barton Trinity and Great Barton. The gate actually slammed behind him. He scowled at it.

It had to be that cheeky cherub. He was locked out of the Gathering Place. Well, there was nothing for it now but to get out there and do his best. He took a huge breath and stepped bravely on to the concrete of the road.

****

Chapter 21

This was where he had left the world, where his car had gone half way up along the old wall. After the fiasco of his last visit to this place, he'd not expected to see it again. Be brave man, get out there. Be a hero Thomas, he told himself. To ease his nervousness, he concentrated on Gina Herbert.

Where was she? They did not seem to be able to find her. So, she must be hiding. Where though? Was she in fact back here? Was it possible they knew something and were not telling him? If he lived to be five thousand years old, he would never understand the Gathering Place. Then he laughed. You do not live Thomas. Exist maybe. This business of eternity was a bit of a wonder to him still. Time, it seemed had no relevance once you left your earthly body. Was that the secret?

The sun was shining and the hedges were bright with the paler green of new leaves. It must be spring time. Clumps of daffodils grew in great masses along the green grassy verges, their heads showing yellow, but as yet not fully open. There had not been daffodils growing that he remembered, in fact there were clumps of primroses just beginning too. Change, always change. Why could things not always stay the same? He sighed. Silly of him, there needed to be change. You could not live in the past. He smiled. The past? That was over and gone. There was only the now. It had been a foolish thought.

Traffic drove by, first one way then the other. So much more than there used to be when he lived. He stood and thought for a long time. What was the point of leaving him on the road to his home? Well of course, it was not his home. That had been made clear. Thomas stared in the other direction along the road to Barton Trinity. He had a sudden intense feeling that he should go back there and not bother searching anywhere else. He turned and began to walk towards the village.

A voice called his name and as he turned, saw the figure of a man, "Thomas. Wait for me."

Thomas watched the man running along the road. It was the man with the silver hair he had seen on the pathways. The one who walked around and who'd been with the Buddhist priest. Thomas felt a chill. Who was this man? What was he? The waiter at the mansion had a look of him too. "How nice to see you again." the man said.

Thomas smiled but said nothing. This man had seen him inside the Gathering Place, yet had barely been civil. "I see you do not remember me from life," the man said pleasantly and did not seem to mind at all that he was not remembered. "I am sorry. I just do not remember, although I have seen you in the Gathering Place." Thomas was apologetic. "Please, the fact that you don't remember me, does not matter in the slightest," the man said, "I have seen you inside the place of course. It took a while to remember where I had seen you previously."

Thomas nodded, still wary, "We must have met at some point and I can only apologise once again for my poor memory."

The man nodded, "I am called John Blaine and you of course are Thomas Beck. We met a couple of times in London. We worked at the Ministry. I remember you as being very quiet and reserved."

Still there was no recognition but the man knew him from work. He seemed pleasant, and yet? His smile was wide and there was an air of friendliness and warmth about the man now. Thomas was still uneasy. "I have been sent out to help find somebody. We should travel together." John Blaine said, "It seems you have been sent out to seek a soul. She is not easy to find. I have searched long and hard. The Gatherers followed her across the country but it seemed she might have come back here."

"Who is the person you seek?" Thomas asked "It is the same one for whom you are searching"

"Oh, you mean Gina." Thomas smiled, he was more at ease now. So, this man had been sent to help. "Of course." the man turned away and looked all around, "It would be better if we were to stay together." He paused for a moment, "You must be very well aware; there are others who search and not so caring as you and I."

He smiled his warm smile and Thomas felt that he should have no more worries, indeed felt guilty for having had any doubts. His fears were now fading away. Cadamiel however, had said he must be careful. The Gatherers had been unable to find her and he and John had been sent out together. That was good. He did not see the man look at him. Did not see the eyes darken and the calculating glance. Had he done so Thomas would have been very much afraid and run, as fast as he could, screaming for the Great Angels to come with sword and shield. He would have had reason to fear.

The man watched Thomas carefully. He would have done anything to find the woman Gina. The woman Salema told him it would help his cause, make him great before those who guarded the Great Gate if he found her, and brought Gina to her. She offered him figs but he had refused, said he hated figs. The woman had laughed so hard at that, had found it vastly amusing, but he listened to what she had to say. She told him that if he chooses, he could go back to life and have everything. All he had to do was search and get Thomas Beck to help him. She offered everything and it blew his mind. He'd agreed. Life, was now more important than the Great Gate above. Life and huge wealth would soon be his. It had been promised. That was all he ever wanted in life, but wealth had always eluded him.

Yes, he had known Gina Herbert. He had been her head of department at the Ministry and he had an affair with her, then when he was tired of Gina saw to it, she lost her job. He had vaguely known this man Beck, but had not liked him. He gestured in the direction of the village.

They walked along the road together. However, neither saw the flash of white that appeared from time to time. Fariel drifted behind them watching carefully, eyes looking out for the dark shapes. Fariel knew of the duplicity of John Blaine. He, too, needed to be protected. Yet, it was doubtful he could be saved now. The angel would try very hard to rescue the man.

Thomas and his companion walked on along the road towards Barton Trinity. His uneasiness was gone, he felt comfortable. His idea, John Blaine said, of going back to Barton Trinity was indeed the right one and felt this was the place to start. The gatherers said that she might have been seen by another who was being gathered in. It was only a glimpse the man had said. He thought she was someone he'd been to school with, name of Gina, who had been married once to a friend of his, but they had divorced. He had thought she was coming in with him.

The man with the silver hair chatted continuously, holding Thomas attention. He said the idea of going to her house was a good one, since she'd lived there and would leave a sense of her being behind. Thomas looked at him. A what? "A sense of her being, you know; it's like opening a wardrobe or a drawer and getting a scent of the clothing inside. People leave that same sense of their being behind. Traces of their life. She would be drawn back to where she was happy, or if she left something undone," he stopped and looked around, "or if there is nowhere else to go."

Now Thomas was uneasy again. She had never been a happy person. Maybe, as a child for a short time, certainly not as a teenager and a woman. He frowned. The Gatherers who came for him had not mentioned that they came because of his scent, sense of being, whatever it was this man called it. In fact, they simply said they had lost him. The girl who was murdered by the men in the car had just been lost when he found her and they had come rushing to him when the street boy was lost and somehow found himself inside the Portal. He felt a sudden prickling sensation on the back of his neck. This was wrong. Yet what was he to do? Fear touched him and he looked towards Blaine who smiled gently back.

Thomas saw a movement by the evergreen hedge and looked carefully but it was only a sheep, and yet, there was something. He felt a coldness steal over him. He could smell them. They were here. Somehow his attention had been taken from his surroundings. He'd lost concentration and they had caught up. Please, let them not see him, let them go somewhere else, but he knew they would not. He decided to ignore the chattering of the other man. Keep watching, he told himself, be ready to shout for help if you see anything.

They were almost at the village now. Thomas could see the churchyard had become even bigger, more gravestones, than when he was last there. John was guiding Thomas gently into the churchyard. Not exactly grasping his arm and pulling but just touching and guiding. He is manoeuvring me into position Thomas thought fearfully, becoming increasingly alarmed. He glanced across toward where his own remains lay, but there were now many more headstones hiding his. He saw movement. There was a flash of something white across the way and he was sure there was an angel behind a large headstone. Was it Fariel? Let it be Fariel. A thick mist was coming down, but he saw another flash of white, then another. Thomas took a deep breath. Relief flooded through him. Angels.

He glanced to see if his companion noticed but the man was busy talking. More movement to the far side but it was dark movement. Yet he was not frightened now. The angels were gathering. This was something big. He counted the flashes, five, and then another five. Yes. They were gathering. His heart lifted and his fear was gone.

He knew that when something happened it would be fast and he had to be ready. He turned to look at John Blaine who was hurrying him across the graves.

Thomas made up his mind. He stopped suddenly and the man went past him swiftly. He stopped and asked crossly. "What is the matter with you? Come on we are almost there. She is here somewhere. I know it. I can feel her presence."

He knew for certain now. The dark ones wanted him and Gina and this man was helping them. Was he one of theirs? Thomas moved forward slowly, then caught a glimpse of a dark shape in the mist ahead. They too were arriving. He shivered, that was a huge shape. Something big was happening. "No," he said, "No, there is no reason to come this way. We should go to her old home. If as you say she has left a sense of her being there we will find her. I do not like this place. There is something wrong here. I feel we could be in trouble. Come on, let us go."

Blaine looked as if he might argue and kept glancing over Thomas shoulder. Thomas looked back and saw the dark shapes but also the flashes of white, still partly hidden behind the gravestones. The faceless ones were here in a big group. This was important to them. Was it revenge for the vortex? To the right he had a quick glimpse of more angels. The angels were in two groups now He was not alone. Slightly apprehensive he moved forward towards the main gate. He knew now. Blaine was one of them. He was going to hand him and Gina over to the faceless ones. That was it.

The man grabbed his arm, "Why do we have to go there? I feel sure she is here. In fact, am certain."

"Look over there," he pointed, "There she is. We have found her." He shouted loudly, "She is here."

A woman, thin and pale stood by a gravestone. Thomas peered through the mist. "No." He said sharply, "Definitely not. That is not Gina. That is somebody else."

He was glad. This was no spirit. She was a living woman tending a grave of a loved one. He could see the faded flowers on the ground on top of a plastic bag. The fresh flowers were in a small urn. "It is her." Bone stood in front of him; He shouted, "It is Gina."

Thomas snapped back, "You do not have to shout. It is not Gina. That is somebody else. That's a living person. Let us go now."

He had seen the dark shapes go towards the woman, and then the heads turned in Thomas's direction. That was why Blaine had shouted, to catch their attention. The man grabbed at Thomas arm, but he pulled away, "I am not staying here."

"You will stay," the man shouted, "You have to stay with me. I will not lose everything now."

Thomas would not allow them to take him. No. He moved swiftly forward leaving the other behind and raced for the gates, was out and running towards the green and crossing it to the other side, then he ran the couple of hundred yards to where the gate lodge had been in the old days. The lodge was still there but there was little more than four walls and a roof left of it now. Some of the windows were in one piece, the rest cracked and broken. The place was crumbling and deserted.

Bedraggled tattered wet ivy clung to the walls. He raced between the posts where there had once been gates, saw the notice which said, Keep out. Dangerous structure. He saw too the bulldozer and the tools and realised it was about to be torn down. Glancing swiftly behind he saw there was nobody following and slowed down. He looked at the overgrown garden, the trailing ivy. Rain was coming down in a fine mist.

Why would she come here he wondered? Yet, it was the only place. It was where she was born and lived for a time, where she must have had some happiness. The small panes of glass on the ground floor were almost all broken. Everything was damp with moisture. There was movement inside the ground floor of the lodge and he caught a fleeting glimpse of a frightened face, then it was gone. Gina. "Come out Gina," He called, "quickly. It is time to go."

There was a moment's silence, and then a woman's quavering voice called back, "Go away. I am tired of running. Leave me alone."

"Come on Gina. You know me." he called softly glancing behind. Nothing. "I don't know you," she called back, "Who are you? What do you want with me? Leave me alone. Let me have peace. I don't want to go with those faceless things. They have been following me, and they are too frightening to be from anywhere good. Why have they sent you in your white suit? You too are trying to trick me."

"Do not shout, speak softly. You know me Gina. I am Thomas Beck." he said quietly.

He saw her move forward towards the broken window. She peered out. "You are trying to trick me into coming out," she whimpered. "Come over nearer the window Gina. You know me. You remember when you had bad times all those years ago. I helped you. Remember?"

He saw her face at the broken window then, and at last recognition dawned, "I know you. You are Thomas. Don't let them take me," she pleaded, "Those people with no faces are trying to take me away with them. I won't go. Help me."

"They won't take you. I won't let them. Come out now and hold on to me and we will go together."

He could see a mass of dark shapes across the green. If they ran for it now and made the Portal and the gate, it would be over. The Portal meant safety.

The light was going. Darkness was coming down and it was a deepening swiftly. Two young people crossed the green laughing, arms linked, walking towards the gate lodge Did they not see how dark it was? Did they not know the thing that was happening here? The rain had stopped now. "Go home. Go home," he shouted into the ear of the girl, "It is not safe."

The couple came on still laughing, but the girl stopped suddenly. "It's got very cold." She shivered, "I don't want to go in the old Lodge tonight. They say it is haunted now," She looked around nervously, "Let's go to the pub."

The young man put an arm around her and looked around, "Yeah," he said, "It feels kind of funny here tonight." They hurried towards the Inn on the Green.

It was so dark now Thomas could barely see her shape as she came out to meet him. She came to him slowly at first, a thin frail woman in a light dress and coat. Gina crossed the patch of worn lawn, then ran swiftly towards him. He reached a hand to her and she grasped it, then she stared in horror over his shoulder. Thomas looked behind and saw Blaine and to his horror a big group of the faceless ones. He put her behind him flinging out a hand. "Go from here," he shouted, "Go from this place now. Get away from her. I command you."

He waited for the Vortex. It did not come. He stared at the huge shape of the Scavanger who stood just behind the man Blaine Thomas was panic stricken now Blaine laughed, "We are not going anywhere. We have come for what is ours. Give her to us. If you do not give her, we will take her and you." He laughed again, "We are taking you anyway."

"You cannot take me," Thomas was frightened but would not let them see, "I am already taken and belong. You cannot touch me and if you cannot touch me you cannot take her. I will hold on to her forever."

"We can take her." the harsh voice of the huge dark shape said behind Blaine, "She is ours. We own her soul. She gave it to us in her youth with the man, with more than that man and with other things and now she rightly belongs with us. If you hand her over it will go easier with you."

A female laughed shrilly, and then another joined in. They all began to shriek and laugh, moving slowly forward. Thomas shuddered. It was a dreadful sound. He stepped back slowly, moving Gina back with him, not letting go of her hand, wondering where he could go now. The group of faceless ones moved forward spreading out like a fan. He could smell them too. The smell of something which had rotted and died a long time ago.

They seemed to be following Blaine's movements as his hands gestured this way and that. So, Thomas watched him, all the while moving backwards. What to do now? They moved in closer. Thomas was afraid, the light was almost gone now and Gina behind him was desperately pleading. "Please Thomas, please don't let them take me. Please."

"Get away." Thomas shouted, "You will not have her."

Thomas watching the man realised his appearance was changing now, becoming darker, yet not completely blending in with the dark shapes. He had chosen, of his own accord, to become one of them and now Thomas could not see very well as the darkness seemed to pour in from somewhere behind them. They moved inexorably, ever closer and just when Thomas thought they would be dragged away to that terrible place, the group stopped and seemed to be looking behind them.

Light suddenly streamed out from somewhere behind him and there they were. Thomas almost yelled out with the relief which flooded over him. A group of Great Angels came swiftly in between him and the faceless ones, led by the Archangel Michael, hair flowing, wearing breastplate and carrying flaming sword and shield, with three more angels directly behind dressed also for battle. Behind these came a great hosts of angels prepared too, to do battle with the forces of evil.

The largest of the faceless ones shouted in a hoarse voice, "So, Michael, we meet again. You are come with your demon fighters and your legions,"

It hissed and growled at them. As the three moved out from behind the Archangel it snarled, "So, Mae, Leo, and Loath, you think to destroy us. You shall not take the woman from us. She belongs to us."

The Archangel Michael smiled grimly, "No Haagen, you shall not have her. You will go back to your pits. Go, or be driven."

"Go Thomas and take the woman with you." The Great Angel Loath called, "Go now. You have fought well but battle now is ours. Take the woman Thomas and run now."

Thomas grabbed Gina and they ran towards the road out and away from the town of Barton Trinity and straight into a pair of the faceless ones. The two tried to reach for her but Thomas held on tightly to her arms. Then they tried to grasp him but as they reached out for him both screamed and leapt back as Fariel flew swiftly in between them, arms outstretched pushing at them.

One screamed, "I burn."

"I too," the second shouted, and curved away from Fariel. Both stood uncertainly for a few seconds but then moved forward again. Thomas released Gina to fight them off. They tried to get behind him to take her but there was the sound of wings and a pair of Great Angels came in between. Two Gatherers came running. He pushed Gina towards the angels and they grasped her arms and fled. Gina was gone now and the Scavengers fled before the might of the Great Angels and Fariel. They stood now swords aflame and shields held high. Fariel called to him, "Return now, Thomas to The Portal and to the Gathering Place."

The angel flew with him as he ran toward the Portal. As they reached it Fariel said, "Now Thomas, enter the Portal and thence to The Gathering Place. Cadamiel waits."

A pair of gatherers came running as he moved towards the Portal. He stopped. He was not going back yet. The angel Cadamiel stood by the Arch and watched him. Thomas stood just outside and stared back. He shook his head; he was going back to the battle. Cadamiel smiled and nodded. Thomas turned and went swiftly back. He ran like the wind. Nothing would keep him away.

****

185

Chapter 22

He met them again on the road back. A female terrifyingly big, yet she did not touch him. He knew now that if they touched him, they could not hold him but if he touched them, they could take him. More of the Faceless ones came screaming to help her. He backed away, turning to run towards the church. If he could get inside, would they follow? Was there not sanctuary there? Thomas could hear them behind him and he ran as fast as he could. Then he was in the churchyard and the wall of the church was before him. He turned. There were even more of them now, hundreds upon hundreds of them. They came forward hissing and screaming. His back was to the wall and still they came on. He tried to force his form through the church wall but could not. They had not managed to get hold of Gina, but were now determined to have him.

Several of the Great Angels came in a rush and they pushed forward slowly but surely towards Thomas, thrusting the flaming swords at the Scavengers who fled in all directions but re-grouped quickly.

The angels placed Thomas in the centre of the group and pushed forward again, shields high, flaming swords thrusting at the faceless one. There were a lot more of the bigger dark ones now, Thomas saw. They, too, carried long flaming torches that blazed out a foul flame. The smell of it was something Thomas thought was like carbide, something mineral. Sulphuric? He was not sure. The smell was suffocating. Thomas moved forward and then back with the Great Angels. He could not see a lot hidden deep in their wings.

More of the dark ones came and even more of the Angels. It seemed now that they filled the sky and the land as they battled. Thunder roared across the sky and lightning flashed. First the Angels pushed forward, then the Dark ones. The struggle was immense. Then, when it seemed as if all might be lost, great hosts of angels poured out across the skies. The Dark ones fell slowly back.

Thomas, released from the protection of the huge wings stared at them in horror. He could not believe there were so many of the dark ones, or that some were so big. Then he saw even greater flights of angels lined up in a great arc across the sky, as a huge hand stretched out to fill the sky and covered the Angels and they gathered in strength and force, driving down and pushing the faceless ones back and down into the ground. Thomas stood by the wall of the Church "What is that?" he whispered.

He stared up at the mighty hand which seemed to cover the earth. Then the darkness faded away and the light came again.

A deep voice filled the land and the air and echoed and re-echoed. "I am who I am. The first and the last. The Alpha and the Omega. All ye of the darkness, hear and obey. Return to that place to which you were sent. This is my creation. Mine alone. Hear and obey my command."

Then there was silence and the last of the faceless ones melted silently away into the ground and it was over and all was quieter still. The darkness was gone and still there was silence. No bird sang. No creature moved. It seemed as if the whole earth and the heavens stood still in amazement at what it had seen.

John Blaine was no longer. Whatever he was now Thomas did not know. The faceless ones had taken him. Anonymous now, as one of their kind, he was gone. They had faded away with him leaving no trace. He was theirs and they would keep him. Thomas felt a deep sadness for the man. They had made him promises. Those promises were empty, worthless.

Now Thomas walked unsteadily along the road and saw the young couple walking arm in arm. Had they seen or heard nothing of all this? He shook his head. Worlds apart. He entered the Portal. It was not cold inside, in fact it felt pleasantly warm. His tiredness seemed to slowly drain away. He walked until he saw the gate. It was open, but there were two Great Angels guarding it. Each held a flaming sword. This was not usual. They were protecting the gate. Why? Thomas slowed down.

Would they let him in or stop him? He was still apprehensive of them.

One of them spoke, "Come forward and enter here, Thomas Beck quickly now."

The second said, "Welcome back into the place which is yours by right."

The first spoke again, "You have done well, Thomas. Come now."

The second said, "Quickly Thomas, enter now. The gate must be sealed before they reach it. Do not doubt they will come again and try to enter. Even an order from the Almighty will only stop them for a short period. It is their nature, quickly Thomas. Run."

Both angels were looking at something behind him, each raised a flaming sword and stepped outside pushing whatever it was away. Thomas ran between them; he did not want to see what was behind him. Once inside he stood and turned. The angels had moved back inside now. The gate was closing. Something was outside, screeching. They raised their swords and ran the flames across and along the edges of the gate. It glowed red and the noise from outside stopped. They turned to him then. One said. "This gate is sealed for all time, it will never open again, but there will be another to replace it. Come now and return to that place which had been allocated to you in the Gathering Place." one said "We will follow behind," said the second. To his astonishment, both gave him a small bow.

Thomas walked along the pathway. There was warmth and light and his exhaustion was gone. He came out on to the plain and the Great Angels left him. They did not look to see if he was all right. Thomas felt slightly aggrieved that they never said thank you. He had worked so hard to get Gina for them and they could not be bothered to even look back at him. He sniffed. Mind you, they had said he had done well and gave him a little nod of their heads that was a big thing. Yes.

They could have said goodbye though, instead of haring off on their great big wings. After all he had done them a big favour. But then, he thought, they are different. Angels are not people. They don't have the same thoughts or anything like human beings. Then, neither did they serve man. Their service was to another. Yet in a way they did a service for people, "Oh, well," Thomas muttered to himself, "What do I know?" he scratched his head, "Half the time, I don't even know what I mean myself."

He walked towards his small house where his own angel waited by the gate. "You have done well," Cadamiel told him, smiling.

Thomas puffed out his chest waiting for more praise, but there was none. The angel left then. Thomas bent his head. I should be humble, he told himself. The thing that needed to be done was done. Nothing more would be said. I should be used to their ways by now. I should remember why I am here. I am the one who owes a debt. Not they. Therefore, I am the one who makes payment.

Thomas walked to the door of his little house head bowed and pushed open the door. He lifted his head and then stepped back startled by the sight. Tears came to his eyes. The walls of the little room were ablaze with light. He walked around, eyes searching the room. Then he saw his book on the table. The dirt and dust and tarnish was gone and the book glowed like fire. The jewels dancing with light. Was it done? What happened now? Would somebody come and say? Would they come and tell him? Thomas was overjoyed. Mike was gone now too. Soon he would be on his way. There was a sound behind him. Cadamiel had returned. "There is a small task awaiting your attention," The angel said, "This must be done before all light shines for you." Cadamiel pointed to a corner and Thomas saw that a tiny patch on the cover of the book was not glowing. One tiny dirty spot, he felt disappointed. Then the angel told him what must be done. Thomas stared, could not believe it. "Why, why do I have to do this thing." he demanded.

The angel's large gentle eyes looked into his, "You have done great work Thomas. There is however, the one, the final act, which you may feel is one of humiliation. But humility, Thomas is an act of great sacrifice, a putting of yourself last and all else before. There needs also, to be an act of forgiveness, before you can have the light to shine for you in all its glory. This will be a culmination, a celestial point. It must be done."

Thomas nodded. A lump came to his throat, tears filled his eyes, "It will be done," he said.

Cadamiel spoke to tell him of the task before him, then said, "Earth is now in darkness. You will be sent out in safety and return to it for a short period and do that which is asked of you and return with that soul. This task is yours alone. Be assured again that you can do this in safety. Go now with the blessing and full protection of the angels." Sometime later Thomas returned. He had handed over the soul to the waiting gatherers. Now he felt wonderful. Cleansed and refreshed. Young again, like a child. I am new he thought. This must be it. He went into his little house. All was alight.

There was a sound behind Thomas. He turned slowly. Two Great Angels stood there. Two great, dazzling white angels. They were smiling. "Thomas dear soul. It is time to go to your reward. We are here to take you on to all that you have earned. Your work in this past time has indeed been great." one said. "You showed great courage in protecting the woman, in holding her from those who would destroy her and showed humility in the bringing forth of the other woman," said the second, "The Book of Life that was yours, is now completed. All that should be done has been done. Your work has been pleasing to heaven."

Thomas Beck stood looking at the angels. I feel like a child again he thought, full of joy and wonder. Now was the time. He was going on to the dazzling gates up there.

They each held out a hand towards him and he grasped them. He realised he was holding his book and it felt soft as clouds. All three walked through the door of the little house and they lifted him high. Thomas neither saw or heard anything, except the rush of a great wind as they rose higher and higher. Light seemed to pour through him. Then all sound was gone. There was a glory inside his head. A shining wonder and a great love. A love such as he had never known.

They crossed the great gulf towards the colours of eternity and his body filled with such joy as he could not have believed possible. His mind was free and clear. A living wonderful thing. The sense of freedom and lightness was so strong, it was as though he could fly and curl and weave in the immensity of space. Then the veil of mist parted and he could see the Great Gates. He had thought it was made of gold. Not so. The gates were huge, made of pearl, banded with gold and studded with precious stones. It dazzled. There were three great golden sunbursts emblazoned on the gates. One each side and one in the centre.

Two huge Angels stood, one each side of the gates, flaming swords held aloft, the flames blazing upwards. The gates began to open in the centre and Thomas heard the music, felt the glory, felt himself become one with the light. The great central sunburst remained suspended in mid-air. A tall figure came toward him smiling. The Archangel Michael took Thomas's book. Long silver hair flowed down on to the breastplate covering shoulders and chest and a double set of wings that stood high and wide. He lifted the book high and it burst into flames and was gone, leaving no part of it behind. The great Angel smiled and beckoned him forward. "All has been done. Enter here," it said, "Enter and behold all that you have earned. See too all those you have loved and have come before you to welcome you."

Thomas stepped forward. I am here, he thought. I never believed this was all here. Now I know. There was no anger left now, no pain, only the now and the joy, the glory and the love. So much love and wonder too. And peace, a peace unknown in all his seventy years. This was what it was all about.

Now he could see figures inside behind the light. They were calling to him. His parents, Amalie. Thomas was sure he could see his grandmother. James was here, smiling. Was that Robert? So many people smiling at him. Waving to him. Something else, the most amazing thing. He understood everything. Every single thing. The entire Universe. All. He had made it. The Great Gate closed behind him.

****

The Final Chapter

Two women, one young, one very old, sat together in the comfortably warm sitting room of the house in the Avenue, in what was still called the village. The heavy drapes were drawn against the night. Outside, the sky was brilliant with stars and it had begun to freeze. It was going to be a very cold January night. They were listening to the older woman's favourite piece of classical music. She loved Greig, found it very soothing at the end of the day. She lay back in her big soft chair eyes closed, seeming to be asleep. Only her small hand lifting to her face or hair occasionally showed she was awake and listening. The younger woman watched her smiling and thinking she should make their bedtime drinks, but was too comfortable to move her long legs from beneath her.

These days Barton Trinity was no longer a village. It had grown and spread and was now a large town. It spilled out on to the back road and the main road to Great Barton. Soon they would meet and whilst the Village would always be called that, it would be part of the town. Where once she could walk through the village in less than ten minutes, the older woman needed to travel by car now. There was also the fact of her great age. She was now ninety-two years old, a tiny pretty old lady with soft white curls who looked twenty years younger than her age. She was dressed in a red wool dress and wore a pair of pretty red embroidered pumps on her small feet. Rings adorned her fingers and her nails were the same colour as her dress. Valerie Drew was, even in very old age, still, a beautiful woman.

The younger woman sat reading. A very attractive woman in her early thirties, she had the same neat features as her grandmother. Her mass of pale gold curls, usually worn up high on her head now tumbled down over her shoulders. She glanced occasionally at her grandmother. If I look like her when I'm old I will be one happy woman, she thought. Then again will I even get to be ninety-two? Sara Duval smiled. She was a lot taller than the old lady and wore well-fitting trousers in shining bronze material with a silk knitted low necked beige top. A fine gold filigree necklace filled in the neckline.

Valerie Drew opened her eyes glanced at the photograph of the smiling white-haired old man who was her second husband Mel. There was no photograph of her first husband Thomas Beck who had managed to end his life in a car he had been told not to drive. But then, she did not think very much about that man now. He had been dead for over thirty years. So very, very long ago and yet in her mind it could have been a matter of weeks. So much had happened to change her life for the better.

Her dearly loved second husband Mel too was gone these past seven years. He had reached a good age, eighty-five. How she missed him still. Those last years were the happiest of her life. I wonder, Valerie thought, how it would have been if I had met Mel first? No use wondering. It had not happened. Imagine, she thought, she'd had to wait until she was over sixty years old for that kind of happiness. It had been worth the wait.

Her granddaughter, Sara, sitting opposite was reading a medical journal. Sara was now a GP with her own practice in Barton Trinity. She lived with Valerie and looked after the old lady who was, given her age, still very active. They had a woman who came in daily. But Valerie still cooked their evening meal and always filled the dishwasher afterwards and tidied the kitchen. "Let me do it darling," Sara pleaded many times. "I like to be useful. I can't bear to sit around, you know that," her grandmother told her, "Besides, you are always exhausted after the long afternoon and evening sessions at the surgery and I like looking after you." She smiled at her beautiful grandchild remembering the small plump golden-haired little girl. Sara had never married, but there was a young GP in the practice who seemed very interested in her.

They had supper every Friday evening with Sara's mother Kate, who was a widow and still lived next door. Kate's beloved Jack had also died a few years earlier. Kate Duval, worked as the practice manager in the purpose-built centre. The twins, Kate's sons were also doctors; but lived and worked in London, one a Consultant Neurologist with a private practice in Harley street, the other a Specialist in Paediatrics. Kate was somewhat bemused by the fact they all followed each other into medicine.

Tonight Sara, Kate's daughter was restless and uneasy and wondered why. There was nothing she could think of to make her feel like this. The afternoon at the surgery had been quiet. There had been time to relax over a cup of tea and cake which one of the receptionists had made and iced for Kit Morley, the practice Nurse, who had reached her fortieth birthday.

The doors were closed and secured and all were gone at half past eight on the dot. So, whatever was making her feel like this she did not know and certainly did not like the feeling. She tried to concentrate on the article in the journal. Sometimes too her psychic feelings, which she subdued, came back and she hoped this was not one of those times.

Sara glanced over to her Grandmother who sat back in her chair, eyes closed smiling to herself. My lovely grandmother, she thought. Then a thought struck her and it was like a piece of flint in her heart. How much longer will I have her? She is ninety-two years old and in good health for a woman of her age. In fact, she was in better health than a lot of sixty-year-old patients whom Sara saw on a regular basis. The last illness she had was what? When? Good lord, she could not remember.

Valerie opened her eye and looked at her granddaughter smiling, "I think I might go up now, my darling. I am a little tired tonight. I'll have my shower in the morning, I can't be bothered tonight. I'll just wash my face and put on a bit of cream."

Sara kissed her: "Sleep well. Would you like a hot drink?"

"No thank you Sara. I'm fine. I'll drift off quite happily." Valerie climbed the stairs up to the bedroom she had shared with Mel, and was now hers alone. She remembered the way her first husband had insisted on single beds, because he said she was restless and kept him awake. She smiled to herself. She looked at the photographs on her dressing table. Her boys, David and Jonathan. Boys no longer. Two elderly men in their sixties, both grandparents. Both handsome still. Roberts sons. Her heart contracted. She had loved him so much, so wildly and passionately. Oh Robert, what did we do. Our sons, our wonderful sons, and you hardly knew them. The worst part of it now was that she could not even remember Robert's face. Tears came to her eyes and she gave a gasping sob. "I loved you so madly, but it all ended so dreadfully." She brushed the tears away. Robert had been madness and passion. That was all spent now. Then of course, there was Mel. Mel was sanity and true happiness.

Mel had come to her that day when Thomas was killed and had never really gone far away. He had got a full-time career in to help with his mother who was still alive and came in to be with her every day. He had been kindness and goodness itself when the twins Jonathan and David went back home and Kate got married. Kate had wanted to know if she should put off the wedding, "Why would you want to put it off?" Valerie had asked, "Your Father would not have wanted that. He would want you to be happy. If you are worried about what people will think, don't bother. People think what they want to, no matter what you do. You can't change that."

Mel had been the one to give her daughter away. His mother was gone to her rest then. She had suffered from dementia for years. She had a bad chest infection and had opened wide the windows in her bedroom one cold wet night and in her weakened state developed pneumonia and died.

A month after her funeral they were in Valerie's kitchen drinking tea when Mel stood up and looked out through the window to the back garden. His back was turned. Mel said something she did not quite hear. "Sorry, I didn't hear what you said," she told him.

He said it again and again she did not hear. "Mel dear, I think my hearing is not as good as it was. Turn around so I can hear you."

He turned swiftly, spilling some of his tea, face pale and she felt suddenly quite worried. "What is it?" she asked. "I love you," Mel said, "I've always loved you. I want to marry you and make you happy. I know it's too soon, but I just can't keep it to myself any longer."

His face went from pale to flushed then pale again.

Valerie was unable to speak. Her mouth opened and closed but no sound came out. "Sorry," he said, "I'll go. Sorry. It was too soon. Sorry."

He had put down the mug and left the house, almost running, and Valerie wondered if she had imagined the proposal.

She sat on her king-sized bed smiling to herself, remembering. She had sat that day in the kitchen for a long time thinking, then had made up her mind. She did love him, in fact if she was honest had loved him since before Thomas had died, but never allowed herself to think about it. He had been a rock in bad times. She would marry him. He was the best man she had ever met in her life. He had asked nothing more than to sit with her and have a cup of tea and talk and been there to help in every possible way. He'd never asked anything in return, only ever given to her and her children, even going so far as to offer financial help if it was needed. Valerie had made the decision then. She had gone upstairs and put on a little lipstick, combed her hair and gone after him.

He was standing in the back-garden staring at the fence. "Mel." she said and he turned swiftly, "Yes. I will marry you. I love you too. I will be so happy to

195

marry you. Privileged. It is not too soon. My life has been pretty rocky at times and I think you have a good idea the marriage was, to say the least, troubled. But I must tell you everything about my life, the mistakes I made."

He protested, "There is no need."

"There is every need," she said, "I made the mistake once of believing there was no need to say any more when Thomas said that to me, but there was a need. Not telling him everything was a huge mistake. I was so very wrong. So, I want you to sit down and listen. Then and only then can you decide whether you still want to marry me. I want to tell you about Robert and the twins too."

They had sat and she told him everything. She'd not meant to deceive Thomas, had not known when they married that she was pregnant. Her stupidity, she said, was in thinking he would never find out that Robert was the father of the twins, not he. Valerie told him of the good years they had in the early days and the wretched misery of life when he did eventually find out. The punishment that went on forever.

Mel had simply said to her: "Thank you for telling me, but that is in the past and the past in another country. It has nothing to do with us. We have to look forward to the future together, and even if it is only for a few years it will be worth it and I promise, I will do everything to make you happy." He had. That had been the beginning of twenty-five years of great happiness.

Valerie sat at the dressing table and looked at her reflection. The pretty white-haired elderly woman who looked back at her seemed to be smiling as if she were looking from some other place and just for a second, she thought she saw Mel's reflection beside hers. Then, for a fraction of a second, saw another face had appeared with them both. Was it? Thomas? No, that could not be. Not him. She shrugged. It was imagination. Why would either of them be there? But I am not going yet. She had a few years left even if she was ancient.

She opened the bottom drawer in the dressing table and took out the box, inside which was the tissue wrapped fine silky negligee and nightdress worn on her wedding night for Mel all those years ago. She had felt a little foolish in it and had never worn it again. She'd put it away to treasure it. He had made her feel like a young bride. Valerie giggled and decided to wear them again. Why not?

She let the pale pink silk slide down over her tiny body, drew the negligee around her, climbed into her bed, then lay down. She'd not drawn the drapes and could see the moonlit sky through the big window. It was one of those frosty brilliant nights when the sky took on that particularly beautiful velvety midnight blue colour. Then a falling star trailing its long tail slid across the sky for a few seconds. Valerie took a deep breath and contentedly closed her eyes.

Downstairs, Sara switched off the music. She read for another half hour then got up and put her magazine away and looked around the big room. Nice and tidy. She went to the kitchen to heat some milk. It might soothe her, help her sleep because the feeling of uneasiness inside her would make for a night of wakefulness.

Sara sat back in her chair and sipped her drink. Tomorrow was her day off, maybe she would take Valerie out somewhere. They could have lunch and if her grandmother felt up to it, do a little shopping. Sara placed her cup in the kitchen sink. She checked the doors and windows. She thought, just for one moment there were two men dressed in white suits out on the avenue. Imagination, just like when she was a child. Sara turned and ran upstairs, then stopped outside her grandmother's door. It was slightly ajar and the lamp on the dressing table was on. Had she forgotten to switch it off again? She pushed gently against the door and saw the old lady asleep, moved inside to switch off the light on the dressing table but stopped, looking back towards the bed. Something was not quite right. What was it?

Sara walked back to the bed. Was she breathing? She smiled. Of course, she was. I'm just being silly she thought. It's just this odd feeling. I'm unsettled. Sara went to walk out and close the door. No. The colour on her grandmother's face was not right. She was too still. She slowly moved to the bed and touched the small hand. "Oh no," her voice broke, "Please. No."

She switched on the bedside light and touched the old lady's face, felt for a pulse. Nothing. She was not cold, yet not as warm as she should be. She raced for her medical bag to get her stethoscope. Coming back quickly into the bedroom she turned the old lady on to her back and listened for a heartbeat. Nothing. No breath sounds. The mouth had slackened and dropped. The eyes were slightly open. There was nothing she could do now. No point in using CPR on the small body. She reached out and took the tiny hands and placed them on Valerie's breast, closed the eyes, then kissed the little face she loved so much.

Valerie opened her eyes and looked up at her granddaughter. She smiled at Sara's tearful face, then raised a hand to push away the stethoscope. "What are you doing darling, did you think I died and gone to heaven?"

She laughed, then stopped. Her hand seemed to go right through Sara. She stood up easily, not slowly and stiffly as usual, reached out a hand to Sara and again the hand passed through the young woman. She stood still. "Has it come?" Valerie said wonderingly, "Has it come so quickly?"

She looked down at the bed and at her own body lying there, at her beloved Sara, sitting on the edge, listening for her heartbeat with tears pouring down her face.

My heart no longer beats, Valerie thought. I no longer live and breathe. It has come to me so softly and silently and I am here and my body lies there. She looked down at her body again. How small it seemed. My remains, she thought. It had come so swiftly. She used to wonder in low moments how it would come and now it was here and was such a surprise. Valerie looked at her weeping granddaughter. "Don't cry, my darling. Mel promised to come and find me. He did and I did not realise, but then so did..." She paused, "I am very happy. Goodbye my darling."

Sara touched her grandmother's face, then bent down to kiss her. She was getting colder now. She thought, I had to let you go. How could I do anything else at your age. She picked up the bedside phone and called Kate. "Mummy. Can you come now? Please."

There was a short silence, "It is Mum?" Kate asked. "Yes, I'm so sorry."

"I'm coming now," her mother said.

Sara again kissed the beautiful serene old face again and went down stairs to let Kate into the house. She opened the front door to find her mother was already standing there in her fleecy pyjamas. Kate reached for Sara and they hugged, shedding tears and then went inside and closed the door.

Valerie stood by the bed. Was this what they called an out-of-body experience she wondered? It felt good. No, it felt great. She was as light as a feather. There had been a moment after she had closed her eyes to sleep when she felt a little odd and then it seemed as if the light went out. She looked closely at her tiny body lying on its back and thought. It came and I hardly noticed. It was not even an experience. She had just gone to sleep, that must have happened when the lights went out. How very easy it had been. It was of course, the end of life. The end of my life, she thought. So, if I am still here, then is there a beginning? A new beginning?

She had always believed, known, there was a hereafter and tried hard to make up for the stupidity of her youth. She moved barefoot across the room and sat on the window seat. So, what now? Would she stay here in the house which had given her so much pain and then so much love or would she have to move on somewhere. Hmm. That was something to think about.

There were voices from downstairs. It sounded like her daughter Kate. She looked out through the window and saw the two men dressed in white suits coming along the Avenue. Aha, they were coming for her. Sara, as a child had told her about the men in white. So, they really existed, were not just a child's imagination. Yet, her granddaughter had not mentioned them since childhood.

But what about Kate? Poor Kate, she would be so very sad, and Sara? Kate had met somebody, a nice man whom Valerie met when they went for coffee a couple of weeks ago. Perhaps they would make something of it. Perhaps Sara and the young doctor? Her sons too, they would be sad and her lovely grandchildren. Ah well. Valerie hoped they would not be too sad. She smiled, looking around the bedroom. She supposed she'd have to be on her way. Her way, yet to where? There must be somewhere. Valerie made her way to the bedroom door which was closed. She put out a tentative hand to touch the wood of the door and it simply passed through. She giggled This was great. She could flit about wherever she wanted. She stood at the top of the stairs. There was little left behind to worry about. Her children and grandchildren were all happy, had good lives. She wondered if she would see Robert, or even Thomas again but it was just a thought.

She slipped down the stairs, watched Sara as she spoke on the phone, with Kate beside her. She kissed at her daughter's cheek, "Goodbye my darling girl, we will meet again someday," then gently touched at Sara's shoulder and slipped through the front door and out into the frosty January night. It did not feel at all cold. She saw the two men dressed in white suits coming towards the black enamel gates and dived behind a large shrub. Well, she was not going with them just yet. She was going for a last stroll through the town. She turned the corner and saw another of them leaning against the wall. She was caught. "Hallo Valerie." Thomas said straightening and walking towards her. "Thomas." She gasped.

He came forward into the light of a street lamp holding out his hands. He looked younger, and more handsome. and best of all, he was smiling. "What are you doing here?" she asked. Valerie felt no fear of him now, only curiosity, "Why have you come, why not Mel?"

"Mel is waiting," he said smiling and she saw him now as he had rarely been in life, a calm lovely man, "But since I owe you a debt, I was sent for you. I did you a great wrong. Now I come to ask you to forgive me. I made our lives together a revenge on you. I am sorry. I would like to take you onward. Will you let me do that? It will be my final act."

She looked at him, eyes wide with surprise, "I, forgive you?" she asked, "No, that can't be right. I caused it all, but if that is what you want, need, then I forgive you and you must forgive me."

He kissed her cheek, then took her hand, "I forgave you a long time ago. Come now, we must meet the Gatherers. They will take you to the angels, who will tell you all you need to know."

"Ah," Valerie sighed delighted that there would be angels and she was going to the right place.

He handed her over to two Gatherers waiting by the gate. "We will meet again sometime." he told her.

She smiled back at him, a dazzling beautiful smile. At last. She had waited a long time for his forgiveness.

The gatherers took her into the gathering place. A short time later Valerie, seated on a seat waiting for her angel guide, watched two enormous angels leading a man from one of the little houses. They held the hands of the man dressed in white who looked very familiar, and then all three rose into the air. Was it Thomas? She nodded. Yes, coming for her had been his final act. Then she stared in astonishment at the beautiful angel moving toward her. Her mouth opened but she could not speak. This was so wonderful, so amazing. The angel seemed to float like gossamer toward where she sat waiting. "Hello Valerie," the beautiful creature said, smiling, "I am your angel guide whilst you are here. I am called Cassiel. Welcome home."

Two other angels, standing a little distance away, looked at her, then at the figures rising into the distance toward the Great Gates. The angels Cadamiel and Fariel watched a while, then Fariel left. The Angel Cadamiel, hands folded inside the sleeve of a dazzling white robe, glanced toward the Great Gate high above, bowed it's silver head and smiled. All was as it should be. It was done.